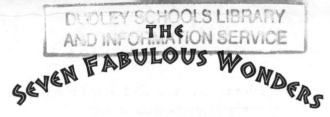

THE
SEVEN FABULOUS WONDERS
OF THE ANCIENT WORLD

THE GREAT PYRAMID ROBBERY
featuring The Great Pyramid at Giza

THE BABYLON GAME
featuring The Hanging Gardens of Babylon

THE AMAZON TEMPLE QUEST
featuring The Temple of Artemis at Ephesos

THE MAUSOLEUM MURDER
featuring The Mausoleum at Halicarnassos

THE OLYMPIC CONSPIRACY
featuring The Statue of Zeus at Olympia

THE COLOSSUS CRISIS
featuring The Colossus of Rhodes

THE CLEOPATRA CURSE

For more information about Katherine Roberts, visit
www.katherineroberts.com

First published in Great Britain by HarperCollins *Children's Books* 2006
HarperCollins *Children's Books* is a division of HarperCollins*Publishers* Ltd
77-85 Fulham Palace Road, Hammersmith
London W6 8JB

The HarperCollins *Children's Books* website address is:
www.harpercollinschildrensbooks.com

1 3 5 7 9 8 6 4 2

Text copyright © Katherine Roberts 2006

Illustrations by Fiona Land

ISBN-13   978 0 00 711284 5
ISBN-10   0 00 711284 X

OTHER BOOKS BY KATHERINE ROBERTS

The Seven Fabulous Wonders series

The Great Pyramid Robbery
The Babylon Game
The Amazon Temple Quest
The Mausoleum Murder
The Olympic Conspiracy
The Colossus Crisis

The Echorium Sequence

Song Quest
Crystal Mask
Dark Quetzal

Spellfall

www.katherineroberts.com

Katherine Roberts

THE CLEOPATRA CURSE

HarperCollins *Children's Books*

EGYPT

Mediterranean Sea

to Rome & Greece

Rosetta

Alexandria   Canopus

Pharos
Island

ship
canal

Lake Mareotis

Nile Delta

Pelusium

desert

Giza Pyramids

Memphis

N

W   E

S

River Nile

Red Sea

desert

0   Km   50

0   miles   50

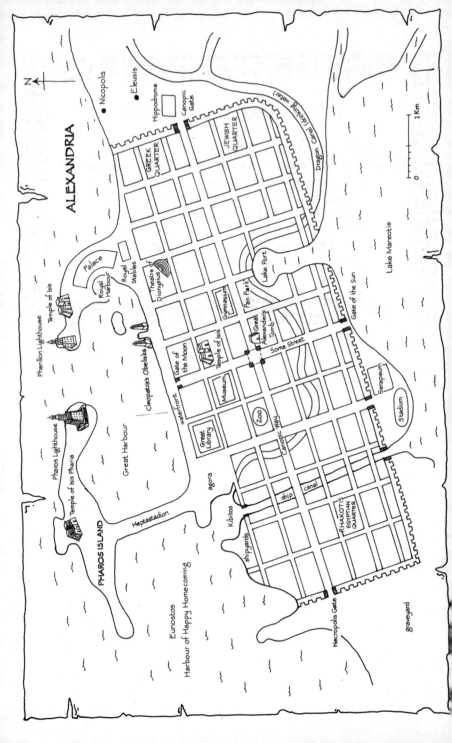

ALEXANDRIA

N

• Nicopolis
• Eleusis
Hippodrome
Canopic Gate

GREEK QUARTER

JEWISH QUARTER

Dragon Canal (drinking water)

Lake Port

Lake Mareotis

Gate of the Sun

Serapeum

Stadium

RHAKOTIS EGYPTIAN QUARTER

ship canal

Zoo

Canopic Way

Great Library

Museum

Gate of the Moon

Temple of Isis

Cleopatra's Obelisks

waterfront

Theatre of Dionysius

Royal Stables

Royal Harbour

Palace

Temple of Isis

Pharillon Lighthouse

Gymnasium

Pan Park

Greek Alexander's Tomb

Soma Street

agora

Great Harbour

Cleopatra's Obelisks

Pharos Lighthouse

PHAROS ISLAND

Temple of Isis Pharia

Heptastadion

Eunostos Harbour of Happy Homecoming

Kibitos

shipyards

Necropolis Gate

graveyard

0   1 Km

CURSE OF AGATHODAIMON

O Mighty and Dreadful Demon of Alexandria,
Wake from your slumber to avenge one who has been wronged!
Take the power of the false Queen Cleopatra –
Make her horses fall and her chariots crash,
Take her royal throne and her stolen gold,
Remove her name from the coins of this land,
Take those she loves away from her,
Then send your serpent to end her wretched life!

Chapter 1

CURSE

THE CHARIOT WRECK had been a bad one. Blood soaked the sand all around, making a black stain in the moonlight. As Zeuxis crept closer, he saw a horse's hoof buried under the splinters of wood and leather. The horse would be dead by now. A racehorse with three legs was no good to anyone. But the smashed chariot had a second life as fuel for Alexandria's biggest lighthouse, the Pharos, which was why Zeuxis, lighthouse boy, got the job of clearing up after race days.

He picked up the hoof and held it sadly. He didn't like it when the horses got hurt, but on the whole he didn't mind this part of his work. At least it got him into the Hippodrome, even if it was in the middle of the night, when the races were over and the crowds had gone home. His imagination provided the rest.

Still holding the hoof, Zeuxis balanced on the balls of his feet and closed his eyes.

He crouched in the lead chariot, driving four black stallions at full gallop. His breath came faster as the chariot took the final turn on one wheel. He could almost feel the reins of his excited team tugging at his hands, hear the roar of the crowd: "Zeuxis! Zeuxis for the Blues!" His heart pounded with the thrill of the race...

Voices banished the dream. With the speed of someone used to being punished for being caught in the wrong place, Zeuxis took cover behind the central barrier. Although he had permission to be in the Hippodrome tonight to collect the wrecks, he had already lingered a lot longer than he should have done. He ought to have been halfway back to Pharos Island by now with his load of fuel. If the lighthouse's fire went out before he got there, he'd be in a lot of trouble with the Keeper.

He peered through a crack in the barrier, curious. People did not normally come to the Hippodrome on official business at night. So, whoever they were, they were up to no good.

In the moonlight, he made out two men in the uniform of the Royal Macedonian Guard. They flanked a boy a few years older than Zeuxis, who wore a hooded cloak and carried himself very arrogantly.

As Zeuxis watched, the older boy knelt near the starting gates and dug a hole in the sand with his dagger. Jewels glittered on its hilt as he held out an impatient hand. One of the guards passed him a rolled-up strip of lead, secured with a nail. The boy dropped the lead into the hole and covered it up again. He scuffed his sandal over the top to hide the place, smiled, and marched back to the main exit. As he did so the moonlight fell on his face, and Zeuxis' heart missed a beat. He could be wrong, but he didn't think so – who else but a member of the royal family would have a Macedonian escort? He prayed to all the gods of Alexandria that the guards wouldn't look his way. But the men exchanged a glance and hurried after their charge, shaking their heads.

Zeuxis let out his breath. He ought to take the wreck back to the lighthouse and forget the whole thing, count his blessings that the gods had answered his prayers and he hadn't been caught. But this was an opportunity not to be missed. The gods could equally as well have meant for him to see what he had just seen.

Staying low, he sidled along the barrier until he reached the place where the older boy had dug his hole. The starting gates loomed over him, and a shiver went down his spine.

Hooves thundered all around him as the chariots raced to secure the favoured lead position on the course. He'd drawn the best position, the inside gate with a straight run, but he had to watch the others. If their horses were fast enough, the outside drivers might try to cut across and force his team into the barrier...

He shook away the vision and examined the ground. Even though he'd been watching, it was difficult to tell the exact spot where the boy had buried his roll of lead. Lacking a dagger of his own, Zeuxis used a broken spoke from the chariot wreck to dig in the sand. Splinters pierced his palm. He sucked away the blood, wrapped a corner of his tunic around the spoke, and tried again.

He had to dig three holes before he found what he was looking for. Gingerly, he picked up the roll of lead and blew off the sand. Without unrolling it or removing the nail, he slipped it into his inside pocket. Then he filled in the holes and scuffed his sandal over the top like the boy had done. Satisfied no one could tell where he'd dug, he gathered up an armful of splintered wood and leather and hurried back to where he'd left his cart at the rear entrance.

The donkey, which the lighthouse boys had named Cleo after the Queen of Egypt as a joke, brayed a welcome. Zeuxis fondled her long ears. "What's the matter, old girl? You know I wouldn't leave you here with the ghosts. We've someone to visit before breakfast, so move those furry little legs of yours." He loaded up the wreckage as fast as he could and clucked his tongue. The donkey shambled at an eager trot towards the city.

The roll of lead felt as if it were burning a hole in his pocket, but the guards at the gate barely glanced at Zeuxis as they waved him through. "Better hurry, Lighthouse Boy!" they called. "Your fire's looking dim."

Zeuxis grinned. The guards liked to tease him about the Pharos' fire going out. But as he passed through the gate, he could see it shining like a bright star over the roofs of the city. Reassured, he dragged the donkey through the late-night party crowds.

When they reached the public park, where he usually took a forbidden short cut to reach the long sea wall that led across to the island, Cleo pricked her long ears and speeded up. But Zeuxis grabbed the donkey's rein and pulled her head round. "No, Cleo, you'll have to wait a bit longer for your breakfast. I'm not carrying this thing round with me all day."

The donkey didn't like it, and told him so by braying and going sideways. A plank of precious wood fell off the cart.

Zeuxis gritted his teeth. "I'm in charge here," he said, picking up the wood and showing it to Cleo. "Not you!"

The donkey lowered her head and gave in. Zeuxis replaced the plank on the cart with a smile. He never had to resort to hitting Cleo. She was too clever for that.

He checked the fire at the top of the Pharos again. He still had time. Zeuxis thanked the gods for giving him this opportunity to bring his dream a bit closer, and dragged the reluctant donkey into the narrow streets of the Egyptian Quarter.

Chapter 2

WITCH

THE CART AND its load of fuel would not fit between the overcrowded Egyptian houses, so Zeuxis tied Cleo to a post at the corner of the main street. He warned the donkey to behave herself, and darted up an unlit alley. Even at this time of night, flickering lamplight showed on the flat roof of the third house on the left. The muffled jangle of a sistrum rattle and low chanting came from within.

He tapped on the window blind.

Tap-tap-tap. Pause for a count of three. *Tap-tap*. Repeated three times. The code his friend had taught him.

The sistrum stopped, leaving a deep silence. A shiver went down Zeuxis' spine. Then a woman's head peered over the edge of the roof and called down in accented Greek, "I've told you kids before, I don't sell spells to the likes of you. Clear off!"

"It's me, Lady Wernero," Zeuxis called back, annoyed at the waver in his voice. "I've got something to show you. It's important."

The woman squinted down at him. "Lighthouse Boy? What are you doing here at this time of night?"

"Please, Lady, let me in. I've found another curse, and I think this one's still got power."

The head disappeared. After several tense moments, the door was unbarred. "Quickly," the old woman hissed, checking up and down the alley. "Inside."

Zeuxis slipped past her and blinked around the single room that formed the ground floor of Lady Wernero's house. Bunches of dried herbs hung from the rafters. Priceless rugs from Persia covered the dirt, five or six deep, so that walking across the room felt like walking on a layer of sponges. Coloured glass vases glittered in the corners, with shells and other things from the sea glimmering inside them. Statuettes of animal-headed Egyptian gods peered from the shadows, and a stuffed crocodile guarded the stairs. Every time Zeuxis came here, he saw something stranger than last time.

He eyed the crocodile uneasily, wondering if it would come to life if he tried to get past it to look for his friend.

"Well?" Lady Wernero snapped. "Let's see it, then."

Zeuxis fumbled in his tunic pocket and pulled out the roll of lead. It was warm – from his body or something else…? He could hardly bring himself to touch it.

At once, Lady Wernero's entire attitude changed. Long black hair streaked with silver fell around her face as she took the curse in her cupped hands. She touched her nose to the roll of lead and inhaled deeply. "Ahhhh! A powerful one, too. How did you find it?"

"I... er... saw it when I was collecting the chariot wrecks."

She darted him a quick glance from her black eyes. "You should be more careful. If the people who planted this had seen you dig it up, you could be crocodile bait by now."

Zeuxis hid a grin. "If I was careful, you wouldn't have a live curse to play with, would you?"

"Less of your cheek, my boy!" Lady Wernero snapped. "One does not 'play' with curses. Particularly not ones with *this* sort of power. Now, I think I'm going to need some help with this."

Zeuxis' heart thudded. Did she mean him? "Er, I really ought to get back now," he said, backing towards the door. "The fire will be getting low and I've still got to take my load of fuel up the ramp."

Lady Wernero chuckled. "I didn't mean you, Lighthouse Boy, don't worry. You'd be worse than useless if something escaped when I unrolled this thing. My granddaughter will help me. You can stay and watch, or go as you like." She gave him a sly look. "I just need you to answer a few questions about this curse before you run away."

She'd caught Zeuxis looking at the stair again. He blushed and Lady Wernero nodded, as if she knew every thought in his head. He wouldn't have been surprised if she did.

"Ahwere!" she called. "Ahwere, I know you're up there, listening! Get dressed and come down. We've a live curse to unroll and your little friend down here is scared without you to hold his hand."

Zeuxis' blush spread to his toes. But he couldn't leave now, or Ahwere would think he was a coward. Also, he was curious. He'd found curses for Lady Wernero before. Racehorse owners routinely buried the little rolls of lead in the Hippodrome to make their rivals crash, so he often came across used ones kicked up in the wreckage, and brought them to the witch so she could salvage whatever power was left in them. But before tonight, he'd never found one with its power still intact. The lighthouse fire would have to wait a bit longer.

He perched on a rug beside a statue of the Egyptian god of the dead, Anubis. The god regarded him from its golden jackal-eyes, making Zeuxis shudder. Midnight in the Egyptian quarter was spooky at the best of times, even without a curse to unroll.

Then Ahwere came downstairs and he swallowed his nerves and tried to look brave.

The girl wore a plain dress of white linen that made her look like a priestess. Her favourite amulet hung from a thong around her neck, and she had taken time to line her eyes with kohl. Her hair was thicker and glossier than her grandmother's, but the sly look was the same.

"You'll be in trouble!" she whispered, folding her brown legs beside him on the rug. "Aren't you supposed to go straight back to your precious Pharos so you can feed the wrecks to the fire and get your cart back across the city in time to collect the morning pile of muck from the royal stables?"

"Fuel," Zeuxis muttered. "It's lighthouse fuel, not muck. And I'll be there."

"It's still muck, whether it comes from a racehorse or a donkey." Ahwere giggled. "It only burns so well because Queen Cleopatra feeds her racehorses so many potions. She thinks she's such a witch. But she knows nothing! She's just a stupid Macedonian princess wearing kohl and wigs, worshipping Isis and pretending to be an Egyptian. I've heard she's not even that pretty under all the make-up and jewels, and her skin burns if she goes out too long in the sun. I can't understand why every male in this city is head over heels in love with her."

"I'm not," Zeuxis mumbled.

Ahwere gave him a sideways look. "You'd be licking her gilded toenails along with the rest of them, if she ever offered to let you drive one of her chariots. People are even saying she's bewitched the Roman envoy – I bet it's not magic she used on him, though."

"Ahwere!" Lady Wernero called. "Don't be so crude. Get over here and hold this for me, while I take out the nail. We're ready to unroll it."

While they had been talking, Lady Wernero had lit a brazier and added handfuls of herbs that made the smoke turn purple. It smelled foul, but Zeuxis knew better than to say so. He held his nose and watched while Ahwere gripped the edges of the lead with her neat fingers.

Her grandmother carefully worked out the nail, chanting under her breath in Egyptian. A prayer or a spell? There wasn't much difference, apparently. Zeuxis eyed the statue of Anubis, and wondered if the god of the dead could hear her.

It grew colder in the room. The purple smoke thickened and his eyes watered. He stifled a cough. Ahwere was looking at him over the curse, smiling at his discomfort. She didn't seem to be afraid. Holding curses for her grandmother was probably something she did every day. But she had her amulet to protect her. Zeuxis tried to appear casual, though he could feel invisible talons gripping his throat.

"That's it. It's coming free at last... Concentrate, Ahwere! Then we'll see what this thing is meant to do."

Zeuxis could not breathe. The rug tipped under him and the room spun. The grip on his throat tightened.

The nail came out with a loud pop, and Lady Wernero quickly dropped it into the brazier. As the flames flared up around it, the invisible talons left Zeuxis' throat. He spluttered, coughed, sucked in a breath that felt like swallowing sand, and threw up over the priceless Persian rug.

Lady Wernero did not notice. She snatched the unrolled curse from Ahwere and frowned at the Greek letters scratched into the lead.

Ahwere giggled at Zeuxis' attempts to hide the mess he'd made. "What's the matter, Lighthouse Boy? Can't stomach the smell of a curse being unrolled? I'd have thought your sense of smell was dead after hauling all that muck up your lighthouse every day!"

"Fuel," Zeuxis croaked. He wiped his mouth, unable to explain. He hoped it *had* been the smoke.

Lady Wernero's eyes widened as she finished reading the curse. She looked thoughtfully at Zeuxis. "So, you just happened to 'find' this in the Hippodrome? Yet live curses are notoriously difficult to find once they've been buried – that's the whole idea, or the rival charioteers would just avoid them. I don't suppose you happened to see who planted this thing?"

Zeuxis wondered how much to tell her. Looking into the witch's black eyes, he decided on the truth.

"I think it was Prince Ptolemy, Lady."

Ahwere stared at him with new respect. "You saw Queen Cleopatra's brother plant a curse in the Hippodrome, and you *dug it up*?"

A nervous giggle rose in Zeuxis' throat. He swallowed. Put like that, it did sound a rather stupid thing to do.

Lady Wernero nodded, as if the news didn't surprise her. "Then you were more than lucky to get here alive. Are you sure no one saw you?"

"I don't think so," Zeuxis said, turning cold at the thought that the Macedonian guards might have been watching him. "The prince left pretty sharpish."

"Mmm, maybe. But they'll know soon enough that someone dug it up, when it fails to work as it should next race day. You're playing a dangerous game, Lighthouse Boy – and don't give me that old story about wanting to save horses' lives. Plenty of horses die and chariots crash without curses to help them on their way. What do you want in return?"

Zeuxis sighed. Was he so transparent? "I need something," he said. "A favour."

"Ah, now we come to it! Spit it out, Lighthouse Boy. What can I do for you? A spell to make your donkey trot faster? Or one to make the Pharos' fire burn brighter, so you don't need to haul so much muck up the ramp? Or perhaps a love charm?" Again, that sly look, directed at her granddaughter this time.

It was Ahwere's turn to blush.

Zeuxis straightened his shoulders. "If you're just going to make fun of me, then I'm going home."

"What's the favour, Lighthouse Boy? Quick! Before I change my mind."

Zeuxis wet his lips. The witch knew him too well. All the way back from the Hippodrome, he'd been thinking about what the curse might be worth. "I want... I want a spell to make one of the queen's charioteers ill while he's training in the park," he said. "Nothing too bad, mind! Just so he needs someone to drive his team back to the stables."

"That someone being you, I suppose?" Lady Wernero asked with a sigh. "I wondered what you'd come up with next in your quest for fame and fortune."

Ahwere laughed out loud. "Be serious, Zeuxis! Racehorses aren't as easy to handle as donkeys, you know!"

"I know that." Zeuxis blushed again. But Ahwere's ridicule just made him more determined. "I know I can do it. I just need a chance to show people I can. Please, Lady Wernero? Just a small spell. It'd be easy for you, and if I show the queen's Master of Horse I can drive a chariot, then maybe he'll let me train with the other boys when my work at the lighthouse is finished for the day, and then maybe one day I'll get a chance to…"

"Race in the Hippodrome," Lady Wernero finished for him with another sigh.

"I'm good enough! I know I am! Plenty of slave-boys start out driving chariots. And when they win, they earn their freedom."

The old woman shook her head. "Have you any idea how long those boys train for? They're riding chariots before they can walk, learning the balance of it. Their fathers and their grandfathers drove chariots. It's in their blood. They don't just take anyone."

"It's in mine, too!" Zeuxis insisted. "Or why do I dream of doing it so much? My father could just as easily have been a charioteer as anything else. Anyway, the boys can't train for that long, because when they grow up they get too heavy. Most of the drivers aren't much older than me."

Ahwere had stopped laughing. She knew the story of how Zeuxis had been abandoned as a baby on the Pharos steps and raised by the Keeper as a lighthouse boy, but he could tell by her face that she thought it unlikely his father had ever driven chariots.

"Most of them don't *get* to be any older than you," she said. "They get trampled to death beneath the hooves of their team, or crushed by the wheels of a following chariot, and that's the end of their dreams! I thought you knew that better than anyone, collecting up the wrecks as you do."

Zeuxis raised his chin, determined.

"I know it's dangerous. I know the risks. But I don't want to be a lighthouse boy all my life. There's this old man who works with the donkeys. He's been doing it for fifty years... *fifty*! I'd go mad. I'd rather be trampled to death in a race in the Hippodrome tomorrow, than still be dragging Cleo and her cartloads of muck up the lighthouse ramp when I'm fifty! It's so OLD."

Lady Wernero smiled. "I'm fifty-three. It doesn't feel so old when you get there, young man, believe me, and you might be surprised how appealing working with muck can seem when you're about to be run over by a chariot." But she re-rolled the curse, shut it away in a box, and rummaged in a corner of the room.

"You're not going to give him the spell?" Ahwere said, alarmed.

"He's brought us a very powerful curse. At the very least, we can trade some of its magic for another Persian carpet to replace the one he's just ruined."

Ahwere shook her black hair. "But Zeuxis can't handle racehorses! It's crazy."

"Then he'll find out, won't he?" Lady Wernero thrust a twist of papyrus into Zeuxis' hand and gave her granddaughter a stern look. "And I don't want you interfering when he uses this, understand?"

Ahwere pulled a face. She tried to talk Zeuxis out of his plan, describing all the terrible injuries that could happen to a charioteer. Zeuxis closed his ears, slipped the spell into his pocket, and headed for the door.

"Don't you even want to know what Prince Ptolemy's curse says?" Ahwere called after him, angry now.

"No, I don't!" Suddenly, all he wanted was to get out of the house and its choking purple smoke, away from the god of the dead, the stuffed crocodile, and the sly black eyes of the Egyptian witch and her granddaughter.

"Well, *I* want to! It says— Ow!" She sucked her fingers as her grandmother slammed the lid of the box and tucked it under her arm so Ahwere could not try to open it again.

All the way down the alley, the back of Zeuxis' neck prickled. Lady Wernero's spells always worked. He didn't have any worries on that score, even though he'd never dared ask her for one before. But... that invisible hand at his throat. Had he been imagining things? Or had the curse somehow touched him as it unrolled, despite Lady Wernero's precautions? And Ahwere! Did she really care what happened to him, or did she just think he was useless, like everyone else seemed to? It wasn't fair.

Just because he was an orphan, forced to work with donkeys all hours of the day and night, didn't mean he wasn't good enough to be a racing driver. But now he'd finally have a chance to show them, show them all.

Leaping bravely into the runaway chariot, he gathered up the reins and brought the royal team around the exercise track at a perfect hand-canter. He stopped the chariot with a salute in front of the queen's Master of Horse, who smiled in relief and clapped Zeuxis on the back, praising his courage and skill...

His dream evaporated as he reached the place where he'd left the donkey. Cleo was still waiting patiently as donkeys do. But the cart was empty. Someone had stolen every last piece of precious wreckage Zeuxis had been sent to collect for the Pharos' fire.

The demon wakes to avenge one who has been wronged

The human world again!

They think they can summon a demon whenever they like, as if we do not have more important things to do. But I admit this particular curse looks more imaginative than most. Perhaps it is worthy of my attention?

The problem is how to proceed. Gone are the days when a demon could simply blast in and destroy whole cities. Even the chariot wreck will not be easy, since the curse is no longer buried beneath the track where chariots race. What the curse is doing here in the Egyptian Quarter, I have no idea. But humans are peculiar at the best of times, and the foolish boy who dug it up might well prove useful. Of those who touched the curse tonight, he is the least protected against magic.

Chapter 3

SPELL

THE FAMOUS PHAROS lighthouse of Alexandria stood on a rocky island to the west of the bay, linked to the city by a sea wall seven stadia in length called the Heptastadion. The lighthouse had three tiers. The lower levels, where the boys and donkeys lived and the fuel was stored, had been cut into the rock and were underground. On top of these sat a square tower with round windows, where the Keeper had his rooms. A ramp spiralled up the centre for the donkey carts. The round upper section housed the winch mechanism that lifted fuel to the fire at the top. Mirrors and sheets of glass reflected the firelight far out to sea, warning ships off the rocks and guiding them into safe harbour – but only as long as the fire received constant fuel, which was not always easy in a country where trees were so scarce.

For being careless enough to lose his entire load to thieves, Zeuxis suffered three lashes of the whip and was confined to duties in the tomb-like buildings beneath the lighthouse until he proved he could be trusted again. The Keeper shook his head sadly as he ordered the punishment. He had the scarred hands and cheeks of one who had fed the fire as a boy, and took every mistake very seriously.

During the next seven days Zeuxis fretted at his duties. He patted the muck from the royal stables into cakes and set them to dry in the sun. He groomed Cleo and harnessed her for old Aelian to take out on fuel-collection duty. Worst of all, he knelt in the small space behind the mirrors at the top of the lighthouse with boys half his age, working the winch and feeding the flames. His cheeks blistered from the heat, the whip cuts on his back stung when his sweat ran into them, and he stank all the time. But, desperate to get off the island, he worked twice as hard as the others and did not complain. He was afraid Lady Wernero's spell would run out of power if he didn't get a chance to use it soon.

On the eighth day, the Keeper relented. When he rang the gong to wake the boys in the grey time before dawn, he beckoned Zeuxis across. "I want you to take Cleo to the royal stables this morning," he ordered. "Aelian's back is playing up, so you're on muck collection duty until further notice."

Zeuxis could barely hide his grin.

The Keeper gave him a sharp look. "That doesn't mean you get to collect the fuel from the Hippodrome, even if there are ten wrecks next race day! You still have to earn back that trust."

Zeuxis bowed his head. "Yes, Master. I understand."

He began to back away, fingering the spell he kept in his pocket day and night. But the Keeper touched his shoulder, forbidding him to leave.

"Ah, Zeuxis," he said, his stern tone gentling. "I know it's hard to be a slave, and the hardest time is when you grow from boyhood to manhood. I punish you for your own good – you realize that, don't you? It's thirteen years since I found you on the lighthouse steps, and one day the Pharos will need a new Keeper. Someone who knows the routine and will keep the fire burning through peace and war, famine and plenty. The Pharos lighthouse gives Alexandria her power. Without its light to guide ships safely into harbour, Queen Cleopatra would be ruling an Egypt without trade, and without trade from across the Mediterranean we would be nothing but a collection of Egyptian fishing villages like those Great Alexander found here three hundred years ago, when he built our fine city. You're one of my brightest boys. I don't want to lose you to the lures of Alexandria's darker side."

Zeuxis froze. *He can't know about the Egyptian Quarter, he can't! He must think I left the cart unattended to join one of the parties.* He made himself take a long, slow breath.

The Keeper lowered his hand with a smile. He seemed to think Zeuxis' reaction was the shock of hearing that he was being groomed for the position of next Keeper of the Pharos – which it was a bit. He'd always assumed that the Keeper had to be of pure Macedonian blood, and that an orphan of unknown parentage didn't stand a chance of ever being more than a slave. But his moment of pride was short lived. How could he be Keeper of the Pharos if he was going to be a racing chariot driver?

"The temptation won't be there in the daytime," the Keeper said. "So bring me back a good load of fuel from the royal stables. The queen's horses should be eating well at the moment, with the next race tomorrow."

Zeuxis had not counted on the next race being so soon. But he'd been on the island for seven days, and the fun-loving citizens of Alexandria didn't like to wait too long for another dose of their favourite entertainment.

"Today," he whispered to Cleo, as he led the donkey along the waterfront past the fishermen landing their catch, while the sea was still silver and magical with the dawn. "They won't be exercising the horses in the park tomorrow, so we'll have to use Lady Wernero's spell today."

The donkey huffed at him, as if to ask where he'd been over the past week. Zeuxis pulled her ear in apology. He didn't feel ready to drive his first ever chariot, and he dreaded to think what his punishment would be if he lost the load of fuel this time. But it had to be today, because tomorrow was race day, when the curse he'd dug out of the Hippodrome wouldn't work as those who had planted it expected. Someone might start making enquiries, which would ruin his chances.

For the first time, he wondered if he might have ruined Prince Ptolemy's chances in the race by digging up the curse. He felt a bit guilty, but only a bit.

"I need magic more than Prince Ptolemy does, don't I, Cleo?" Zeuxis muttered. "He's rich and he's got an army to look after him. I'm poor and I'm a slave. All I've got is my wits."

And a spell bought with a stolen curse.

Stop thinking about it, Zeuxis! he told himself firmly, not realizing he had come so far across the waterfront. The sentries at the gates of the royal stables gave him a strange look. But there were advantages to being the lighthouse boy. They already thought him a bit mad.

Zeuxis hurried Cleo around the back of the stables, where the muck got thrown out. It was nearly sunrise. He'd have to load up quickly, or he'd miss the chariots going out to exercise. Already, he could hear the first teams being harnessed in the yard, neighing and stamping their hooves, while the grooms shouted at them to behave.

At least Cleo was behaving herself. She liked coming to the royal stables, where she could snatch mouthfuls of the best hay, or grain from the manger of an empty stall. He grabbed a pitchfork and helped the queen's grooms load the cart, working as fast as he could and keeping one ear cocked for the rumble of chariot wheels in the yard.

"Hey, slow down, Lighthouse Boy!" a groom called Dameos said with a laugh. "You'll do yourself an injury! Where've you been skiving to, anyway? We've had that old grump who's bin working the lighthouse for ever, over here collectin' our muck."

He meant old Aelian. And Dameos was right. Fifty years was for ever.

Zeuxis grunted something about being sick and kept forking. He liked Dameos. The boy was always cheerful, whistling as he worked. Sometimes they'd sneak off together to taste some of the fizzy beer the grooms made with the leftover barley from their horses' mangers. But he had more important things to do today.

"You are in a strange mood today, aren't you?" Dameos said. "What's wrong? Get another beatin'?"

Zeuxis straightened before the boy could see the whip scars under his tunic. "That team going out," he said, pointing to four black stallions pawing the yard and snorting at the groom who held their heads. "Who drives them, usually?"

Dameos laughed again. "You want to keep away from *that* team, Lighthouse Boy! Those horses are crazy. Didn't you collect the big wreck, last race day? Only one of the horses survived, and he's completely mad – the big stallion on the right. See his eye rolling? He hasn't forgotten the crash yet, probably never will. The others are new, youngsters who haven't been tried. They're meant to be fully race-trained, according to the trader who sold 'em to us, but if you believe that you'll believe anything. They're right wild in the stables. The queen's champion charioteer is comin' down to try 'em out in the park. That is, if he ever turns up. We all reckon he's still in the palace, changing his underwear."

The other grooms chuckled.

Zeuxis gripped his fork harder and sneaked another look at the waiting chariot. The sensible thing would be to work Lady Wernero's spell on one of the charioteers driving a well-trained, docile team. But those blacks... they were beautiful. They were wild. They were exactly like his dream. They were youngsters fighting their harness, like him.

The Pharos *would* need another Keeper one day. But right now, Zeuxis had more important things on his mind.

He closed his eyes and sent a silent prayer to the gods. Then he untied Cleo and clucked his tongue to get her moving.

"Hey!" Dameos said. "Where are you going? We haven't finished loading you up yet."

"Poor Cleo's got quite enough to drag up the lighthouse ramp," Zeuxis said. "You must have mucked out extra well this morning."

Zeuxis got Cleo as far as the park gates by holding a handful of sweet-smelling hay in front of her nose. Once she was inside, he let her eat it and promised her lots of lush grass if she behaved herself. Cleo blinked at him, as if in disapproval. But she didn't argue.

He led the donkey further into the park. Several chariots were already on the practice circuit, which had been raked overnight by slaves. Everything looked orderly. The horses arched their necks and trotted with a springy step. The charioteers smiled and called out jokes to one another. A sea mist curled around the horses' hooves.

Then, with a wild neigh and a rattle of hooves, the blacks cantered past Zeuxis and through the gates with their heads in the air and their mouths wide open, fighting their bits. The charioteer looked quite a bit older than the other race drivers. He was obviously used to being obeyed, for he yelled at Zeuxis to keep "that stupid donkey" out of the way and lashed out at them with his whip as he barged past, making Cleo throw up her head and snort.

Almost wishing he had asked Lady Wernero for a more serious spell, Zeuxis untwisted the papyrus and – his heart banging – threw it into the chariot as it drew away from him.

The queen's champion did not notice. He was having too much trouble with the blacks, who had seen the wide open space and the other chariots ahead of them. The wild-eyed stallion kept going off to one side, fighting his traces. The three colts were better matched, but upset by the stallion. Even Zeuxis could tell they were hardly race-trained. The chariot disappeared behind some trees and emerged on the other side ahead of the one it had been following, going at a fast canter.

Was the spell working? Or was the queen's champion just having a bad day?

The grooms lined up at the park fence to watch, grinning. The other charioteers trotted their teams off the track, out of harm's way. Now only the blacks were going round, faster and faster, their coats covered in white foam. Their driver's furious face passed Zeuxis in a blur. He'd dropped his whip somewhere round the back curve. He still had control, of a sort, but he didn't look as if he could stop in a hurry.

"What did I tell you?" Dameos called, winking at Zeuxis. "That'll bring old Clytius down a bit. Uh oh, look sharp. The queen's coming, and it looks like she's got the Roman envoy with her. *Now* there's going to be trouble!"

The grooms melted back into the stables as the glittering gates of the palace swung open. A troop of soldiers in the uniform of the Royal Macedonian Guard marched out, followed by a line of slave girls strewing rose petals on the path. A battle-scarred but dashingly handsome officer in Roman uniform came next, laughing at something the queen had said.

Zeuxis clutched Cleo's rein. *Forget it*, he thought. *Just take the fuel back to the lighthouse and forget the whole thing.*

The spell had probably dropped out round the back. He'd have to come and look for it later, when the chariots had gone. Except now a cordon of Royal Macedonian

Guard blocked the way to the waterfront so that the common citizens on the quay could not approach their queen. Trapped, Zeuxis led the donkey behind the trees. He clenched his fists, which were suddenly sweating with tension.

The gods must mean him to be here, after all. Either that or they meant to punish him for meddling with the prince's curse.

Zeuxis hadn't seen Queen Cleopatra in years, and then only at a distance as she rode through the city. She'd still been a girl then. Now she was definitely a woman. She emerged on foot, accompanied by a host of slaves carrying huge, ostrich-feather fans to keep her cool and fringed parasols to shade her pale skin from the sun. She wore a white dress that reminded him of Ahwere's, set off by a collar of blue, red and green. A black wig covered her pale Macedonian hair, braided into a hundred plaits and fastened with silver bells that tinkled as she walked. Her eyes had been lined with kohl, and her cheeks stained with berry juice. Whatever Ahwere said, the Queen of Egypt was very beautiful.

The queen watched her chariot thunder past with narrow eyes.

"What do you think, Mark Anthony?" she said to the Roman, who was also watching the horses with interest. "Faster than any of Caesar's horses, I bet."

"But rather out of control, Your Majesty," the envoy pointed out.

Queen Cleopatra frowned at her Master of Horse, who had been supervising the training session. "I thought you said Clytius could manage them?"

The Master of Horse cleared his throat. He looked uncomfortable. "I'd hoped the stallion would calm the colts' enthusiasm, Your Majesty, but the wreck must have affected him more than I thought. We'll obviously have to try a steadier horse with them and sacrifice some speed... BRING THEM IN NOW, CLYTIUS!" he bellowed as the chariot galloped past for the second time.

This had no effect on the speed of the chariot. With a pang of guilt, Zeuxis noticed that Clytius was holding his stomach and trying to control his runaway team with just one hand. The spell had not fallen out, after all.

Queen Cleopatra laughed. She stood on tiptoe and whispered something in the Roman envoy's ear.

He smiled and said, "I think your champion is suffering from more than bad wine, Your Majesty. The man looks ill to me."

"I agree with Mark Anthony, Your Majesty," said the Master of Horse, giving the envoy a grateful look. "My advice is that you scratch this team from tomorrow's race and enter the greys instead."

The queen laughed. "Oh, don't be such a spoilsport! Let me have a *little* fun. Lots of teams run away in the excitement of the Hippodrome. They'll still beat my brother Ptolemy's horses. They'll be fine."

The Master of Horse said stiffly, "If you run those blacks in the Hippodrome tomorrow, Your Majesty, they'll never run again, and nor will half the other horses in the race. There'll be enough wrecks to keep the Pharos supplied with fuel for the remainder of your reign."

"I'm your queen, remember?" Cleopatra said softly, giving the envoy a wink. "You have to do what I order you to, and I want to show Mark Anthony what Caesar will be up against if he insists on sending his horses to race in Alexandria's Hippodrome."

"And I'm your Master of Horse. When it comes to the safety of the horses you placed in my care, *you* listen to *me*, Your Majesty," the Master of Horse insisted. Before the queen could protest, he climbed the fence and yelled at the champion charioteer, who was going round for the third time, "PULL YOURSELF TOGETHER, CLYTIUS! I SAID BRING THEM IN!"

Queen Cleopatra frowned after the vanishing chariot, and Mark Anthony hid a smile.

"In my opinion, that man of yours Clytius is too old for racing," he said in a low tone. "Maybe you ought to consider retiring him?"

"He's still the best," Cleopatra insisted. "I know what you're up to, Mark Anthony. Convince me to retire my champion, so that Caesar's team will have more of a chance – I'm not stupid."

"Then you should stop inviting Clytius to your parties. Everyone knows when charioteers start drinking as much as he does, it's because they've lost their nerve."

The queen smiled and fluttered her eyelids. "Clytius hasn't lost his nerve yet. And if I stopped inviting men to my parties, I'd have no fun at all... would I, Mark Anthony?" Her voice softened, bringing a flush to the envoy's cheeks.

The guards were trying to ignore the way their young queen was flirting with the Roman envoy. Some of them watched the runaway chariot. Others watched the ships sailing out past the Pharos, their faces impassive. They were alert for a possible attack on the royal party by Prince Ptolemy's men, but none of them seemed to consider the lighthouse boy, hovering in the corner of the park with his donkey and cartload of muck, to be much of a threat.

It was now or never. With trembling hands, Zeuxis tied Cleo's rein to a tree and left her grazing. He slipped through the bushes to the far side of the park, his mouth dry with excitement and terror. There was another audience down this end – curious members of the public, who had heard the commotion and come to see what was happening. The other charioteers walked their teams up and down while they waited for the circuit to be cleared. They seemed to be enjoying the spectacle of the queen's prize charioteer made to look a fool.

Clytius was in a bad way. He flopped over the front of his chariot, making little attempt to do much except keep the horses from crashing into trees. The exercise chariot was more solid than a racing one or it would surely have turned over by now. The horses were getting tired, and the slack reins actually did him a favour. Without him hauling at their mouths, they calmed down a bit and dropped back to a trot.

Lady Wernero's spell couldn't have worked more perfectly. As the chariot came abreast of Zeuxis, Clytius toppled gently out the side into the grass. The horses sprang forwards again with the unexpected change in weight. Before he had time to think about it too much, Zeuxis ran alongside them, judged the distance, and jumped in.

He gathered up the reins, his heart pounding so hard he was sure the horses would sense his terror and play him up. But he'd driven stubborn donkeys for so long, the reins felt natural in his hands. By the time he'd reached the trees, his nerves had steadied. Gently, he took up the pressure of the horses' mouths. At first the platform felt strange, jolting under his feet. But he'd imagined this so often during his nightly visits to the Hippodrome, he soon gained his balance.

Feet spread... legs slightly apart... knees bent... reins taut... the horses leant against his hands and used his weight to balance themselves. The stallion was pulling off to the side still, but the colts were listening to him.

Zeuxis tightened the stallion's rein a little and called to the horses in a soothing voice. "There, I've got you, steady, steady round the turn, that's it, you're all right, I won't let you fall..."

The words were nonsense, but it didn't matter. The colts' ears flickered back to catch the sound of his voice, and the stallion gradually calmed and arched his neck and snorted. Zeuxis' mouth stretched into a grin. He raised his chin, feeling the wind in his hair, the powerful horses tugging at his arms, the chariot alive beneath his feet. It was every bit as wonderful as his dream, and more. The trees became the marble pillars of the Hippodrome. The track shimmered and turned into the famous racecourse.

The finish post flashed past in a wild surge of cheering, and he drove the black team on a victory lap, smiling and waving at the crowd as they threw rose petals into his hair—

The horses shied as the chariot jerked sideways, nearly throwing him out. Zeuxis stumbled against the front plate, bruising his knees, as the queen's Master of Horse grabbed the stallion's bit with a thunderous expression on his face. He hadn't realized he'd driven so far so quickly. The colts skittered to a halt, blowing and snorting as they recognized their master's smell.

Zeuxis' nerves returned with the enormity of what he'd done.

"Get out of that chariot at once, Boy!" roared the Master of Horse. "What do you think you're trying to do? These are the queen's most valuable racehorses!"

Zeuxis untangled himself from the reins and staggered off the platform, his cheeks burning. His knees wobbled and his arms were trembling. He'd driven half a circuit of the park at a mere trot, and he could barely stand!

But this was the chance he'd been waiting for. All his life.

With an effort, he stood straighter. "I… er… the charioteer fell out round the back, and I thought they would bolt, so I just thought I'd bring them round to you. I'm sorry, Sir, I didn't mean any harm."

The Master of Horse frowned and gave him a closer look. "You just thought you'd bring them round…? Who are you? I don't remember seeing you training with the other boys."

"Zeuxis, Sir."

"I didn't ask your name. I asked who you are."

"He's the lighthouse boy, Sir," one of the guards called. "Comes to collect the muck from the stables." He nodded to the cart Zeuxis had abandoned.

"An islander." The Master of Horse lost interest and flicked a hand at the guards. "Get the boy out of here. He shouldn't be allowed to hang around the royal park like this."

"But Sir! I thought if I proved I could drive them, you would—"

The Master of Horse was already in the chariot, trotting the subdued black team round the circuit to pick up Clytius, the muscles in his back bulging as he held the horses in check.

"Please!" Zeuxis protested as one of the guards put a hand on his arm. "Let me stay a bit longer. I want to tell your queen something. It's very important."

Queen Cleopatra, who had been giggling at something Mark Anthony had said, turned her attention to Zeuxis. She looked him up and down with a haughty expression, reminding him a bit of Ahwere. "Well?"

Desperate, Zeuxis said the one thing that might interest her.

"Y-Your Majesty," he stammered. "I think I know what made your charioteer ill."

The queen glanced at the envoy. "You know what's wrong with Clytius?"

"Not exactly, but I think I know why it happened."

Mark Anthony watched this exchange with an amused expression.

Queen Cleopatra scowled as she realized how unregal it looked to be seen talking to a common slave-boy. "Is this some sort of joke?" she snapped. "Will someone get this boy and his donkey out of my park before I lose my temper."

"A curse, Your Majesty!" Zeuxis shouted, as the guard took his arm again. "I saw your brother Prince Ptolemy plant a curse in the Hippodrome!"

The guards were hustling him away. But the queen's head swung round so fast, the bells at the end of her plaits jingled. She told Mark Anthony to go on ahead to the palace, then ordered the guards to bring Zeuxis to her. "When did you see my brother?" she hissed.

"I... ah... saw him plant a curse in the Hippodrome, Your Majesty."

"So you said. I'm not deaf. When?"

"After last race day, when I was clearing up the wrecks."

The queen frowned and glanced at the park, where her Master of Horse was returning with the sick charioteer. "Mmm, I wondered... it's not like Clytius to lose control of a team, whatever Mark Anthony might say. So! My brother has decided to play me at my own game, has he? Well, we'll see about that." She beckoned to her slave girls, and hurried to catch up with the Roman envoy.

"But, Your Majesty!" Zeuxis called after her. "If there is a curse, shouldn't we at least warn your Master of Horse about it?"

Cleopatra gave him an amused look over her shoulder. "You're already in quite enough trouble with my Master of Horse, as it is. You were extremely fortunate my prize blacks didn't run away with you and injure themselves."

"But I only wanted to help. See, I want to train as a charioteer, and—"

The queen laughed. "Go find my brother, then. He may need someone to race his donkeys!"

The slave girls giggled and even some of the Royal Guard smiled.

"Save your breath, Boy," said the guard who had hold of his elbow. "And thank your stars the queen didn't order you thrown into prison for interfering with her best racehorses in front of the Roman envoy like that."

Zeuxis had no choice but to let the guard escort him and the donkey back along the waterfront. It was only when he was dragging Cleo across the Heptastadion to the island that he realized he'd forgotten to retrieve Lady Wernero's used spell from the chariot.

"It didn't even work, Cleo!" he whispered, tears filling his eyes. "I drove that team, and the Master of Horse saw me, but it still didn't do any good! I'll be a lighthouse boy for ever!"

Chapter 4

PRINCE PTOLEMY

AS HE WENT about his lighthouse duties, Zeuxis replayed over and over in his head what had happened in the park. He should have thought it through more carefully. He should have told the Master of Horse about the curse he'd seen Prince Ptolemy plant in the Hippodrome. Then maybe the queen would have taken him more seriously. Instead – idiot! – he had left Lady Wernero's spell in the chariot where the grooms were sure to find it. He'd be in a lot of trouble if someone had seen him throw the spell at Clytius and realized what it was.

The queen had seemed interested enough when he'd mentioned her brother, but he should have realized the Queen of Egypt would be too high and mighty to talk to a mere lighthouse boy. Did he dare try to talk to the Roman envoy, Mark Anthony? What would he say to him, if he did?

For the first time in his life, Zeuxis wished he'd paid more attention when the Keeper tried to teach them about politics. He knew that a few years ago Queen Cleopatra had refused to marry her brother Prince Ptolemy (which the Egyptian priests said she must do if she wanted to be crowned Pharaoh), and had thrown him out of the palace. Prince Ptolemy had taken his bodyguard to start his own army, leaving Cleopatra with the rest of the Macedonian Guard in the royal palace across the harbour. Cleopatra named herself Queen of Egypt, ignoring the fact that under Egyptian law she had to share the throne with her husband-brother, and the two had been at each other's throats ever since. If Cleopatra had really bewitched the Roman envoy, as Ahwere claimed, then he bet she was doing it for some political reason.

Maybe he *should* ask Prince Ptolemy if he needed a driver? Except he had no idea where to find the prince, and now he wasn't even allowed out to the Hippodrome until he'd won back the Keeper's trust.

Why did he always make such a mess of things?

Anxious about Lady Wernero's spell, Zeuxis completed his chores as quickly as he could, hoping to be early for evening stables, when the royal grooms would clean the stalls again and provide a second load of muck to be dried into fuel for the lighthouse. Even so, the sun was sinking into red clouds over the western harbour by the time he dragged Cleo and her cart back across the Heptastadion.

"Come on, come on!" he muttered, tugging impatiently at the donkey's rein – not the right way to persuade a donkey to cooperate. Cleo brayed in protest, stuck out her head and planted her hooves.

"*Move,* you stubborn thing!" Zeuxis shouted. "Or I'm going to be in a lot of trouble, and not just with the Keeper this time—"

"That's no way for a charioteer to treat his team," said a quiet voice behind him.

Zeuxis whirled, his heart thudding. He had to look twice at the cloaked figure standing against the low sun. "Ahwere!"

The Egyptian girl smiled and stroked the donkey's neck. "Who were you expecting? The queen's Master of Horse? I saw you this morning in the park with those wild black horses."

Zeuxis scowled. "I suppose you were watching for me to make a fool of myself so you could have a good laugh."

"Grandmother only forbade me to interfere. She didn't say I couldn't watch. Actually, she sent me to look out for you. She got worried that someone might have confiscated the spell she gave you, and then she said you must have got scared and decided not to use it. But I knew you would try eventually. What kept you?"

Zeuxis thought of the weals on his back. He shrugged – carefully. "Keeper gave me other duties. I have to do what I'm told, and now I'm late. If I don't get this load of muck back on time, I won't be allowed to collect the wrecks from the Hippodrome." *And that'll be worse than a whipping.* "If I do a good job, maybe he'll let me go out there tomorrow night, after the races."

Ahwere looked sideways at him. "So, you haven't heard?"

Zeuxis' heart thudded again. "Heard what?"

"Tomorrow's races have been cancelled. Some vandals broke into the Hippodrome this afternoon and dug up the course. It's a real mess, holes everywhere. Strange thing is, even though it was broad daylight, the guards claim they didn't see who did it." She gave him another sideways look.

"It wasn't me, if that's that you're thinking," Zeuxis said quickly. "I'm in enough trouble as it is."

"Maybe more than you think."

"What do you mean?"

Zeuxis' voice rose. The night fishermen, preparing their nets and lanterns on the quay, gave Ahwere curious looks. They were not used to seeing the lighthouse boy with anyone, let alone a girl.

Ahwere leant across the donkey's neck and whispered, "Grandmother thinks she's seen a ka-demon."

Zeuxis wet his lips. He hardly dared ask. "What's a… *ka-demon*?" The Egyptian word felt strange on his tongue.

"It's an ancient spirit of our ancestors. Thousands of years ago when the pyramids were built, people were supposed to be able to talk to them. They don't show themselves much these days."

"Ha!" Zeuxis said, though he shivered. The sun had gone down and the Egyptian night wrapped them in eerie purple shadows. "Your ghost stories don't frighten me."

Ahwere pulled the donkey to a stop, a little frown between her dark eyes. "You believed in Grandmother's spell, or you wouldn't have been able to use it. So you must believe in ghosts. Some people say it's the kas of our ancestors that make curses come true."

Zeuxis thought of those invisible talons at his throat when Prince Ptolemy's curse had unrolled. He shivered again. As if he didn't have enough to worry about.

As if she'd read his mind, Ahwere continued, "Grandmother thinks the curse we unrolled summoned it. She's going to try to send it back to the spirit world, but she says you should be extremely careful over the next few days, just in case."

"In case of what?" Zeuxis said, a bit alarmed despite the fact he didn't really believe in Ahwere's demons. Spells were one thing. Ancient Egyptian ghosts, quite another. Except for what had happened when that curse had unrolled... no! He had been imagining things that night. Anyone would have done in the witch's house at midnight.

The girl frowned again. "I don't know. Grandmother wouldn't say. She just said to warn you. But I don't think that curse was worded simply to make a rival chariot crash. She won't tell me what it says, and now she's hidden it somewhere. I'll have to wait until she goes out before I can find it and sneak a look."

The mention of chariots reminded Zeuxis of the spell he'd used on Clytius. He wet his lips. "Ahwere... we might have something else to worry about. I, er, threw your grandmother's spell in the chariot this morning, and with all the excitement I forgot to get it back again—"

"Oh, that!" The girl dug something out from under her cloak.

Zeuxis let out his breath in relief as he recognized the crumpled piece of papyrus, muddied with half a hoofprint.

"Good job someone's looking out for you," Ahwere continued with a smile. "It fell out in the park. Got no power left now, of course, but I'll take it home anyway. These things are best burnt after use, so people don't start asking awkward questions. You'd best get going."

They had reached the Gate of the Moon, which guarded the main road into the city from the waterfront. Before she headed through it, Ahwere paused to give him another of her sideways looks. "It wasn't your fault the queen's Master of Horse wouldn't listen to you this morning. You drove that chariot better than their champion did."

Zeuxis walked on air the rest of the way to the royal stables. He didn't even shout at Cleo when, passing the park gates, the donkey shied at a rustle in the shadows and trod on his toe.

Dameos was waiting for him at the muck heap. "Are you *crazy*, Lighthouse Boy?" he hissed as they forked the royal dung into Cleo's cart. "What did you think you were doing, driving Clytius' blacks this morning? The Master was furious when he brought them in. Checked them over himself. If there had been one tiny cut..."

"But he didn't find any cuts on them, did he?" Zeuxis said, smiling, still warm inside from Ahwere's compliment.

He'd driven the queen's chariot better than Clytius had.

"No." Dameos gave him a funny look. "That's the strange thing. I expected him to be down here tonight to give you a piece of his mind, but he's up in the palace with the Roman envoy, comparing notes on different training methods. And tomorrow's races have been cancelled, anyway, so it doesn't matter that Clytius is sick. Some idiot dug—"

"—holes in the Hippodrome. I know."

Dameos stopped forking muck and frowned at him. "Lighthouse Boy, this is serious stuff. You don't realize how much we need to win next race day. Prince Ptolemy's Greens won last time after our chariot got wrecked. Every time the Greens win, more people go over to the prince's side. There's no way he'd beat the queen's army in battle, of course, but getting enough supporters on his side here in the city could cause a riot. You're probably too young to remember, but last time we had a serious riot, half the city was destroyed and thousands died in the fighting before the Guard restored order."

Zeuxis gave his friend a calculating look. "That must have been before you were born, as well."

Dameos flushed. "Well, I heard it from the other grooms…"

Zeuxis laughed. "Sure it wasn't the *whole* city, and that the people weren't killed by ka-demons?"

"By what?" Dameos said.

"Never mind. Just help me load this muck so I can get out of here."

Zeuxis whistled as he completed the loading. He wasn't worried. Actually, he half hoped the queen's Master of Horse *would* come to tell him off. Now he had spoken to the Roman envoy and been given a chance to consider Zeuxis' skill with the black team, perhaps he regretted missing his chance to train Zeuxis as a charioteer. But no one came.

Zeuxis sneaked a look into the stables on his way out and saw the black stallion that had caused all the trouble in the team this morning staring out into the night with rigid neck and pricked ears, barley spilling from the corners of his mouth.

"Don't worry, lad," he whispered, feeling a pang of sympathy for the horse as he remembered the hoof he'd found in the Hippodrome. "You don't have to race tomorrow."

It was fully dark by the time the guards let him out of the palace complex. Clouds hid the stars, but the harbour gleamed with the reflections of torches burning along the waterfront. In the distance on its island, the Pharos light shone across the sea brighter than them all.

Zeuxis paused at the park gates, smiling as he remembered this morning. He *had* driven well. It hadn't been as easy as he'd thought, and he obviously wasn't fit enough to race yet, but he knew he had connected with the horses. Maybe tomorrow, he'd bring Cleo across early and see if he could talk to the Master of Horse again. Maybe the Master was even thinking of hiring a new boy to replace Clytius and drive for the Blues—

As he was dreaming, two figures in dark cloaks sprang out of the park and grabbed his elbows. Cleo shot sideways, and a clod of muck fell off the top of the cart.

"Hey!" he said, thinking at first that it was Dameos and his friends playing one of their jokes.

The dagger poking into his ribs said otherwise. "No noise, Lighthouse Boy," hissed its owner. "Be sensible, and no one need get hurt."

Zeuxis' knees turned weak as the other man took hold of the donkey's bridle and dragged her round, leading her back towards the Greek Quarter. The men were familiar, and he knew where he had seen them before. They were the two Macedonian bodyguards from the night in the Hippodrome, when he'd dug up Prince Ptolemy's curse.

In his terror, Zeuxis could not think what to do. Did he call for help and risk that dagger slipping between his ribs? Cleo had no such worries. She resisted, clearly thinking of her supper waiting at the other end of the waterfront. The man holding her swore as the rein ripped through his hand.

"Just bring the boy and leave the donkey here," hissed the one with the dagger.

"No!" Zeuxis said, recovering his wits. "You can't just leave the cart out here," he explained, wetting his lips. "Or someone'll steal the load of fuel, and the Pharos' fire will go out."

His captors glanced at each other, and then at the Pharos. They hesitated.

"I'll make her come," Zeuxis said. He reached for Cleo's bridle, only to have his arm jerked back and the dagger poke him harder in the ribs. "I promise I won't make trouble," he added, heart banging. "You work for Prince Ptolemy, don't you?"

"How d'you know that?" growled the man with the dagger.

"Doesn't matter," said the other. "The boy'll know soon enough, anyway. Right, Lighthouse Boy. You lead the donkey nicely, and we don't use force. We don't want to be responsible for the Pharos fire going out. But no tricks, understand? The prince wants to talk to you."

Zeuxis' heart hammered faster. But he allowed the men to escort him into the unlit streets of the Greek Quarter, where the poorer people of Alexandria lived and worked. This could not be coincidence. Perhaps the prince's spies had seen him with the blacks this morning, and been impressed? Perhaps Prince Ptolemy was looking for a new charioteer? They obviously didn't know Zeuxis had been in the Hippodrome when the prince had planted his curse, or they'd have known how he recognized them.

A new variation of his dream took shape in his head, sparked off by the queen's comment this morning that he should ask her brother if he could drive his 'donkeys'. He would persuade Prince Ptolemy to train him as a charioteer. Then, when he beat Clytius and the Blue team in the Hippodrome, it would serve the queen and her Master of Horse right for not listening to him.

"Zeuxis! Zeuxis for the Greens!" roared the crowd as he rounded the final turn three lengths in front, and Prince Ptolemy beamed down at him from the royal box—

The dagger poked him in the ribs again, reminding him he was not a champion charioteer yet.

The prince's men took him to a shabby house built right up against the city wall. There were no torches outside, nothing to show that this was the dwelling of the co-ruler of Alexandria. Zeuxis' nerves returned as he secured Cleo's rein to the post they indicated.

"Someone should stay out here to guard the fuel," he said as his escort took his elbows again.

"Don't push your luck, Lighthouse Boy," they growled. "The prince has his guards, don't you worry."

Zeuxis saw a shadow move at the end of the street, and the glint of a sword in the starlight. He wet his lips again. With the wall towering behind the house, it wasn't going to be easy to get out of here. And now he'd stupidly brought Cleo and her cart along, too. He could hardly change his mind and run now, leaving the donkey behind.

They went up some stairs, past several more cloaked guards, and along a narrow passage into a room with peeling plaster that showed a hunting scene of the marshes. Around the walls, boys in canoes fired arrows at ducks and geese, bordered by fading pictures of lotus flowers. The ceiling had been painted with flying swallows. The shadows cast by the torches made them appear to move, making Zeuxis dizzy.

As he was staring up at the ceiling scene, the boy he'd seen planting the curse in the Hippodrome walked in.

Today, Prince Ptolemy wore a wide collar of blue and red jewels, and a circlet of gold held back his hair. The sword hanging at his belt made him seem very grown-up, though he lacked the muscles to wield it properly.

He looked down his nose at Zeuxis and flicked a hand at the two guards. "Make the slave kneel."

"Kneel before the rightful Pharaoh of Egypt!" growled one of his escort. Not giving Zeuxis any time to argue, he pushed him down with a firm hand.

Zeuxis bit his lip as he bruised his knees on the floor. But he raised his gaze to meet that of the prince and said, "Your Majesty, I—"

"Silence!" said Ptolemy, scowling at Zeuxis. He considered him a moment, then said, "You will answer my questions truthfully, and speak only when you're spoken to. Afterwards, you will not speak of this interview to anyone, or my spies in the city will know, and next time they will take you to a much less pleasant place. Do you understand?"

Zeuxis nodded, his mouth drying again. This wasn't going the way he had hoped.

"Right. Let's begin with what you and my sister spoke about this morning." Prince Ptolemy paced the room as he spoke. "You were seen speaking to her after you stopped her runaway chariot in the park. Quite frankly, I find both of those facts hard to believe. But my spies are usually truthful in these matters, and they tell me my name was mentioned. Well?" He snapped, swinging round on his heel and coming to stand over Zeuxis. "Out with it! I like to know what people are saying about me behind my back."

"I- I asked the queen if I could drive for the Blues," Zeuxis said, annoyed at the way the prince made him nervous enough to stutter. "Her charioteer fell ill…"

"Yes." The prince's lip twitched up at one corner. It was a sneer, rather than a smile. "So I understand. Clytius is too old for the game, anyway. I hear the old fool puts a feather down his throat and throws up his food after he's eaten to keep his weight down. Might as well put our baby brother in charge of her chariot, for all the use old Clytius'll be if he carries on like that! A charioteer needs to be strong as well as light in weight. A baby would probably do better, actually." He laughed at his own joke.

Zeuxis said nothing.

"What else did you talk about?" snapped the prince.

"N-nothing." Zeuxis looked at the floor. That stain on the wood under his knees looked horribly like blood.

"Are you quite certain, Slave?" The prince's sword scraped out of its scabbard and was suddenly – frighteningly – under Zeuxis' chin. "Nothing about the Roman envoy, for example?"

Zeuxis drew a ragged breath. "I d-don't pay much attention to politics, Your Majesty," he said. He did remember the Keeper telling them some stuff about the expanding Roman empire, but Rome was a long way across the sea. Roman politics had nothing to do with Zeuxis' life in the lighthouse or his dream of racing in the Hippodrome, so he hadn't really listened.

The prince scowled. "What about curses, then? You know about *them*, don't you, collecting up the wrecks like you do?"

The guards were quiet behind him. Zeuxis thought of Ahwere, and made himself breathe deeply. In, out, in… "C-curses, Your Majesty?" he said with as much innocence as he could manage. "Is that why you think the queen's charioteer got sick? Did someone plant a curse against him?"

He'd overdone it. Now Prince Ptolemy would cut his throat. But the prince's arm trembled with the effort of holding the heavy sword at such an awkward angle. When he saw Zeuxis had noticed, he jammed the weapon back into its scabbard and settled for giving Zeuxis a hard stare. "I warned you, Lighthouse Boy! I ask the questions, you answer them. So, you told my sister nothing about curses? You just asked to drive for her? And that's how my name came up?"

"Yes, Your Majesty. See, I want to be a charioteer, and I know I can do it if only someone would give me a chance—"

The prince cut him off with a flick of his hand. "And what did Cleopatra say?"

"She said to ask you if I could race your donkeys!" Zeuxis said, straightening his shoulders.

His knees were hurting and he was fed up with being treated like a criminal by a boy only a few years older than him, prince or not. The Keeper never treated his lighthouse slaves like this, not even when they were being disciplined.

One of the guards put a warning hand on his shoulder. But the prince's scowl turned into another cold laugh.

"He has spirit, this lighthouse boy! And it proves he's telling the truth. That's exactly the sort of thing my sister would say. My donkeys, huh? I'll show her, come next race day! My chestnuts are in fine mettle, and they'll be all the better for a few extra days' training. They'll leave that uncontrollable black team of hers standing at the start – if Clytius even gets them as far as the starting gate!"

Zeuxis breathed a bit easier. "Sir, Your Majesty... if you need another driver..."

The prince's scowl returned. "That's enough, Lighthouse Boy. No doubt her prize charioteer's illness explains why my sister had her men dig up the

Hippodrome to postpone tomorrow's races. I expect she hopes to give Clytius a chance to recover. She was probably looking for curses as well, of course, but even if she found what she was looking for, it won't change anything now." He pulled a face at Zeuxis and flicked a hand at the guards. "The boy knows nothing. Take him back where you found him."

"But Your Majesty, I really am good with horses, and—"

"If he says another word, kill him." The prince turned on his heel and walked out of the room.

"Shut up, stupid," muttered one of the guards, pulling Zeuxis roughly to his feet. "You see that bloodstain? That's all what's left of the last man Prince Ptolemy interrogated in here. You're extremely lucky."

Zeuxis looked at the bloodstain and swallowed hard.

Numb, he let the prince's men escort him back outside, where to his relief Cleo and her load of fuel were safely waiting, and back through the dark streets as far as the waterfront. When his escort had melted away into the shadows, his knees wobbled and he had to sit down at the side of the road. He touched his chin where the prince's sword had been, and thought of that final cold order.

If he says another word, kill him.

Though he hadn't felt the blade cut his skin at the time, his finger came away bloody. He took a gulp of night air, and threw up in the gutter.

The donkey huffed at him, reminding him her supper was long overdue, and so was the evening load of fuel at the lighthouse.

"I don't want to drive for Prince Ptolemy anyway, Cleo!" Zeuxis whispered, using her rein to pull himself to his feet. "He's horrible. Anyone who can plant a curse deliberately to make horses die doesn't deserve to be Pharaoh. I don't blame Queen Cleopatra for throwing him out of the palace. I hope she kicks him out of Alexandria altogether."

The demon takes the power of the false queen

So, this is Alexandria's famous lighthouse, which makes Queen Cleopatra so powerful in the human world! It is very cold and damp. The outer door is locked because it is the middle of the night. But locked doors do not stop a demon.

I can smell the boy who dug up the curse, sleeping in an underground dormitory, but I do not need him for this. I am more interested in the second tier of the lighthouse, where its Keeper lives. This part of the curse should be easy, at least.

Remove the Keeper, and the light that protects the queen's ships will die.

Chapter 5

NIGHTMARE

Zeuxis lay pinned to his pallet in terror as the monstrous ka-demon Ahwere had told him about coiled out of a corner of the underground dormitory on a cloud of darkness. He thought it might have a snake's body with a man's head, but all he could see for certain were its green eyes that gleamed in the shadows.

It had to be a dream, except he couldn't seem to wake up. The ka slithered slowly closer, stopping at each pallet to wave its huge head over the sleeping form huddled there. It spent a long time hovering over old Aelian in the corner, who waved his withered hands at it and mumbled something in his sleep. The ka moved on. Now just two empty pallets lay between the monster and Zeuxis – those belonging to the boys on night duty up at the fire. For the first time in his life, he wished he were up there with them.

"Go away," he whispered. "Leave us alone."

The ka paused and raised its head. Then it turned from Zeuxis' pallet, slithered up the steps and straight through the solid wood into the lighthouse's second tier, taking its cloud of darkness with it.

Zeuxis sat up with a start, still sweating and breathing hard, as he had been in his dream. He blinked at the steps. Nothing, except shadows cast by the single torch the Keeper left alight at night so that the younger boys would not be frightened of the dark. Aelian was snoring again. The others all seemed to be asleep.

Feeling a bit stupid, he pulled his blanket tightly around him and closed his eyes. As his breathing slowed, he thought he heard the splash of oars and men's voices outside. He smiled. No doubt that was what had disturbed him in the first place. Rather than waking him, his tired body had translated the noises into a nightmare.

"You and your ghost stories, Ahwere!" he whispered.

The next thing he knew, the door of the lighthouse stood open. Light and salt air blew in from the sea, showing him a line of empty pallets. He'd overslept and no one had woken him. In his frustration, Zeuxis didn't stop to think how unusual this was. Now, thanks to Ahwere's stupid ghost stories, he'd missed both breakfast and his chance to catch the queen's Master of Horse doing his pre-race checks in the royal stables.

In a foul mood, he dragged Cleo out of the donkey stable and backed her between the shafts of the cart. His head was so full of his own concerns, it took him a while to realize something was wrong in the lighthouse. Boys raced all over the place, disturbing Cleo, who tossed her head and backed crookedly. When Zeuxis shoved his elbow into her chest, she flattened her ears and brayed in protest. Then she trod on his toe.

"You little beast…!" Zeuxis yelled, dragging his foot free. "You're as sly as the real Cleopatra!"

Old Aelian tutted and limped across. "Gently, lad," he said, stroking the donkey's nose. "She don't know what's happened, do she?"

"Know what?" Zeuxis muttered, still cursing the donkey for treading on his toe.

"'Bout the Keeper, of course." When Zeuxis looked confused, the old man chuckled. "You're about the only one who ain't heard. Last night, it was. He was out checking the torches on the second tier when one of the statues broke off. Keeper must've been leanin' on it at the time. Fell right down with it into the sea! If it weren't for the Romans' boat, rowing round the cliffs at the time, he wouldn't still be with us. They brought him in half drowned this morning. They're up there with him now. Our Keeper owes them his life, I'd say."

Zeuxis' heart missed a beat. "The Keeper fell off the *lighthouse*?" he said, peering up at the towering bulk of the Pharos. Then, with a little chill brought on by the memory of his interview with Prince Ptolemy: "Did you say Romans?"

A balcony ran between the first and second tiers of the Pharos. At the corners, statues of sea creatures – half men and half fish – blew trumpets to the four winds. It was one of these that had broken off and caused the Keeper's fall. Although tourists thought them wonderful, Zeuxis had stopped really seeing them years ago. Now he squinted up at the damaged one with fresh eyes. With its trumpet and arms fallen into the sea, all that was left was a man's head and a scaly body ending in a fish's tail.

His spine prickled as he remembered his nightmare.

"Yes," said Aelian, mistaking his reaction and frowning at the harbour. "Another ship's just arrived from Rome. Word is they've come to join the envoy, Mark Anthony, except it seems their arrival last night was a bit of a surprise. I only know what I heard this morning, but Queen Cleopatra's refusin' to let them move their troops into the palace, so they rowed across to our island in search of fresh water and supplies – lucky for our Keeper!"

The politics passed over Zeuxis' head. He was still looking at the sea-creatures on the corners of the Pharos. A nightmare because somewhere deep down he'd remembered them, or…?

Aelian's hand touched his shoulder, making him jump. "You've gone white as Alexandria's streets, lad! Don't worry, things'll work out. It could have been a lot worse. If he'd fallen on the other side, he'd have hit the rocks and no one could have saved him. Better get the morning load in, then hopefully Keeper'll be up and about to tell us what to do. The fire must stay lit, anyhow. We'll just carry on as normal, till Keeper tells us otherwise."

Zeuxis pulled himself together. The monster in his dream hadn't had a fish's tail, he was sure of it. And the Keeper wasn't dead.

"Yes," he said. "Yes, we must keep the fire burning. The other boys shouldn't be running about like that... who's up at the winch?"

"Still the two from last night, I think," Aelian said, frowning up at the lighthouse.

"They'll be half asleep! Hasn't anyone sent up replacements?"

The old man scratched his head. "Well, the Keeper usually decides who goes... I didn't like to, in case it was wrong."

Zeuxis closed his eyes. Aelian was five times his age, but he didn't seem to have a clue. His initial panic gave way to an unexpected sense of responsibility as he thought of what would happen to the ships sailing along Alexandria's treacherous coastline if they let the Pharos' fire go out before dark. Remembering what the Keeper had told him about the importance of the Pharos and having to take over one day, he straightened his shoulders and took a deep breath. He hadn't counted on that day being so soon, but he had no choice. None of the other boys were old enough to take charge.

"Who usually goes up in the mornings when I'm out collecting the muck?" he asked.

"Let's see... he changes the rota about so much, I forget..."

"Never mind." Zeuxis spotted two of the younger boys running across the cliff and yelled, "You two! Get up the ramp, and take over winch duty. You're to stay there till I bring the muck back and send someone else up to take over from you, right?"

The boys pulled faces at him. But when Aelian clapped his hands and told them the Keeper would hear about it if they didn't do what they were told, they cast sideways looks at Zeuxis and went, grumbling under their breath.

Zeuxis smiled. It felt surprisingly good to be obeyed. He sent Aelian inside to make sure everyone got some breakfast, and finally persuaded Cleo to reverse between the shafts so he could fasten her harness. He checked the sun. It wasn't too high yet. He might still catch the Master of Horse, if he was quick.

But it seemed everyone and everything had turned against him since he'd dug that curse out of the Hippodrome. When he reached the Heptastadion, he found the end of the causeway blocked by a pole and guarded by two men in the uniform of the queen's Royal Guard, who called for him to halt and started to search the cart.

"It's empty," Zeuxis said.

"We'll be the judge of that, Lighthouse Boy," one of them said.

"What's this about? I'm late already. The Keeper had an accident last night. He's sick in bed and I have to get back and organize the fire rota."

The guards gave him an amused look. "Very high and mighty, aren't we, all of a sudden?"

"If the fire goes out and ships get wrecked on the rocks, it'll be your fault," Zeuxis said, impatient.

"And if those Romans we saw rowing across to your island last night cause any trouble, it'll be our fault," the first guard said, rattling the axle with his spear to make sure there was no one clinging on underneath. "He's clean." As he stepped back, he looked a bit disappointed.

Zeuxis shook his head as they pulled the barrier out of the way. "Why doesn't the queen want the Romans in the palace?" he asked, trying to remember exactly what Aelian had said. "She let their envoy in, didn't she?"

The guards smiled. "It must be nice to be an innocent lighthouse boy with nothing more to worry about than the Pharos' fire," one remarked.

And the other said, "If you were Mark Anthony, would you want your every move reported back to Caesar?"

Zeuxis flushed, thinking of the way the queen had flirted with the Roman envoy in the park. "Are they here to help Prince Ptolemy to get his throne back – is that it?"

The men had turned their attention to a group of island women, on their way across the Heptastadion to shop at the market place. But when Zeuxis said this, they laughed aloud.

"Help the *prince*? I think that's rather unlikely, considering what we think he's done to their missing centurion! More likely, they've come here after Prince Ptolemy's blood."

Zeuxis frowned. "What did he do?"

The guards finished searching the women's baskets and waved them through. "You ask too many questions, Lighthouse Boy," said the first one. "If I were you, I'd collect your muck, tend your fire, and keep out of them Romans' way. We're just here to make sure there's no trouble. The last thing we need is some other idiot taking it into their head to kill a Roman, like we think Prince Ptolemy killed that centurion they're looking for. Queen Cleopatra knows what she's doing. She doesn't need Caesar's help to get rid of her brother, and Egypt doesn't need Caesar's armies trampling through her fields, like they will be if any more of his countrymen die in mysterious circumstances."

"Prince Ptolemy killed a Roman centurion?" Zeuxis said, shivering. He touched the scab on his throat where the prince's sword had nicked him. He found it difficult to believe the older boy had won a fight against a trained Roman. But maybe Prince Ptolemy had ordered his bodyguard to kill the centurion – he could believe that.

The second guard gave his comrade a warning look and said, "It ain't common knowledge yet, so don't go spreading it about."

"I'm not stupid," Zeuxis said, frowning.

The guards looked at him as if they weren't so sure. Then the first one smiled and patted him on the head, the way he hated. "Don't worry so, Lighthouse Boy. From what I hear, these Romans have come to challenge our queen in the Hippodrome, not by force of arms. They've got horses on that ship, brought specially across from their homeland. But even if Queen Cleopatra lets them race, they won't stand a chance against Clytius and the Blues, not if they use the most powerful curses in the world!"

Zeuxis went very still. He stared at the new ship anchored in the bay, his breath coming faster. "They've brought racehorses with them? Are you sure?"

The guards laughed. "It seems Alexandria's Hippodrome is a challenge their Caesar couldn't resist. We've got nothing to worry about, though. Even your old donkey there could beat a Roman racehorse!"

Cleo tossed her head, and Zeuxis smiled at the image of her pulling a chariot in the Hippodrome.

"Come on, old girl, move yourself," he said, clucking his tongue to make her trot. "We've got to get back to the lighthouse before those Romans leave. I've got an idea."

As he made his way along the waterfront, Zeuxis kept half an eye out for Ahwere. He wanted to tell her about his dream of the ka-demon. But there was no sign of the Egyptian girl, which was just as well. He wasn't sure he had it straight in his own head yet.

When he reached the royal stables, it seemed he hadn't been the only one to suffer a disturbed night. While he helped him load up the cart, Dameos told him some garbled story about the queen's black stallion going crazy last night and injuring himself in his stall. Probably a nightmare about the wreck it had been involved in, Zeuxis decided. The poor horse would be better off for the rest – and if the queen's Master of Horse wasn't going to let him drive for the Blues anyway, what did it matter? Anxious to get back to the lighthouse before the Romans left, he thought no more of it.

It did not occur to him to wonder if horses had dreams.

Chapter 6

ROMANS

THE GUARDS ON the Heptastadion were not quite so keen to search the cart on its way back to the island. Zeuxis smiled as he watched them prod the soggy brown straw with their spears at arm's length. He was used to the smell now, but he could remember his disgust when the Keeper had first showed him how to make fuel-cakes out of it for the Pharos' fire.

The guards waved him through with another warning to watch out for the Romans. He promised he would, paused long enough to store his load, settle Cleo, and send two more boys up the lighthouse to relieve the ones on winch duty. Then he hurried up the stairs to the Keeper's rooms.

He would have known something was wrong even without old Aelian's story that morning. The torches spluttered in their wall brackets. No one had swept the ramp. The door to the Keeper's quarters was closed, and raised voices came from behind it.

Zeuxis paused to catch his breath and peer out of one of the round windows that overlooked the harbour. The newly-arrived Roman galley towered over the smaller merchant ships, the eagle standard on top of its mast glittering proudly in the Alexandrian sunshine. A little shiver went down his spine that had nothing to do with demons or dreams.

He put his ear to the wood and listened to the shouting on the other side of the door. That was the Keeper's voice. Obviously, he wasn't quite as weak as Aelian thought. The other voices were softer. They were speaking in Latin, anyway, so he couldn't understand the words. Maybe he ought to go back down and wait until he was summoned?

As he hesitated, the door was pulled open from inside. Zeuxis lost his balance and stumbled into the room. Two Romans wearing formal togas pulled up short, equally surprised. He had an impression of dark hair and clean-shaven chins, before the older one seized his elbow in a fierce grip. "How long have you been listening out there, boy?" he hissed.

At the far side of the room, the Keeper struggled to sit up in bed but was held back by one of the island women, who perched on a stool beside his bed with a basin of bloody water and a cloth.

"Zeuxis!" the Keeper said in relief, flopping back against his pillow. The woman tending him tried to wipe a nasty cut on his forehead. The Keeper thrust her hands away and snapped at the Romans, "Let that boy in! He's one of my slaves. The fire must be tended, no matter what happens. Zeuxis, come over here and report!"

The Roman let go of his arm, but narrowed his eyes after Zeuxis as he went to kneel at the Keeper's bedside.

Now he was closer, he saw Aelian had it right. The Keeper's skin was a pale yellow under his tan, and the cut on his forehead was one of many still bleeding. One leg had been bound in linen and splinted – clearly broken. His left arm was also bandaged tightly to his chest. But when he reached out with his right hand and grasped Zeuxis' shoulder, his voice was as strong as before.

"These gentlemen are Lucian Flavius and Marcus Suetonius, just arrived from Rome," he said with a frown. "They pulled me out of the harbour last night, for which I owe them my life. But they seem to think such service is worth more than I am at liberty to give. They are leaving now." He glared at the two Romans, who nodded stiffly and made for the door.

"No, don't go—" Zeuxis said.

The one who had gripped his arm, Lucian, gave him another narrow-eyed look.

"I mean, I have to talk to you, Sirs!" Zeuxis said, his heart hammering. "It's about your racehorses."

The Keeper frowned. "Zeuxis, I need you here to pass on my orders to the other boys until I'm up and about again! You haven't time to go running about after horses. Aelian tells me you did a good job this morning when everyone was in a panic over my accident, and that you brought in the load of fuel from the royal stables as well. I'm proud of you, but there's still a lot needs doing. It'll be up to you to keep the fire burning while I'm stuck in here. Aelian hasn't the strength in his legs these days for running up and down the lighthouse steps, so he'll have to go back on fuel collection while you stay here to help me."

Zeuxis cast a look at the door, wondering how he could get out of this new corner.

The Romans glanced at each other again, and then back at the Keeper. "We'll leave you to speak to your slave-boy in private," said Lucian smoothly. "Obviously, you have lighthouse business to discuss. Meanwhile, we'd be grateful for some hospitality before we return to our ship. Is there somewhere we can refresh ourselves? I don't suppose you have baths in this lighthouse of yours..." His gaze took in the damp corners of the room. "But a cup of wine and something to eat would be most welcome to us weary travellers from Rome."

The Keeper closed his eyes. When he next spoke, his voice was more civil. "Of course," he said. "Phila, take these gentlemen down to the kitchens and see that they're fed. Send a flagon of my best wine to their ship, and fodder for their horses, too. Never let it be said that the Pharos islanders do not repay their debts."

The Romans smiled, nodded again, and left the room with the woman. They walked like men used to conducting their business in palaces rather than in damp lighthouses perched on windy rocks. But just before the door closed, Zeuxis was certain the younger one, Marcus Suetonius, winked at him.

The Keeper's instructions were long and boring. Zeuxis fidgeted on the stool where he had been allowed to sit, trying to take it all in, but itching to run down to the kitchens where the Romans were taking their 'refreshment'. Would they wait for him? Had that really been a wink from the young Marcus, or had he been imagining it? And how was he going to speak to Ahwere about his dream of the ka-demon, if he wasn't even allowed off the island to collect fuel?

Finally, the Keeper stopped talking. His hand rested on Zeuxis' knee. Zeuxis (who, in his dreams, was already driving the Roman chariot team round the Hippodrome) jumped.

"I know it's a lot to take in all at once," the Keeper said. "I'd hoped to have time to prepare you better. But you're the only one I can trust with this, Zeuxis. Old Aelian's memory is failing him almost as fast as his body. You're growing up fast. Your actions of this morning prove it. If you manage to keep the Pharos' fire burning until I am fit enough to take over again, you'll have earned your freedom."

These words broke through Zeuxis' dream of winning in the Hippodrome. "You'll set me free?" he whispered, going very still.

"You'll no longer be a slave," the Keeper corrected. "I'll pay you a wage for your work instead. You will, of course, remain at the lighthouse until you've completed your training."

Zeuxis sighed. No different, then. Not really.

"I'll do my best, Sir," he said with sinking heart. What else could he do? He couldn't abandon the lighthouse now, at least not until the Keeper was up and about again.

The Keeper looked hard into his eyes. "Good," he said. "I believe you will. And it won't all be work. The Romans have asked to bring their horses across to the island for training. They're hoping Mark Anthony will persuade Queen Cleopatra to let them race." He smiled at Zeuxis' yelp of excitement, then sobered. "There's one other thing, however."

Halfway to the door, Zeuxis turned, his heart fluttering as he remembered his nightmare. "Last night…" he whispered.

But the Keeper frowned and said, "I want you to be very careful what you say to these Romans, Zeuxis. I know you want to help them with their horses. I'm not blind. I know why you enjoy collecting the wrecks from the Hippodrome so much. And no doubt they'll be pleased to have someone who's willing to muck out and groom for them. But they are clever men. They haven't come here to race just for the fun of it, and when politics get involved things are seldom what they seem to be. Rome is probably looking to gain support in the city. In the Hippodrome, they'll be the White team, the challengers. Queen Cleopatra's Blues and Prince Ptolemy's Greens will take a lot of beating, but it's not unheard of for an outsider to steal the hearts of the people. With the Red team so weak at the moment, things could easily swing in the Romans' favour. I'm warning you now, so you don't do anything stupid."

Zeuxis bit his lip. "Am I forbidden to help them, then?"

The Keeper sighed again. "No. We'll cooperate until we work out what they're up to. Keep your eyes and ears open. The last thing we want is for Julius Caesar to arrive with his legions and seize Pharos Island by force, while the queen and her brother are busy squabbling over the throne. Equally so, I can't let these Romans have what they want, which is to make our island their military base here in Alexandria."

"They can't do that!" Zeuxis said. His spine prickled as he remembered what the guards on the Heptastadion had said. "Can they?"

"Not if I have anything to do with it," the Keeper said with a smile. "I'm sure Queen Cleopatra will send some men across to defend our Pharos, if it comes to that. But for now, it's best to be civil to these Romans so we don't have our island overrun by soldiers – of any sort." The Keeper lay back and closed his eyes.

Zeuxis hesitated. "Er... Sir?"

"Leave me now, Zeuxis. I've told you everything I can. If you can't remember what I said, ask Aelian and see if he can help before coming to see me again. My head hurts. I need to rest. Send that woman Phila up with some more of her sleeping potion, will you?"

"But I need to ask you something important! Something you haven't told me."

The Keeper's eyelids fluttered open. "Well? Spit it out, boy."

"Last night, when you fell... was it *really* an accident?" He shivered as he remembered the ghostly ka-demon that, in his nightmare, had slithered up the steps into the second tier last night. Before the Keeper fell, or after? Because if it had been before...

"There was no one else on the balcony, if that's what you mean," the Keeper said, looking hard at Zeuxis. "I was careless. I leant over to see the Romans' boat better, see what they were up to. The statue crumbled under me. It was old. Why? Do you know something I don't?"

Zeuxis shook his head. With the sun shining outside, and the city dazzling white and beautiful across the turquoise sea, it felt stupid to tell the Keeper an ancient Egyptian demon might have pushed him off the lighthouse during the night.

That statue could have broken off at any time, he told himself as he hurried down the steps. *It's two hundred years old. I was dreaming, that's all.*

He found the Romans in a small room beside the kitchens, lingering over their wine. When he rushed in without thinking to knock, Marcus patted the bench beside him and smiled. Neither of them seemed surprised he had come.

"Zeuxis, isn't it?" he said. "Sit and have a drink with us."

"I'm not allowed wine," Zeuxis said, eyeing the flagon on the table.

"You're allowed grapes and cheese, though, aren't you?" Lucian said, pushing a platter towards him. "Help yourself. There's plenty."

Zeuxis clenched his fists. He didn't want to sit and eat with the Romans. He wanted to see their horses. But the sight of the food made his stomach rumble. All at once, he realized he was starving. He'd missed breakfast, and it was now well past lunchtime.

He perched on the edge of the bench and stuffed down a piece of goat's cheese, followed by three juicy red grapes.

"That's better," Lucian said. "Now, you wanted to talk to us about our racehorses, I believe? How come you're interested in horses? I didn't think you kept anything larger than a donkey out here on your island."

"I collect up the wrecks," Zeuxis said with his mouth full.

The Romans glanced at each other. "Ship wrecks?"

"Oh, no… chariot wrecks, I mean. The ones that crash in the Hippodrome. Not ships, though we call them by the same word because they make just as much mess."

Marcus chuckled, and Zeuxis almost joined in. The Keeper's warnings fresh in his mind, he caught himself in time.

"So, you know a lot about chariot wrecks," Lucian said, pouring Zeuxis some wine and pushing the cup across. "Useful, but we're hoping not to have one of those. We understand that you collect muck – fuel – from the royal stables. You must see the queen's horses while you're over there?"

"Yes," Zeuxis said. "They exercise around the park every morning at sunrise. She's got this team of crazy blacks. One of the stallions was involved in a wreck last race day – he was the only one who survived, so he's still worked up about it. And the other three are colts barely broken. They're fast, though..." He broke off and shook his head. The wine was making him dizzy.

"Mmm. They must be the ones Mark Anthony told us about." Lucian said something in Latin to Marcus, then topped up Zeuxis' cup with another smile. "And Prince Ptolemy's got a fast team, too, we understand?"

"His chestnuts, yes. I've not seen them race, though. I'm not allowed to watch the actual racing..."

Zeuxis' next mouthful of cheese stuck in his throat. This was not going the way he'd planned. He pushed the wine away and tried to remember why he'd wanted to talk to the Romans. "What about your team, Sirs?" he asked. "Do you need a driver? Because I'm available."

Lucian smiled. "We might," he said carefully. "But I thought your Keeper kept you busy here in the lighthouse. Do you have any experience?"

Zeuxis thought of that single circuit of the park, driving the queen's blacks. "Yes!" he lied. "I've driven

Queen Cleopatra's best team. Your envoy Mark Anthony was there. He saw me. Please let me try out your horses. I could tell you if they're as fast as the queen's, at least."

The Romans glanced at each other again. Lucian narrowed his eyes. "That could be useful to know. But how will we know if you're telling us the truth? You say you used to drive for the Blues. You could be a spy."

Zeuxis realized his mistake. "I... er... didn't drive them in the Hippodrome, as such, just at exercise. The queen's Master of Horse wouldn't let me race them. They already have a charioteer called Clytius, who's too old and heavy really, but he's the queen's champion. He got sick exercising them in the park, and —" He bit the words off. The wine talking again.

"I see," Lucian said, leaning across the table and pressing his fingers together. "Let me see if I've got this straight. You badly want to drive a chariot in a race, but the queen's Master of Horse won't let you. So I'm guessing there's no love lost between you and the Blues?"

"No," Zeuxis agreed, thinking of the way the queen had dismissed him. "I'd like to see the Blues get beaten."

"By Prince Ptolemy's Greens, perhaps?"

"No!" Zeuxis said, touching his throat where the prince's sword had nicked him. "I *hate* Prince Ptolemy! He's a bully and a murderer."

"On that point we are in full agreement, Lighthouse Boy!" Lucian said with a sharp laugh. "I think we might have found ourselves a driver, Marcus my friend! The boy's the right size, and he looks strong enough. All that muck forking, I expect. What do you say we bring our horses ashore and give him a trial?"

Zeuxis' heart swelled with pure joy. He could not stop the grin spreading across his face. Just wait until he told Ahwere he was going to drive the Roman team in the Hippodrome!

But Marcus didn't look so happy.

"It might be better to hire a boy from the city to drive for us," he said softly. "You heard that Keeper. Zeuxis is needed here to work the light. It's one thing to have him help us with our horses, quite another to send him into the Hippodrome to—"

At this point, he changed to Latin again and the two began to argue fiercely in their own language.

"But I *want* to race!" Zeuxis said, staring from one to the other of the chiselled Roman faces. "I know it's dangerous, but I'm not afraid. If you give me this chance, I promise I'll win for you!"

The argument stopped. Lucian looked amused. "Win?" he said. "Bring our White team to victory against the famous Blues and Greens of Alexandria?"

"Yes!" Zeuxis said. In his dreams, there was no other way.

Lucian stared at him with a little wondering smile. But Marcus mumbled, "We haven't seen the boy drive yet. Maybe we should wait until we get our horses ashore, before we decide who's going to race the White team for Rome and Caesar's honour? And we really ought to check with the Keeper before we make use of his lighthouse boy's time."

Zeuxis' heart fell a bit. In all the excitement, he'd forgotten the extra duties the Keeper had given him. In the Keeper's eyes, he was sure "helping with their horses" would not stretch as far as training for the race. And now he was imprisoned on the island again, so he couldn't get out to the Hippodrome to practice, even if they did let him drive.

But Lucian slapped him on the shoulder. "Don't look like that, Lighthouse Boy! Your Keeper owes us a favour or two for saving his life last night. We could do a lot worse than use a local boy to train our horses over here on the island out of sight of prying eyes. I'll have a word with him. Meanwhile, you go with Marcus and help him get the horses ashore. That is, if you've time between your other duties…?"

Zeuxis grinned. "I'll *make* time," he said.

The Roman horses were grey. Three pretty dappled fillies, and one pure white mare as a steadying influence in the team. They came ashore snorting and plunging, and Marcus laughed. Zeuxis led the mare and the darkest of the fillies, whispering nonsense until they jogged sensibly beside of him, staring about the island with big brown eyes and flared nostrils. He wanted to try them straight away, but there wasn't time. Also, they didn't have a chariot yet – the Romans had brought it in pieces on their ship, but it still had to be assembled.

Zeuxis had to be content with making sure the horses were comfortable and had enough hay. He felt sure these weren't the luxurious quarters they were used to. They glowed in the donkey stable, their tails rippling in the gloom like silk. They kept flinging up their heads to neigh at all the unfamiliar noises, making poor Cleo snort in her stall. The other boys crowded round, upsetting the fillies still further, until Zeuxis threatened to send anyone who didn't get back to their work up the lighthouse on night duty at the fire.

The boys melted away. Marcus smiled and went to supervise the unloading of the chariot. Finally, only old Aelian and Zeuxis were left in the stables.

"They're pretty enough," Aelian grunted. "But I don't know what the Keeper's thinkin' of, letting the Romans keep 'em here. With the Nile floods so low this year and the bad harvest, we've hardly enough fodder for the poor donkeys, let alone what these four will eat their way through, if they're racing fit."

"Lucian is going to ask Mark Anthony to arrange for grain to be sent across from the palace," Zeuxis said, stroking the dark filly's neck. The filly huffed at him, and he smiled. "They're named after Roman goddesses, you know. Marcus told me. This one's called Venus. The other fillies are Minerva and Maia, and the white mare's Diana. I'm looking forward to racing them!"

Aelian shook his head. "You take care, lad. I wouldn't trust those Romans any further than I can throw 'em. I'm thinking it was a mighty funny thing last night, the way they just happened to be down in the harbour, pokin' around the Pharos at the exact moment our Keeper fell."

Zeuxis shivered, reminded again of the ghostly ka-demon in his dream. But it made no sense for the demon summoned by the curse to attack the Keeper. He had nothing to do with horses or chariot racing. Or did he, now that the Roman team was training on the island? What if the curse Prince Ptolemy had planted was worded against all rival chariot teams? If the Romans persuaded the queen to let them race, they would be a rival – and so would the boy who drove for them.

He shook the thought away. Ahwere's ka couldn't really exist, could it? Even if it did, he wasn't about to back out now. This was his big chance to show he could drive a chariot well enough to race in the Hippodrome. And he *would* win, curse or no curse.

Chapter 7

TRAINING

ZEUXIS SOON DISCOVERED that the dark filly, Venus, was the fastest. For his trial, Marcus harnessed her on the inside, next to the white mare. Zeuxis could feel the filly's energy tugging at the team, and after one ragged circuit he switched her to the outside position.

This was much better. Since she had further to travel, she could stretch her legs round the corners, and this helped to settle her. The other two fillies, Maia and Minerva, worked well together in the middle. The mare, being steadier, was perfect for the inside, and he left her there. She kept one ear back all the time to listen to his voice, and he had only to breathe "whoaaa" for her to slow the others without him needing to touch the reins. After driving the queen's wild black team, it was amazing.

Zeuxis drove those first few circuits with his head floating in the clouds and a grin stretched across his face.

All the lighthouse boys had turned out to watch, and most of the island families as well. But Zeuxis hardly noticed them. Nor did he notice the blisters forming on his palms where the reins rubbed.

He was driving a chariot!

He was going to race in the Hippodrome at last.

He might have driven the greys round all day, had not Lucian stepped into his path and spread his arms to stop them, laughing. "All right, all right, you'll do!" he said. "You certainly have a gift for driving, and the horses seem to trust you. We'll enter them in the next race and see how you do. But no heroics, Lighthouse Boy, do you hear? We don't want to show our true colours in the first race. There could be some money to be made on bets, if we're clever about this. That'll mean a bonus for you as the driver."

Zeuxis couldn't have cared less about the money. In the weeks that followed, he worked harder than he had ever worked before. When he wasn't organizing the fire rota and fuel collection, or running messages for the Keeper, he was training the grey horses on the makeshift track the Romans had made by spreading sand from the beach on the headland. His days settled into a routine that left him so tired, he hardly remembered lying down on his pallet, before it was time to get up and begin all over again.

In his present bedridden state the Keeper did not interfere, except to interrogate Zeuxis about what the Roman envoys said and did, every time he reported to his rooms. And although the queen's men guarding the Heptastadion were well aware the Roman team was training on the island, they didn't do anything to stop them. According to old Aelian, Queen Cleopatra's grooms and charioteers were treating it as a bit of a joke.

"They've heard you're driving the White team for the Romans," he told Zeuxis. "And they're all laughing at you. Your friend Dameos says they're already calling your team 'the lighthouse wreck'." He paused, his eyes wrinkling in concern. "You're not really serious about racing them Roman horses in the Hippodrome, are you, lad?"

"Yes," Zeuxis said, raising his chin. "I am."

Aelian pulled a face. "Then there's goin' to be plenty of fuel for us to collect after next race day. Just make sure you jump out in time. I don't fancy finding your bones buried in the wreckage."

Zeuxis didn't care that nobody thought he had a chance. The grey horses filled his dreams. When he ran up the lighthouse steps, he could feel the chariot jolting beneath his feet. When he helped Aelian harness Cleo for the fuel run, he imagined he was harnessing the Roman fillies to the racing chariot. When he drove around the makeshift track watched by the curious islanders, he was in the Hippodrome being cheered on by thousands of White supporters.

Ahwere's ka-demon did not make another appearance, so he convinced himself it had been a bad dream and stopped worrying that he couldn't get off the island to ask Ahwere about it. She'd only tease him about being scared of ghosts. He was looking forward to seeing her face when he drove the Roman chariot into the Hippodrome.

The morning before the race, the Romans finally let him try the light leather and wooden racing chariot he'd be using in the Hippodrome. Marcus seemed more nervous than Zeuxis as he checked the harness.

"Just give them a quiet trot round to begin with," he said, putting a hand on Venus' rein so Zeuxis could climb in. "Get the feel of the platform. Then, when you're ready, open them up for half a circuit to clear their lungs. You've got excellent balance, so you shouldn't have any difficulty staying on board, but be ready for them. This chariot's a lot lighter than the exercise one, and they'll want to take off with you. Don't let them. We don't want to run our race today and have nothing left for tomorrow."

Zeuxis nodded. His hands were still a mass of blisters, which didn't get a chance to heal between training sessions. He wrapped strips of linen around them and tied the ends with his teeth.

Marcus watched him in silence. "They bother you?"

"Not when I'm driving," Zeuxis said with a grin. It was the truth. He had to bite his lip against the pain when he was about his lighthouse duties. But when the four white tails were streaming before him and the chariot rumbling under his feet, he felt nothing but the joy and pride of being part of a racing team.

Marcus nodded. The fillies were fidgeting, anxious to get out on the track. But he didn't let go of the reins. "Lucian's coming over from the ship to watch. Don't start to blow them out until he gets here." He glanced over his shoulder at old Aelian, who had just brought the morning's load of fuel back across the Heptastadion through the guard post, and hesitated. "Zeuxis... good luck."

Zeuxis felt sure Marcus had been about to say something else. But before he could ask what, a dishevelled figure burst from the back of the cart and came rushing towards them, its long black hair shedding bits of straw and dung.

This was too much for the fillies, who shot up their heads and flared their nostrils in alarm. Scenting a stranger, Venus reared in her traces and spun round, dragging the rein from Marcus' hand. Even the mare, Diana, snorted and went backwards. The light racing chariot skewed round on one wheel, and Zeuxis had to grab for the side – a side that wasn't there. He flailed for a moment in midair, with visions of falling under the fillies' hooves and being trampled before he even made it as far as the Hippodrome.

"Steady! Steady girls... whoa there..." he said, trying not to let the panic reach his voice.

The mare's white ear flicked back. She steadied, and the dark filly came back down to earth. Zeuxis let them canter a few strides, then slowed them back to a trot and brought them round to face the apparition, which Marcus now held prisoner by the elbow.

It was Ahwere. A dirty, smelly, and very angry Ahwere.

"Let me go, you filthy Roman!" she cried. "I have to talk to my friend!"

Marcus held on to her with an amused smile. "I think you're rather filthier than I am just now, young lady." He frowned at Zeuxis. "Do you know this rude Egyptian girl?"

Zeuxis had to concentrate on the fillies, who were dancing impatiently. He dared not get out of the chariot. He felt relieved Lucian hadn't arrived yet. He was sure the older Roman would not have taken Ahwere's words so lightly.

"Ahwere!" he said sternly, trying not to laugh. A piece of straw stuck out of her Egyptian eye amulet, and she had more in her hair. "This is Marcus Suetonius, owner of these horses. He's a friend."

Ahwere snatched her arm free, brushed off her dress and glared at the Roman. "No Roman is a friend of Egypt! Everyone knows your Caesar has had his greedy eyes on our country for years."

Marcus inclined his head in acknowledgement of this. "Nevertheless, we are here peacefully as Caesar's envoys, and politics had better wait until these horses are exercised." He eyed the fidgeting fillies and looked at the harbour, where Lucian's boat could be seen heading across from the Roman galley. "Since Zeuxis is obviously your friend, you can come and watch if you like."

Ahwere turned her glare on Zeuxis. She noticed the racing chariot for the first time, and her eyes widened.

"You're not *really* going to race them tomorrow, are you?" she said. "You must be crazier than I thought!"

Zeuxis set his jaw and wheeled the fillies round so that the mare had to spin on the spot. It was a dangerous manoeuvre with such a light chariot, but he got away with it and pushed the team into a trot down the road to the headland. The two boys he'd put on fire duty after the Keeper's fall had been caught by Lucian to rake the track. They flicked sand at Zeuxis as he trotted the greys past and teased him about wrecks. He ignored them and calmed the dark filly with a touch on her rein and a soothing whisper.

He'd show Ahwere. He'd show them all.

Lucian arrived and gave him the same instructions Marcus had, but with a stricter warning not to let the fillies get away from him. There were more people watching than usual as he trotted the greys around the circuit.

He had expected the chariot to feel livelier than the exercise one, but it was more different than he'd thought, almost like a fifth horse jittering under his feet. The fillies could feel the difference, too. They tossed their heads and broke into a sideways canter, impatient to go faster. Zeuxis bit his tongue as the chariot skewed across the track, its wheel narrowly missing a rock.

He eased the reins, and the fillies leapt forward. The mare was a little slower. He shouted at her, and she caught up. Now they were galloping, the wind whipping his hair back and making his eyes water. They were going fast, but not out of control, not full speed. "Just half a circuit," he muttered, as the reins tore against his blisters. "Just got to hold them for half a circuit..."

Lucian and Marcus were at the side of the track, watching the horses come with narrow eyes. Zeuxis grinned as the fillies galloped past the two Romans, perfectly balanced, their manes and tails streaming and their hooves kicking sand into his face. He might have imagined it, but he thought Lucian smiled. Ahwere's face flashed past, pale and worried. He couldn't resist a wave as he passed her – then swore as the reins slipped and he lost control of Venus.

Forget the girl, he told himself firmly. But the damage had been done. The joy and smoothness left him. His blisters were bleeding so he couldn't feel the reins. Ahwere's presence reminded him of Prince Ptolemy's curse and his dream of the ka-demon. The chariot lurched and skewed its way around another circuit. Out of the corner of his eye, he saw Lucian frown and Marcus step on to the track, waving for him to stop the team.

Zeuxis clenched his jaw against the pain, tightened the reins and called to the fillies. "Whoaa, steady..."

They were heading for the cliff edge, where the track turned. Only a narrow strip of white rock separated the chariot and the horses from the crashing waves beyond. *Something* – maybe a seagull, maybe not – flew at the dark filly Venus out of the sun. She spooked off the track and barged into Minerva, who bumped against Maia. The mare pulled herself up at once, the fillies jolted round, and the chariot turned over.

Zeuxis rolled to his feet and ran to their heads before they could bolt, but too late. The dark filly was snorting in pain, one foreleg streaming blood where she had foundered among the rocks. Minerva rolled her eye, fighting the traces that linked her to her injured team mate.

Zeuxis' heart sank, but there was no time to think. "Whoa, girls!" he said, over and over. "Whoa, Diana, whoa Minerva, whoa Maia, whoa poor Venus, whoaaa."

Marcus and Lucian were already running towards him, followed by Ahwere, her eyes wide with fear. The Romans took the other reins and quickly unharnessed the two pairs of horses, leading the mare and Maia one way, Minerva and poor, limping Venus the other. Ahwere helped right the chariot.

Zeuxis discovered he was shaking.

"What happened?" Ahwere demanded.

Zeuxis shook his head. Marcus and Lucian managed to calm the horses enough to unhitch Venus. They ordered the boys who had been raking the track to take the other three back to the stable.

Lucian held the dark filly's head, while Marcus examined her leg. Tight-lipped, he confirmed what Zeuxis already knew.

"This filly's not going to be able to race tomorrow."

Lucian gave Zeuxis an exasperated look. "The Whites must race. If nothing else, the boy needs experience of the

Hippodrome. We'll have to get a substitute horse, that's all."

This shocked Zeuxis out of his reaction to the near-fatal crash. "But I've no time left to practise with a new horse! The others won't know how to work with the new one. It'll be a disaster... Sir."

Lucian frowned. "You were never going to win tomorrow, anyway. It'll make no difference."

"But—" Zeuxis closed his mouth. How could he explain his dream?

He, Zeuxis, champion of the Whites, leading the field round the final turn with all Alexandria chanting his name.

Marcus finished his inspection of the dark filly's leg and gave him a sharp look. "This race is just to test the field," he said. "I already told you that."

"If you can't obey instructions, then we'll find another driver," Lucian added. "One who can control his team at full gallop, maybe."

Zeuxis lowered his gaze. "I'm sorry," he whispered, stroking the filly's neck. "That seagull spooked her... it won't happen again."

"There'll be a lot more than seagulls to distract you in the Hippodrome, Lighthouse Boy!" Lucian said. "You'd better learn to hold them." He headed back to his boat, shaking his head and muttering in Latin under his breath.

Ahwere wandered off to the cliff edge, where she crouched to examine the ground, which left Marcus and Zeuxis with the filly and the chariot.

"I really am sorry," Zeuxis said again. "Poor Venus! Lucian's right, it was my fault for not paying attention. Will she get better, Sir?"

"She's not going to die of it, if that's what you mean," Marcus said in a gentler tone. "It'll heal over in a few days if we keep it clean, and I expect she'll come sound again in time for the next race. Don't blame yourself. These are hardly perfect conditions for training. It could have happened to anyone. But I think it's about time you told me the whole truth, don't you?" He glanced at Ahwere.

Zeuxis frowned. "You mean Ahwere? She's just a girl I met in the city. The Keeper doesn't know about her... Please don't tell him!"

Marcus' lips twitched. "It's not my business to interfere in a boy's private affairs. No, I don't mean your Egyptian girlfriend, though I admit she was a bit of a surprise. I mean you, Lighthouse Boy. That's the first time you've ever driven a racing chariot in your life, isn't it?"

Zeuxis' breath stuck in his throat. He stared after the boat carrying Lucian back to the Roman ship and wet his lips. They couldn't replace him now, not when he was so close to fulfilling his dream. "I..." He faltered, wondering if he could get away with an outright lie.

"Lucian Flavius doesn't see as clearly as I do in these matters," Marcus said. "He hasn't been around racehorses so long. You fooled us with the exercise chariot – you've got good hands, and Mark Anthony was happy for us to use you after he saw you handle the queen's horses in the park that day. But today it was like you were learning with every breath. I almost stopped you before you let them blow out. But then I saw your face and changed my mind. You nearly got away with it. That bird flying up was unfortunate, but maybe it did you a favour."

Zeuxis gripped the Roman's arm. "Please, Sir!" he whispered. "Please let me race tomorrow! You were right about the racing chariot being my first time. But I've got the hang of it now. I won't let you down, I promise."

Marcus sighed. "I know you'll do your best, and the truth is we haven't time before the race to find another charioteer willing to work for us. As your Egyptian friend said earlier, Romans have a bad name in this city. Lucian will let you race, even if you are useless. That makes me afraid for you."

Zeuxis bit his lip. "You think I'm going to crash, don't you?"

Marcus patted the filly's neck and gave him a sideways look. "No. I think you're going to try to win. That's what scares me."

"I promised I'd obey your instructions!"

"I know you did, and I believe you will tomorrow. With the substitute horse, I don't think you're going to have much choice. But another day, in the excitement of the race, maybe not."

Zeuxis looked at Ahwere, who was staring out to sea, her black hair whipped by the breeze. Was the Egyptian girl listening to them? "But I thought that's what you wanted?" he whispered. "For us to lose this time and win next time so you'd land a good bet?"

Marcus pressed his lips together and seemed to struggle with something. He said very softly, "Zeuxis, it's only fair you should know that's not the only reason we've entered this race —"

Then Ahwere swung round and the Roman sighed. "Never mind. Let's get this poor filly back to the stables and her leg cleaned up. I've still got to check with the Keeper that you can have the afternoon off tomorrow for the races. I'm not going to tell Lucian Flavius or Mark Anthony our little secret, don't worry. Either you'll prove yourself tomorrow, or you'll make such a mess of things even Lucian will agree we have to find someone else. Can you and your Egyptian friend manage the chariot between you?"

Zeuxis nodded, relieved he was going to be allowed to race tomorrow, at least. "No problem," he said, rubbing his bruises with a rueful smile. "As I just found out back there, it's very light."

Ahwere barely spoke on the way back from the headland. But as soon as Marcus had left the stable after making sure the dark filly's leg was properly bandaged, she rounded on Zeuxis with flashing eyes.

"So *this* is why you haven't been into the city! I've been trying to get across to the island to see you for ages! Old Aelian said you'd been given extra duties, but I thought he meant for the lighthouse, not driving horses for *Romans*!" She spat into the straw, making Minerva jump.

Zeuxis stroked the filly's soft nose. "He did mean for the lighthouse. I only help the Romans in my spare time. It's what I've always wanted to do, you know that. But the night they came I had a dream—"

Ahwere wasn't listening. "You're crazy if you think you're going to survive that race tomorrow!" she went on. "How much training have you had driving chariots? Ten days? Eleven?"

"Twelve," said Zeuxis. "And a half, if you count the queen's blacks in the park."

"Twelve days!" Ahwere shook her head in amazement. "When most of the other drivers have trained for twelve *years*! That Blue charioteer of the queen's, Clytius, has been driving chariots since he was tall enough to see over the front plate. He knows every trick in the book. Racing in the Hippodrome isn't like driving round the park, you know."

"Clytius is much heavier than me," Zeuxis said. "His weight will slow his team down. Also, he's old. He won't take so many risks."

"Oh, and your light weight will make these inferior Roman horses go faster, I suppose?" Ahwere said with a harsh laugh.

"They're not inferior," Zeuxis said, patting Venus. "This filly's just as fast as that black stallion of the queen's. Faster, maybe."

"But she's injured, isn't she? And the mare is slower than any racehorse I've ever seen."

Zeuxis stayed silent, because he knew she was right.

Ahwere sighed. "Well, it's your neck, I suppose. When you trail in last tomorrow and everyone laughs at you, just don't say I didn't warn you."

Zeuxis frowned. "What did you come here for? Because if it's just to tell me I'm going to lose tomorrow, I don't need to hear it. You pong, by the way."

Ahwere scowled and picked a piece of straw out of her hair. "How else was I going to get past those guards on the Heptastadion? I saw they don't really search the muck cart, so I took a risk and hid in it."

"You could have got yourself speared, Ahwere!" He was surprised how much the thought of her getting hurt alarmed him. "You can't go back the same way. There won't be any muck in the cart going out."

"I know that. I'm not stupid."

"I really did have a dream the night the Romans came," Zeuxis said. "I'm not making it up. I dreamt of a monster with a snake's body and a man's head... I think it was that ka-demon your grandmother saw." He waited for her to laugh.

But instead of teasing him, Ahwere bit her lip, suddenly serious. "That's why I'm here." She looked around to check they were alone, slipped into Minerva's stall and whispered, "I came to tell you about Prince Ptolemy's curse."

Zeuxis' hand went to his throat, all his worries about the demon resurfacing. "What about it?"

"I finally got to see what was written on it. Grandmother went out to buy some herbs and stuff for her spells, and I sneaked into her room. It's worse than I thought."

"How do you mean, worse?" A shiver went down his spine. "I thought Lady Wernero made it safe when she unrolled it?"

Ahwere frowned. "She should have done. But it's a very powerful curse. And you're right, the ka's still around. I expect that's why you saw it in your dream. Grandmother makes light of it. I don't think she wants to worry me. But I know when she's afraid. That's why she went out so long yesterday, searching for the right ingredients to make a spell to send it back to its own world."

Zeuxis glanced around the gloomy stalls. The snorts and munching that normally comforted him seemed threatening all of a sudden. Was that a new shadow in the back of the stable, crouched beside the Romans' chariot?

"What did the curse say?" He hardly dared ask. "Did it... did it say anything about the White team, the challengers?"

Ahwere was staring at the chariot, too. She shook herself. "The Whites? Oh, no... no. It wasn't aimed at the Romans. Prince Ptolemy obviously thinks he can take care of them the same way he took care of their centurion, by more traditional means." She paused and said softly, "It was aimed at the queen."

"Queen Cleopatra?"

"Who else?"

"The Blues, then." Zeuxis let out his breath in relief. "If the curse is aimed at the Blues, then the ka-demon you mentioned must be after Clytius' team." He remembered what Dameos had told him about the black stallion going crazy in the night, and shivered again.

Ahwere gave him an exasperated look. "You don't understand, Zeuxis. It's not as simple as that. The prince's curse wasn't aimed simply at the Blue team, though that's part of it, of course. He cursed the *queen,* and that means all of us – Alexandria and its lighthouse and everything else that keeps her in power."

"The Pharos?" Zeuxis whispered, turning cold.

"Yes!" Ahwere pulled out a crumpled and rather smelly scrap of papyrus covered in hieroglyphs. She read quickly, "*Take the power of the false Queen Cleopatra. Make her horses fall and her chariots crash. Take her royal throne and her stolen gold. Remove her name from the coins of this land. Take those she loves away from her. Then send your serpent to end her wretched life.* NOW do you understand?"

Zeuxis bit his lip. "That's bad. But I still don't see why the demon made the Keeper fall into the Romans' boat."

"Are you a complete idiot?" Ahwere snapped.

At Zeuxis' flush, she took a deep breath and said more calmly, "Sorry… I forget you don't know how curses work. If a curse calls on a ka-demon to make a rival chariot crash, then it doesn't say *how* to make it crash. The demon could just send the cursed team out of control. Or it might spook one of the other teams so there is a pile up. Or it might make the cursed team's charioteer ill. Or it might cause an accident by making one of the audience fall out of their seat under the cursed team's hooves... Do you see? The cursed team will crash, yes, but they could take any number of innocent people and horses with them."

Zeuxis swallowed, beginning to see the problem. "Then to remove Queen Cleopatra from power and kill her..."

"...is sure to involve lots of other people in Alexandria getting hurt first." Ahwere stared at him, as if challenging him to deny it.

Zeuxis thought of the seagull that had spooked Venus on the cliff this morning, so that she hurt herself and couldn't race. But no matter how hard he tried, he couldn't work out how that would help to take Queen Cleopatra's power away and end her life.

He shook his head. "Accidents happen in chariot racing," he said, setting his jaw. "You don't need a curse or a demon to make them happen."

Ahwere sighed. "True. And I knew you wouldn't listen to me, so I brought you these to tie on your harness for the race tomorrow." She dug in her pocket and pulled out a string of small silver bells that tinkled in the gloom, making Minerva snort in surprise.

Zeuxis blinked. "Bells? The last thing the fillies need is another distraction—"

"Charms," Ahwere corrected, showing him the tiny scratches on the silver. "I put the most powerful spells I could manage on them. Took me all night. They'll help protect you from that ka-demon Prince Ptolemy released, and any other bad luck that's around in the race."

Zeuxis took the bells, a lump in his throat. "Thank you," he said, feeling inadequate. He wanted to hug her, but didn't dare.

Ahwere gave him a quick smile. "Stop looking at me like that! You can't be the only team in the Hippodrome without Charms of Safe Running on your harness. And from what I saw out there on the headland, you're going to need all the help you can get tomorrow afternoon, Lighthouse Boy!"

The demon makes her horses fall and her chariots crash

The lighthouse boy will be useless in the Hippodrome, of course, which suits my purpose just fine. The rest might require a little more cunning on my part. A chariot race in Alexandria is not only about the fastest horses and the best charioteer, oh no! Human politics make things much more complicated than that.

Blue for the crown and Queen Cleopatra... Green for Prince Ptolemy... Red for the native Egyptians... White for Caesar. Bringing the Blue team down today will be easy enough, but the timing is crucial. If Green wins, the prince gains more supporters in the city, and the queen loses some of hers. White is no threat at this stage, and you can more or less forget the Red team, because they always come last.

An attack today, directed in the right place at the right time, could change the balance of power in Alexandria for ever.

Chapter 8.

HIPPODROME

As HE TURNED THE White team into the Hippodrome for the pre-race parade, Zeuxis felt sick with nerves. This was the first time he'd been inside the great oval enclosure on a race day, and it couldn't have been more different from his night visits to collect the wrecks. The little hairs on his arms prickled with excitement. He shivered, which passed along the reins and made the fillies shiver, too.

Every seat in the tiers was full. Blue supporters on one side and Green on the other, shouting insults across the course. Supporters for the less popular Red and White teams were squeezed together at the far bend furthest from the finish line. Lucian and Marcus, wearing their best togas, were somewhere in the owners' box. He didn't know where Ahwere was. He hadn't seen her since she'd marched back across the Heptastadion yesterday morning, daring the guards to stop her. They had searched her, of course, but she had got away with it and run off into the agora, losing herself in the crowds. Zeuxis hoped she had got home safely. But this was no time to be thinking of the Egyptian girl.

The queen's black colts, driven by Clytius, led the parade for the Blues. The black stallion was not in his team today. Either the horse was still recovering from the night it had injured itself in its stall, or the Master of Horse had talked some sense into the queen.

Following the Blues at an insulting distance, Prince Ptolemy's prized chestnuts trotted round the track. Their driver – a hard-faced boy with a whip scar across his cheek – raised his fist to the Green supporters, who showered him with rose petals and cheered wildly.

The Red driver looked even younger than Zeuxis and held his reins too tightly. His team of four mismatched horses picked up his nerves and jogged sideways. But one or two people cheered as the Red chariot passed the far bend, and the boy managed a smile.

Zeuxis came last in the parade. The noise of the crowd made the fillies roll their eyes. Even sensible Diana snorted and danced sideways. The substitute horse, an ugly brown gelding, laid back its ears and snapped at Minerva, who was harnessed on the outside in place of the injured Venus. Zeuxis jerked the rein to make the new horse pay attention. He didn't know its name, but its bad temper reminded him of Prince Ptolemy.

"Behave yourself, horse!" he muttered, concentrating on keeping his distance from the Red chariot in front of them. He looked for Lucian and Marcus as he drove round the bend, and the brown gelding – sensing he was not paying attention – nipped Minerva on the nose. The filly squealed in protest, and several people in the tiers laughed.

"You find that brown donkey on the ramp in your Pharos, Lighthouse Boy?"

"Looks like it should be hauling muck through the streets, not pulling a racing chariot!"

"Can't the great Julius Caesar even afford matching racehorses?"

Zeuxis set his jaw and did his best to ignore the taunts. Where were all the White supporters of his dream, chanting his name? *It'd be different when he won...*

One of the Green supporters threw a mouldy apple, which hit Minerva on the nose. The filly jumped, snatching Zeuxis back to reality and reminding him of the Romans' instructions. *No heroics. We don't want to show our true colours in the first race.*

At last the parade was over, and they pulled up in a line beneath the royal box to salute the queen. The Red driver wiped his palm on his tunic and gave Zeuxis a nervous grin. "I'm Hippolytus," he said. "Don't worry; they always throw stuff at the outsider. They won't do it in the race. But watch out for that Green driver with the scar. He plays dirty."

Zeuxis smiled back gratefully. "Thanks, I will."

Queen Cleopatra's entire household sat behind her in the box, including her youngest brother, the one

Prince Ptolemy had joked would make a better charioteer than Clytius. Mark Anthony was there in the place of honour, but to Zeuxis' relief there was no sign of Prince Ptolemy himself. The queen rose from her throne and stepped forward, a glittering vision of gold and white, the braids of her wig threaded with blue lotus flowers. She leant over the balcony and tossed something down to her champion Clytius. It was a charm for his harness, a blue ribbon fluttering from a bell inscribed with spells. He caught it one-handed and the Hippodrome erupted in wild cheers, making all the horses dance.

Meanwhile, Mark Anthony studied the chariots and their teams. He gave the substitute gelding a doubtful look and whispered something to the queen.

The queen laughed when she saw Zeuxis driving the Roman team. Her voice carried around the Hippodrome. "As you can see, Caesar has sent his best horses to challenge us! Pity the great emperor of Rome can only afford to employ a common lighthouse boy to drive for him."

Mark Anthony frowned as the crowd burst into fresh laughter. More rotten fruit landed near Zeuxis' chariot, making the fillies flinch. Hippolytus flashed him a sympathetic look.

Zeuxis' hands tightened on the reins. His blisters had broken open again during the parade, and blood seeped through the linen wrappings. "Whoa Minerva, whoa Maia," he whispered.

A trumpet blew, making the fillies jump again. A big slave with oiled ebony skin walked out on to the course carrying an urn, which he offered to each charioteer in turn. The drivers drew out tokens for the starting gates. Zeuxis was last to pick, and his heart sank when he saw he'd been left with the outside position.

"You're lucky," Hippolytus whispered, showing his token, which was the second gate. "At least you'll be out of the scrum."

While they waited for the earlier races to finish, the runners for the prize race of the afternoon retired to the Hippodrome stables. Zeuxis took his cue from Hippolytus, who immediately drove his chariot into one of the wide stalls, dismounted, and hitched his horses to the rail so his groom could polish their coats and check their hooves.

Zeuxis took the gloomiest stall at the end of the row, which was the only one left. He wondered if he should give the fillies some water. The Blue grooms were sponging their horses' lips and nostrils with some sort of herb solution. He unwound the linen from his hands and let the fillies lick the blood off his palms. The mare chewed his hair. The gelding contented himself with chewing the wooden rail.

The noise in the Hippodrome rose to a crescendo as the first two chariots returned, their horses steaming and snorting, and their drivers covered in sweat-caked sand. The Blue grooms cheered when they saw the palm branch in their charioteer's hand. The Green driver was shaking his head. One of his horses looked lame.

Zeuxis got a sudden attack of nerves.

"The waiting's the worst," Hippolytus said with a grin. "Won't be long now. I want to see this race. Back soon." He patted Zeuxis on the shoulder as he went off to the charioteer's balcony.

Zeuxis checked the charm Ahwere had given him, which he'd hung from Diana's bridle because she was the steadiest. He wished he could read the spell, but Ahwere had written it in Egyptian hieroglyphs.

"I just hope it works as well as Lady Wernero's did," he whispered to the mare, giving her a pat. "We'll show them, won't we?"

"You haven't a chance, Lighthouse Boy!" growled a voice behind him.

Zeuxis whirled, his heart thudding. The queen's champion, Clytius, stood behind him with a sneer on his face. He wore leather wrist-guards studded with blue jewels. The queen's charm dangled negligently from one hand.

"You made me look stupid in the park before the Master of Horse," Clytius hissed. "But you won't do so today. I've got a charm against any curse you can throw at me." He jangled the bell in Zeuxis' face.

Zeuxis swallowed back bile. He couldn't be sick in front of Clytius. "Are you in the prize race as well?" he asked, attempting to be friendly.

"No, I'm not – no thanks to you!" Clytius looked down his nose at Zeuxis. "The best prize of the day and

I'm going to miss it, because that curse you threw at me in training seems to have spread to my best stallion! I told the queen I'd still leave you and your Roman donkeys standing, but she's worried about Ptolemy's chestnuts, so she's running the greys. They'll win, of course. No question of that. Even our reserve team is better than any Prince Ptolemy can put together, and the Reds are a joke... though not as much of a joke as your Roman donkeys, of course." He sneered at the mare and swung his charm at her nose to make her jump.

Zeuxis pulled the mare away. He whispered, "B-but I didn't throw a *curse* at you!"

"Don't try to deny it, Lighthouse Boy! I've been in this game long enough to know when I've been cursed. That stomach ache I got in the park the morning you foolishly tried to drive my team wasn't natural. I couldn't work out at first where you'd got it from, though I should have guessed. You come up here to collect the wrecks after racing, don't you? I know what you told the queen. You said you saw Prince Ptolemy plant it in the Hippodrome. Would have been easy enough for you to dig it up and throw it at me in the morning. Just the sort of foolish thing an uneducated slave-boy like you would try! Curses are dangerous, you know."

Zeuxis' mouth dried. "But I told you, I didn't—"

Clytius cut him off. "Enough! I want you to know I've got friends in the Hippodrome, Lighthouse Boy. You're going to regret what you did to me that morning in the park."

The noise of the crowd surged and took longer to die away this time. Clytius looked up with a little smile as the steaming horses returned. "See? Another victory for the Blues." He pushed his finger into Zeuxis' stomach with a laugh. "You don't look too well, Lighthouse Boy. If you want to throw up, don't let me stop you."

Zeuxis lost control of his stomach and was sick in the sand. Clytius stepped clear with a chuckle and went to congratulate his team-mate. On the way, he paused to whisper something to the Green charioteer with the scar.

Zeuxis shivered as the Green driver looked his way and Clytius' words took on a whole new meaning. *I've got friends in the Hippodrome.* The scar-faced boy bared his teeth at Zeuxis and drew a finger slowly across his throat.

The crowd had reached a feverish state by the time the chariots trotted down to the starting gates for the prize race. The Blues had won three out of four races, and the Greens were desperate for another win. Zeuxis coaxed his team into the outside stall and gathered up the reins. The whip felt strange. He didn't normally use it for practice, but Lucian had said he'd need it in the race. He tried it in his left hand, then switched it to the right. Neither felt comfortable. He shook his head and dropped it over the rear of the gate.

The enclosure made him feel trapped. The horses must have felt the same way, for Prince Ptolemy's chestnuts were playing up, refusing to go into the gate next to him.

He could hear the Green charioteer cursing them, and the crack of his whip on flesh. Hippolytus was already in the second gate for the Reds. The Blue team was on the inside, in the best position.

The Green team finally went in, their hooves clattering against the wooden partition. Zeuxis' mouth dried. His stomach heaved again, but he had nothing left to throw up. Thankfully, the brown horse had stopped trying to bite the fillies and was looking at the barrier, ears pricked in expectation. He had raced before. Zeuxis felt a bit more hopeful as he crouched over the front plate of the chariot. Did he risk cutting across in front of the Green chariot? Would he make it?

Before he had decided, the queen dropped a white cloth from her balcony. With a loud twang, the gates opened.

A roar went up from the crowd as the horses leapt forwards. The chariot jerked under Zeuxis' feet and then he was surrounded by flying sand, the thunder of hooves, people cheering...

Wild excitement throbbed in Zeuxis' veins and filled his head, driving out Lucian's instructions about no heroics. The Green team's chestnuts had reared when the gates opened, and started half a stride behind the other chariots. Seeing his chance, Zeuxis steered for the inside.

"*Get out of my way!*" yelled the Green driver, and flicked his whip. Before Zeuxis realized what he intended, the end of the lash had wrapped itself around his wrist, jerking him off balance. The chestnut on the outside of the Green team barged into Diana's quarters, making her stumble. The fillies threw up their heads, the gelding shied, and Zeuxis' race was over.

He fell off the platform into the churned-up sand left by the Green team and watched with sinking heart as his chariot lurched after the others without him. Neck and neck, the Greens and Blues rounded the first turn in front, their drivers slashing furiously at each other with their whips. The Red chariot followed, while the White chariot – driverless – headed for the barrier.

Clutching the whip burn on his wrist, Zeuxis staggered to his feet and called desperately to the white mare. Her ear flicked back and she pulled up the team. She waited for him at the side of the course, snorting and shaking her head, one leg caught over the traces.

People laughed as Zeuxis ran after his chariot. The Blue and Green supporters yelled at him to get his 'lighthouse wreck' off the course before their champions came round again. Hippolytus glanced back. But when he saw Zeuxis was all right, he urged his team after the others.

Cheeks burning with shame and frustration, Zeuxis set about untangling his horses. He was about to lead them back to the stables in defeat, when he remembered what Lucian had said about him needing the experience. Setting his jaw against the laughter from the crowd, he climbed back into the chariot, gathered up the reins, and steered his team back on to the course.

Steering the chariot around the posts while keeping all four horses working together at a gallop was harder than he'd imagined. But, using his voice to keep the gelding going, he caught up with Hippolytus on the final lap. The boy grinned at him as he drew alongside, and raised his whip in salute. Zeuxis eased his team back to a canter. He couldn't win. He was a whole lap behind. Hippolytus eased up, too, and they rounded the final turn together, so they both saw what happened in terrible detail.

The Green charioteer, still fractionally behind the Blue, deliberately drove his wheel up inside his rival's wheel so that the two chariots were locked together. Then he leant over and began to prise out the Blue's axle pin with his dagger. The Blue supporters screamed in protest and the Blue driver used his whip desperately to fight off the attack. The dagger spun out of the Green driver's hand. But just as the Blue driver urged his team forward to escape the trap, a great cloud of sand rose up on a freak gust of wind and blew into his horses' eyes.

The Blue's greys leapt sideways into the Green's chestnuts, which stumbled and went down. The Green charioteer disappeared underneath them, and the Blue driver fell into the gap between the chariots and the central barrier. Somehow, his whip wrapped itself around his neck. He was dragged along the barrier, bouncing like a slab of meat, the hooves of the panicked horses thudding into his body.

"Great Serapis!" breathed Hippolytus, hauling his team clear of the carnage.

Zeuxis hauled on his reins, too, and because they were so far behind they both managed to steer around the wreck. The Blue's horses crossed the line first, but without their driver and with their chariot in pieces behind them. Three of the Green's chestnuts were loose. The fourth lay on the ground near the wreck, kicking frantically. The Green driver was trapped underneath the horse, covered in blood and moaning from the pain of broken bones. The Blue driver lay motionless further up the course in a tangled mass of leather and wood, his face white and his tongue sticking out, the whip still tight around his neck.

Hippolytus glanced at him as they passed. "He's dead," he whispered. "It must have been a curse, the way the sand blew into his horses' eyes like that. Did you see?"

Zeuxis felt sick again. The crowd had gone very quiet.

Then one of the race officials came running up to Hippolytus with a palm branch. The young Red driver looked at it in confusion.

"Take it, then!" hissed the official. "You won. You were the first chariot to cross the line with horses and driver intact. The queen's got a bag of gold for you, only I wouldn't go and claim it just now if I were you. She's not in a very good mood after what that Green driver tried to do to her chariot. Good job he's injured, I reckon, or she'd have broken his legs herself."

As Hippolytus reached out to take the palm branch, some Green supporters climbed over the barrier on to the course and tried to free their trapped driver. A gang of Blue supporters followed, angry at the way the Green driver had cheated by pulling out their chariot's axle pin. They accused the Green supporters of planting a curse to cause the wreck. The Greens said their driver would hardly have locked the chariots together if he'd known there was a curse, and accused the Blues of planting it. Soon there was a fight going on, through which the loose horses galloped, knocking over supporters of both sides and adding to the chaos. The Royal Guard arrived at a run, and began closing the exits to contain the crowd.

"We'd best get out of here," Hippolytus said, putting his palm branch safely under one foot and turning his sweating team back to the stables. "They'll have to cancel the rest of the races now, or there'll be a riot."

It took some time to get back into the city. The guards on the Canopic Gate were not letting anyone through with a weapon, and any person who objected or showed signs of violence was arrested on the spot. They broke up gangs of Blue and Green supporters and sent them home by different routes. At every crossroads, a patrol of the queen's guard waved them through, alert for trouble. Zeuxis stared over his shoulder, his neck prickling as he remembered the way the sand had blown up in the race. He hadn't been able to find Lucian or Marcus before they left the Hippodrome, and wondered what they were up to.

Hippolytus left him in the Greek Quarter, where the Red team stabled their horses, with advice to stay off the streets that night. Still thinking of that freak cloud of sand, and of the Blue driver's body bouncing along the central barrier, Zeuxis drove his weary team back along the waterfront and across the Heptastadion.

He was so tired, he felt numb. His stomach hurt and his limbs trembled with exhaustion. He'd survived his first race in the Hippodrome. But it had not been anything like his dream.

Chapter 9

SECRETS

It was dusk by the time Zeuxis and his weary team reached the Pharos stables. He knew he should report to the Keeper. But the horses had to be seen to first and, typically, there was no one around to help him with them. Even old Aelian seemed to have vanished. Zeuxis sighed. Slowly, hampered by his sore hands, he set to work.

He was still rubbing down the gelding, the last of the four, when the Romans returned. They were arguing and didn't see him in the shadows.

He was about to show himself and reassure them their horses were uninjured, when Lucian said, "I tell you, our plan isn't going to work! You saw what happened today. It couldn't have been more perfect if we'd set up that wreck ourselves. But the queen's men are already in control of the city again. They're obviously well practised in handling crowd trouble, and I'm not at all sure where Mark Anthony's loyalties lie. He was supposed to seduce the queen, not the other way around."

Zeuxis crouched in the shadows beside the gelding and prayed it wouldn't bite him. Fortunately, the race seemed to have mellowed the brown horse's temper, and the gelding was more interested in his hay.

"On the day, there'll be weapons in the city for the supporters to use, remember," Marcus said in a low tone, glancing at the stable doors.

"Won't make much difference. They looked ready to kill one another with their bare fists, but the queen's guard separated them so they couldn't continue the fight."

"But they weren't taking on the soldiers, were they? Maybe with weapons they'll feel more confident. At least we know that the royal palace will be more or less undefended, and the city streets deserted during the afternoon. The queen and all her household were at the races today, and Prince Ptolemy obviously keeps well out of the way. It'll work, Lucian my friend, you'll see."

Lucian sighed. "It doesn't take much to set these Alexandrians off, that's true. All right, I've got an idea how we might make them angry enough to take on the soldiers. We'll need another wreck like that one to trigger the riot, but with an added twist. I'll have a word with Mark Anthony, and the less the lighthouse boy knows the better... Where's he got to, anyway? Looks like he's settled the horses. Probably off with that girlfriend of his, boasting about the race he just came last in!"

Zeuxis held his breath and clutched the charm Ahwere had given him. *Don't come and look at the gelding, please don't.*

"I wanted to talk to you about that," Marcus said, after a pause. "We'll need a new driver for our plan. You saw the boy today. He's useless."

Zeuxis clenched his fists, cheeks flushing. He almost dropped the charm and gave himself away. Useless? They thought he was useless, just because the Green driver had played a dirty trick on him and jerked him out of his chariot at the start?

"Wrong, my friend," Lucian said with a sharp laugh. "You weren't watching closely enough. I saw the fire in the boy's eyes when the gates opened. He was going to cut across – he wasn't ready for the Green driver's tricks, that's all. Next time he will be more wary and know to avoid the others' whips. He has the best hands I've ever seen, and the mare listens to him. If the gelding hadn't been so slow, he'd have caught up with the others much earlier. Our speedy little Venus will be sound by the next race, and today will have given the lighthouse boy valuable experience. He'll do fine for our purposes. We don't need him to *win*, after all."

"You can't send Zeuxis into the Hippodrome again!" Marcus hissed, grabbing the other Roman's arm. "I won't let you. It isn't fair on the boy. And as for his hands, have you seen the state of them recently?"

Zeuxis curled his blistered fingers and edged forward to peer through a crack in the stall. He was in time to see the older Roman frown at his friend. "Caesar orders us to create a major riot in the city, and you're worried about a common slave-boy's blisters?" Lucian said. "You're going soft, Marcus Suetonius."

"He's not just a common slave," Marcus hissed. "He's part of the lighthouse team. If the fire in the Pharos goes out, Caesar's ships will founder on the rocks, same as anyone else's."

Lucian made an impatient sound. "The other islanders will keep the light burning. The Keeper isn't about to let his precious fire go out, don't worry. The boy may well survive the race if he keeps his head, and his blisters will have hardened over by then. There's no telling what'll happen in a chariot race. We can't afford the delay of finding another driver now. We'll just have to work on a need-to-know basis and keep Mark Anthony in the dark about the details so there's less chance of anyone warning the queen." He glanced at the stable doors, as Marcus had done earlier. "I don't think any of his men can hear us out here – we've more chance of being overheard by islanders." At this point he switched to Latin, and the discussion continued in that language.

Zeuxis kept his head down and tried to guess what they were saying. Cleopatra's name was mentioned, also Mark Anthony's, and Julius Caesar's several times. His stomach fluttered as the Romans moved over to the chariot and began to examine the shaft and the harness that Zeuxis had left nearby, ready for cleaning. He prayed they would not look so closely at their horses before they left.

Finally, after further discussion and some sharp words, Lucian marched out of the stable. Marcus muttered something Zeuxis couldn't hear, paused to check Venus' leg, then hurried after his friend.

Zeuxis slid down against the stall, his head spinning. The Romans were planning to create a major riot in Alexandria! Did the queen know? Did Prince Ptolemy? He had to tell someone!

He crept out of the gelding's stall, but stopped in the passage, worried that Marcus or Lucian might see him come out of the stable and realize he'd been eavesdropping. He eyed the lighthouse, now closed up for the night. Were the Romans in there? What if they caught him telling the Keeper what he had overheard?

If he told the Keeper, that would be the end of Zeuxis' racing career.

The realisation dropped like a cold stone in his belly. He hesitated in the stable, torn between his loyalty to the Pharos and his dream of winning in the Hippodrome.

"What are we going to do, Cleo?" he whispered to the donkey munching hay in the corner. Cleo pricked her long ears at the sound of his voice and nudged her harness, which Aelian had left hanging on the side of her stall.

Zeuxis shook his head, reminded of his duties. It was already dark. Who was going to collect the wrecks from the Hippodrome? Or had Aelian assumed Zeuxis would bring them back with him from the races? Didn't the old man realize there was no room on a racing chariot for a load of fuel?

He calmed slightly. The next race wouldn't be for a few days, at least. He did not have to make up his mind tonight. Anyway, what did it matter if the Romans created a riot in Alexandria? If Dameos could be believed, major riots had happened before without Caesar's help, and the Pharos had always survived. The island could be protected easily enough by stopping rioters from crossing the Heptastadion – they already had a roadblock in place. Perhaps Mark Anthony *had* warned the queen, and that was why she'd sent the guards? Zeuxis supposed a really bad riot might damage some of the buildings and statues in the city, maybe even the royal palace itself. But the queen and her Master of Horse had laughed at him when he'd asked to drive for them. At least the Romans had given him a chance. What was more, Lucian didn't think he was useless.

"You're right, old girl," he said, fetching the donkey's bridle. "Someone's got to go and collect up that wreck, and we can visit Ahwere on the way. Maybe she'll know what to do."

Despite what the Romans had said about the Royal Guard being in control of the city, the Egyptian Quarter echoed with shouts and laughter. Knots of triumphant Red supporters, fuelled by fizzy Egyptian beer, fought rival Blues and Greens in the dark alleys. Noisy fist fights accompanied the sound of smashing beer jars. Zeuxis hurried past, not wanting to get involved.

At a bridge over the ship canal, he came across a larger crowd chanting political slogans:

"Down with Queen Cleopatra!" someone shouted.

"Prince Ptolemy for Pharaoh!" agreed a Green supporter.

"May Prince Ptolemy eat sand!" shouted a Blue.

"A curse on all of you!" slurred a drunken Red. "Go home and leave Egypt to the Egyptians!"

Zeuxis shook his head and dragged Cleo into a side street to avoid them, praying he wouldn't come across another fight. His luck held. He tied Cleo at the end of the alley and hurried to his friend's house.

Lady Wernero opened the door a crack and pulled him inside, glancing up and down the alley. "I hope you haven't left a load of wood down there this time, Lighthouse Boy," she said. "This is no night to be out on the streets."

"Someone's got to collect the wrecks from the Hippodrome," Zeuxis said. "But I haven't loaded the cart yet. I'm not that stupid."

Lady Wernero eyed him as if she weren't so sure. "Why are you here, then?"

Zeuxis stole a look around the room. Another statue of an Egyptian god had joined Anubis, but apart from that it didn't look much different from the last time he had visited, when they had unrolled the curse. Except it seemed darker, as if *something* lurked in the shadows behind the lamps...

He shivered. Don't think of that.

"If you haven't been to the Hippodrome yet to find me any more curses, why are you here?" Lady Wernero insisted.

"He has been to the Hippodrome." Ahwere appeared at the bottom of the stairs. "He raced the Roman team today – didn't you?" Her black eyes challenged Zeuxis to deny it.

Zeuxis rubbed his elbow, where the old woman's fingers had left marks on his flesh. "You know I had to race. That's why you gave me your Charm of Safe Running, isn't it?"

Lady Wernero gave her granddaughter a sharp look.

"And you lost," Ahwere continued. "Not quite as much fun as you thought, was it? Maybe next time you'll let those Romans find another driver."

Zeuxis forgot about the shadows and raised his chin. The pain of his blisters, the emptiness of his stomach, and the weariness of his limbs faded as he remembered that one glorious moment when the starting gates had twanged open and the course shimmered before him in the sunlight.

"Next time I'm going to win," he said, swaying slightly from the smell of the witch's incense. "You'll see."

Ahwere blinked at him in surprise. "You're crazy!" she said.

Lady Wernero had been watching this exchange with her sharp eyes. "Sit down, Lighthouse Boy," she said briskly. "You're not going to win anything if you keep this up. I bet you haven't eaten since the race, have you?"

Zeuxis bowed his head. "No, Lady," he admitted.

"Then we can talk over supper."

With some relief Zeuxis sat next to Ahwere on a soft Persian rug, while the old woman bustled in and out of the room, bringing them platters of grapes and fish. He thought again of the Romans' conversation. Perhaps he had got it wrong. They had used Latin much of the time, and perhaps they had muddled the Greek word for 'riot' with something else – maybe they simply wanted him to win next time, which would cause uproar in the city?

Feeling a bit better, he reached for a grape.

Ahwere knocked his hand away and said, "Well? What happened? I heard the Blue driver was killed and the Green driver so badly crippled that he'll never race again. Though I suppose we ought to thank you. Grandmother says it's the first time the Reds have won in the Hippodrome since before I was born. No wonder they're having a party out there."

The noise in the streets seemed to be getting louder and closer. Zeuxis glanced at the door, a bit worried about Cleo, despite the fact she had an empty cart.

"Don't worry, Lighthouse Boy," said Lady Wernero, coming back to join them. "They've more sense than to make trouble near a witch's house." She poured Zeuxis some water and watched him gulp it down. "Now then, let's hear it."

Zeuxis licked his lips, wondering how much to tell her.

"The Romans," he mumbled. "I think they're up to something."

Ahwere sat up straighter and glanced at her grandmother. Quickly, Zeuxis told them what he'd overheard in the stable. "I could have got it wrong," he added quickly. "They switched to Latin halfway through."

Lady Wernero's eyes narrowed. "But they definitely mentioned Caesar's ships?"

"Yes, several times."

"And they're planning to create a major riot in the city next race day by causing another chariot wreck?"

"I don't know… maybe. I think they mean for me to win next time, though, so they can make a lot of money on bets."

"Mmm." The old woman chewed a grape thoughtfully. "Did they say anything about your Pharos light?"

Zeuxis started to say no, then remembered what Marcus Suetonius had said about Caesar's ships being wrecked if the lighthouse fire went out.

Lady Wernero greeted this with another narrow-eyed look. She muttered something under her breath, then heaved herself to her feet and rummaged in a corner of the room.

"I knew those Romans were up to no good," Ahwere said. She grabbed Zeuxis' arm. "You can't drive for them again, Zeuxis. They probably mean for *you* to be involved in the wreck next time!"

Zeuxis frowned and tugged his arm free. He scrambled to his feet.

"Where are you going?" Ahwere demanded.

"I've got to collect the wrecks from the Hippodrome. I'm late already." He wished he hadn't told them about the Romans now. He shouldn't have come. Ahwere thought he was more useless than ever, just because he had fallen for the Green driver's trick with the whip. The Egyptian Quarter was not patrolled as well as the rest of the city, and the witch kept giving him sideways looks as she rummaged through her chests.

"Wait a moment, Lighthouse Boy," she said.

Zeuxis backed to the door. The room had grown darker. His skin prickled in memory. Suddenly, he couldn't breathe. "Please let me go," he whispered. "If I don't get more fuel back to the lighthouse soon, the fire will go out."

Lady Wernero didn't seem to hear. She lifted something from one of her chests and swung round, threading a little Egyptian ankh on to a leather thong. "I want you to wear this," she said, knotting the thong and slipping it over Zeuxis' head. "My granddaughter's Charm of Safe Running seems to have kept you out of danger so far. But that ka-demon is still around somewhere despite my attempts to banish it, and I don't like the sound of what you've just told me. Julius Caesar might well be planning an invasion. Mark Anthony wouldn't be here just for fun, no matter how bewitching he finds the queen. I'm not sure yet how they plan to bring it off, so for now I think you should continue to help them train their horses so they don't suspect anything. I'll try another spell on the ka in the meantime, but Ahwere's right. You can't drive that chariot for the Romans in the next race. Promise me you won't?"

Zeuxis took a breath and opened the door. *The crowd screamed his name as he rounded the final turn in the lead: "Zeuxis! Zeuxis for the Whites!"*

"Does that work like my Eye of Horus?" Ahwere asked, interested.

"Yes," Lady Wernero said. "Come on, Lighthouse Boy. Your promise? Amulets won't protect any of us against Caesar's legions."

The door stood open. Cleo awaited him at the end of the alley, her long ears pricked in the shadows. The gang of noisy supporters seemed to have passed.

Zeuxis ducked outside. "I'm sorry, Lady, I can't give up my dream."

He untied Cleo and ran into the Egyptian night, dragging the donkey after him.

Chapter 10

TRAP

THE STREETS HAD quietened down by the time Zeuxis got out of the Egyptian Quarter, though smashed statues and broken pottery showed that the supporters had been active here as well, despite the patrols.

The guards on the Canopic Gate recognized him and grinned. "Plenty of fuel about in the city tonight, Lighthouse Boy," they said, letting him and the donkey cart through. "Needn't bother goin' all the way to the Hippodrome for it! Take care out there, lad. There's still a few crazies abroad."

Zeuxis promised he would. But threat from a human source was the last thing on his mind as he hurried across the shadowy Hippodrome. Although the crowds and the horses had gone, being on the course brought it all back. He shivered as the little hairs rose all over his body. He had only to close his eyes to see...

...the Blue driver falling into the gap between chariot and barrier, his whip coiling like a live snake around his neck...

Gripping the amulet Lady Wernero had given him, he approached the wreck. The Blue chariot was unrecognisable – a mangled heap of leather and wood, splattered with blood. No one had made any attempt to clear the course, though thankfully the Blue driver's body had been taken away for burial, and the injured horse had gone.

Zeuxis took a breath to steady his nerves and paced slowly back along the trail of wreckage, searching the churned-up sand for the place where the accident had actually happened.

Here.

He knew it as surely as if someone had raised an obelisk to mark the place.

He dropped to his knees and felt around in the bloodstained sand. At first, there was only the sting of grit in his blisters. Then his fingers touched something hard and smooth, and coldness shivered up his arm. He snatched his hand back and stared at the folded piece of lead, buried under the course beside the barrier.

"Another curse," he whispered, shivering. "Hippolytus was right."

"Clever little lighthouse boy, aren't you?" hissed a voice he recognized. "That's the curse that killed the Blue driver and regrettably crippled my best charioteer in the process, but that isn't all it does. Are you going to steal it, like you stole the last one I planted against the queen?"

Ice flowed up Zeuxis' spine. He started to get up, but was pushed back to his knees and held there by a sword point in the back of his neck. The initial terror left him, replaced by a more chilling fear as he realized who was standing behind him.

Prince Ptolemy.

"Stay exactly where you are, Lighthouse Boy," Ptolemy continued. "Now, very slowly, pick up that curse and unroll it."

Zeuxis' mouth dried. "But I can't…" he whispered, thinking of what had happened in Lady Wernero's house when she'd unrolled the last curse he'd found. "If it's still got power, it's very dangerous!"

Prince Ptolemy laughed. "I know it's *dangerous*, Lighthouse Boy. But only for you, not me. It's worded to trap anyone who tries to interfere with it, and I knew you'd come back tonight to look for it. The other drivers told me how you threw my last curse at the queen's champion in the park. No wonder my dear sister didn't find it when she had her men dig up the Hippodrome… you'd already stolen it for your own ends!" The prince chuckled. "Not that I object to your use of it, actually. Clytius is an arrogant fool and deserved all he got. But you've unleashed a powerful demon by using it in such a stupidly wasteful way, and you're going to pay for that."

Zeuxis tried to think past the chill of the sword at his neck. He supposed Clytius must have spread the story of his unnatural stomach pain around the races, and now Prince Ptolemy thought Zeuxis had stolen *his* curse to use on Clytius in the park. It was almost funny. "B-but you don't understand! I took the curse to—" he began, and shut his mouth, thinking of the Egyptian ankh hidden under his tunic. The less Prince Ptolemy knew about Ahwere and her grandmother's involvement the better.

Prince Ptolemy's chuckle vanished as quickly as it had come. The sword whistled past Zeuxis' ear, shaving off a curl of hair. Zeuxis cringed, afraid that even if the prince only meant to scare him, the sword might slip.

Ptolemy's guards gripped Zeuxis' elbows, picked him up and slammed him against the central barrier, where they held him facing their master. Prince Ptolemy used the point of his sword to flick the curse towards him. Zeuxis flinched as it bounced off his foot, little shudders going through him as he stared at it. *Worded to trap anyone who tries to interfere.* How? By calling on the ka-demon, like the last curse he'd found?

"You're scared of that thing, aren't you?" the prince asked, interested. "More scared of it than you are of me?"

Zeuxis wet his lips. "If you don't let me go, I'll scream," he whispered. "The Royal Guard—"

"—is busy in the city tonight," Ptolemy finished for him. "Go ahead. If anyone hears you, they'll just think it's stray supporters. They're not going to come and investigate, not when they've got their queen and the Roman envoy to protect." He shook his head. "My sister has no idea how to rule these people. I will do much better when I am on the throne of Egypt. Crucify a few, maybe, like the Romans do, to set an example, and make the rest pay taxes for their race days. *Then* we'll see how troublesome they are in the evenings, when none of them can afford to buy beer."

He considered Zeuxis, stroking the hilt of his sword. "I misjudged you, Lighthouse Boy. Not only did you get away with lying to me at our last meeting, but it seems you've somehow talked the Romans into letting you drive their chariot for them. It seems you need a lesson in loyalty to your city, your country, and your rightful Pharaoh. Secure his hands!"

This last order was for his men, who lashed Zeuxis' wrists together with a leather thong.

Really frightened now, Zeuxis yelled as loudly as he could. But at a nod from Ptolemy, one of the soldiers stuffed a rag into his mouth and tied it in place.

The prince smiled at him. "He's a little more scared of me now, I think," he said, using a corner of his tunic to pick up the curse. He stepped forward and forced the roll of lead between Zeuxis' palms.

Zeuxis gasped as the curse turned his arms numb as far as his elbows. His head spun. He felt sick again, and wished he hadn't eaten Lady Wernero's grapes. He fought the heaving sensation in his stomach. If he threw up now, the gag would make him choke.

"Mmm, nasty blisters." The prince took the long end of the thong binding Zeuxis' wrists and wrapped it around Zeuxis' fingers, fastening them together so that he could not drop the curse. He tugged the knots tight, staring into Zeuxis' eyes all the while. He smiled coldly and scraped the edge of his blade down Zeuxis' arm. "If you won't unroll it for me, you can hold it safe so nothing interrupts us while we talk. I have a few questions for you, Lighthouse Boy, and don't think you can lie to me this time. People never lie to me a second time."

Zeuxis believed it. His legs trembled so much, he was glad he was kneeling down. "Ummm... ummmm...?" he mumbled through the rag.

Prince Ptolemy chuckled. "What was that, Lighthouse Boy?"

Zeuxis mumbled again, wanting to ask how he was supposed to answer questions when he'd been gagged.

The prince smiled at his men. "Ah! The prisoner wants to talk already. But I haven't even asked my questions yet." He leant close to Zeuxis and put his sword under his chin. His voice lowered, chillingly. "I don't think you quite understand me, Lighthouse Boy. I already know the answers to the questions I'm going to ask you. All I require from you is a simple confirmation – yes or no. It's a very easy game. Even a stupid lighthouse boy like you should manage to get it right."

He stepped back and smiled.

"First question! Did you steal the curse I planted against my sister? Nod your head for yes, shake for no. If your answer is correct, nothing more happens to you. If it's wrong, then I'll teach you a further lesson in loyalty until you get it right."

Zeuxis swallowed bile round the gag. Dizzy with fear of giving a "wrong" answer, he nodded.

The prince smiled at his men again. "See? Splendid! He's getting the idea already. Second question! Did you steal my curse to throw at Clytius so you could drive his team?"

Zeuxis hesitated.

"Yes or no?" the prince snapped, touching his sword to Zeuxis' bound fingers. They were so cold by now from holding the roll of lead that he couldn't feel the blade, but the sight of it pressing into his flesh made him tremble.

He nodded, praying it was close enough to the truth to satisfy the prince.

"All right…" Ptolemy said, looking hard at him. "I'll give you the benefit of the doubt on that one. Third question! Are you helping the Romans do more than race chariots?"

Zeuxis shook his head.

Ptolemy frowned. "Could be true, I suppose. They certainly didn't seem too upset when you lost that race today. They're up to something, though, that's obvious. Now, concentrate, Lighthouse Boy, because this one's important. Last question. Did the Romans come to Alexandria to seize power?"

Zeuxis hesitated again. If Caesar invaded Egypt like Lady Wernero thought he planned to do, it would serve the prince right.

"Yes or no?" The sword drew blood. Zeuxis closed his eyes, summoned all his courage, and shook his head.

"Liar!" Prince Ptolemy screamed. "Hold him tight! He needs to know I'm not joking."

Zeuxis' head spun again. There was something behind him, something that lifted the hairs on the back of his neck...

The soldiers' hands tightened on his arms as the men glanced at the tunnel that led to the Hippodrome stables.

The prince frowned, following their gaze. "Company?"

"Thought I saw something move in there, Your Majesty," said one.

Zeuxis tried to see behind him, but he was below the level of the barrier. At a snapped order from Ptolemy, the soldiers shoved his head back round.

The prince frowned at the tunnel Zeuxis couldn't see. He shook his head. "Probably a drunk supporter in there. Don't worry. Whoever it is will have more sense than to get involved."

He bent over Zeuxis, and his voice lowered again. "Listen to me carefully, Lighthouse Boy. A charioteer's skill is in his hands. Without good hands to communicate with his horses, he is nothing. You might think yours hurt now from those blisters, but imagine not being able to hold the reins at all. Your career as a driver would be over before it's begun. I'm afraid I don't believe you when you say the Romans didn't come to Alexandria to seize power, and I told you that people only get one chance to lie to me. You have ten fingers. I'm going to cut off one finger for every wrong answer you give me. So you'd best start telling me the truth, because that's one finger gone already..." The sword dug under the little finger of Zeuxis' left hand, and blood welled out.

Zeuxis' stomach heaved. Prince Ptolemy's eyes glinted with cruelty. You didn't need to be very strong to cut off a finger. He struggled and screamed through his gag – it came out as a muffled whimper. The stars brightened. A wind blew up out of nowhere, swirling sand into the prince's eyes. Ptolemy dropped the sword with an oath.

Zeuxis' ears roared, and through the sand he thought he saw Ahwere's white face. *Help me*! he cried through the gag.

The sand whirled faster. A vast darkness rose up and descended over him like gigantic wings. Someone called his name, high and scared: "Zeuxis! Zeuxis, look out!" The last thing he saw was the monstrous ka-demon from his dream, its huge mouth opening to suck him out of the world.

The demon removes those who interfere

Interfering Egyptian witch! She has given the boy an
amulet so I cannot touch him.

At least Prince Ptolemy and his men are out of the
way. I must have scared them when I went for the boy.
I'll soon work out how to get around the witch's petty
spells. Then I will show her, and anyone else who dares
interfere with my work, that when you summon a demon
you don't get rid of us that easily.

Chapter 11

BETRAYAL

Zeuxis woke wrapped in a blanket, lying on something hard. A musky scent filled the air around him. His ears still hummed, and he could not see a thing. His hands were numb from the wrist down. He shuddered. He couldn't remember what had happened after the wind and the sand.

Afraid of what he might find, he carefully moved an arm. It stopped against the blanket, but his bonds were gone. A feather pillow had been placed beneath his head. He kicked at the blanket until it came free. The blackness was so complete, he wondered if he had gone blind, though his eyes felt normal. He pressed his numb hands to his face, and his panic eased at the feel of fingers against his cheek. He rolled each one against his face in turn, counting under his breath.

One... two... three... four...

When he reached ten, Zeuxis clutched the pillow and trembled with relief. Prince Ptolemy must have been disturbed before he could carry out his threat. Or had he been bluffing all along? What had happened? Where was he? Why couldn't he *see*?

A new fear crept over him. What if the Royal Guard had come to investigate when he screamed, found his unconscious body, and thought him dead? What if they had buried him alive, sealed up the entrance and—?

"Stop it, Zeuxis!" he whispered. "They don't bury slaves in tombs with fine blankets and pillows and *incense*, for the gods' sake."

He giggled at the thought, then froze as something scraped in the darkness behind him. A huge, misshapen shadow rose up the wall, rippling over strings of carved Egyptian hieroglyphs.

The ka-demon!

He fumbled for the amulet Lady Wernero had given him. Even as the scream rose in his throat, the shadow shrank to human size, and he realized it had been cast by a lamp in a girl's hands. He swallowed his cry as Ahwere's voice whispered, "Zeuxis? Don't be afraid. It's me. I've brought you something to eat."

The sight of his friend made him tremble all the more. He clutched the amulet to his chest and, although he tried to sound brave, her name came out as a sob. "Ahwere..."

"Sorry, I didn't think you'd wake up so soon, or I'd have come earlier. Grandmother said you'd sleep for ages with what she put in the brazier." His friend set down the lamp on the rock shelf that served as his bed, and dropped a bundle smelling of cheese and olives beside it. She smiled at him as she untied the knot.

Now Zeuxis could see the source of the scent that was making his head spin. A brazier he recognized from the witch's house smoked in the corner. He gazed round the painted walls, saw the little tunnel Ahwere must have crawled through to get in, and shivered. No light showed at the other end. Either it was still dark outside, or the entrance was blocked.

"Where are we?" he asked.

"In the graveyard," Ahwere said, confirming one of his fears. "It's a hiding place we use sometimes: an Egyptian family's mausoleum. I'm sorry we had to bring you here, but it was the best way to protect you from that curse you were holding. Grandmother's going to unroll it and make it safe. It shouldn't take her long. It can't be as dangerous as the last one you brought us, because she said she'd manage without me. But you can't leave this place yet. Prince Ptolemy's men are still searching for you..." She hesitated and lowered her gaze. "I'm afraid your Pharos will have to wait a bit longer for its fuel."

Zeuxis sat up and almost brained himself on the rock. "The fuel!" he said. "I almost forgot! Cleo—"

"Your donkey's fine." Ahwere pushed him back down. Zeuxis was surprised how easily she managed it. He must be weaker than he'd thought. "But we have to stay here till Grandmother comes to tell us it's safe." She paused again, and her certain tone faltered. "Why do you still want to drive that chariot for the Romans, Zeuxis? You could have been killed in that race!"

Zeuxis blinked at the Egyptian girl. Was she really concerned for him? "They all laughed at me last time," he admitted. "The brown horse was too slow, but next time we'll have Venus back in the team. I need to show everyone I can do it."

Ahwere heaved an exasperated sigh. "You're crazy to want to risk your life for those stupid Romans!"

Zeuxis scowled. "At least they gave me a chance to drive, which is more than your proud Queen Cleopatra ever did."

"I told you, she's not *my* queen. She's Macedonian, not Egyptian like the true Pharaohs. I don't know why Grandmother's so sure she... never mind." Ahwere stared at the entrance and said more softly, "I wanted to come to the races to watch you, but I didn't dare. When I went back across the Heptastadion after seeing you training on the island that day, the guards confiscated my papyrus: the one I'd used to copy the curse against the queen. Lucky for me, they couldn't read hieroglyphs! I ran before they realized what it was, but the queen must have translated it by now. Grandmother was worried her men might recognize me."

Zeuxis took a handful of olives. He didn't know how long he'd been unconscious, but it must have been some time. His stomach gurgled at the smell of the cheese, and he stuffed it down. A large jar of water stood in the corner. He reached for it and drank thirstily. The olives were stuffed with some sweet herb he hadn't tasted before. Regretting the way he'd snapped at his friend, he made an effort to be more cheerful. "These are good. What did you put in them?"

Ahwere didn't reply. "What was Prince Ptolemy doing to you in the Hippodrome?" she asked.

Zeuxis shuddered in memory. "He planted that curse to trap me – he guessed I'd dug up his last curse against the queen. He wanted me to unroll it, but I refused. So he threatened to cut off my fingers instead! Then there was a wind, like in the race before the wreck, and all the sand blew up..." He remembered something else. "I thought I saw you. Were you there? Did you see what happened?"

Ahwere passed him some more olives. She didn't seem hungry. Surrounded by the hieroglyphs, with her black hair shadowing her face and the lamplight glinting from her amulet, she looked more than ever like an ancient Egyptian priestess.

"It was the ka," she said, in the end. "I don't know why, but I think the demon that escaped when we unrolled the first curse you brought us – the one Prince Ptolemy planted against the queen – came back. It blew sand in the prince's eyes and frightened his soldiers away. You fainted. I saw it all from the tunnel. After you left our house so suddenly like that, Grandmother was worried. She sent me after you, but you ran off so fast I lost you. I decided the best thing to do was to go out to the Hippodrome and wait for you to come and get the fuel – only I didn't expect to find you in the clutches of

Prince Ptolemy's thugs!" She shook her head. "Lucky for you that ka came, actually, because I couldn't think how I was going to rescue you on my own."

"It was you they saw in the tunnel," Zeuxis said, remembering.

Ahwere nodded. "I was careless. I didn't think they'd see me in the shadows."

"You were lucky Prince Ptolemy didn't send his thugs after *you*!"

This time, she laughed. "Zeuxis, I do believe you care about me!"

"Don't. This isn't funny," Zeuxis said, clenching his hands to see if the feeling was coming back. He shook his fingers in frustration. "There's still something wrong with my hands. They're numb."

"They'll get better soon," Ahwere said. "I expect it was from holding that curse so long. It probably didn't have much power left, but all the same... I wonder what's keeping Grandmother?" She glanced over her shoulder at the entrance to the tomb, where a glimmer of grey light showed. "She should have finished by now."

Zeuxis' heart gave a jolt. "That's daylight, isn't it? I've been in here all night! I have to get back to the lighthouse. The Keeper needs me to organize the fire rota, and the Romans are expecting me to exercise their team. I don't want them to find another driver to replace me, not now Venus is recovering." He swung his legs off the shelf and tried to stand up. He swayed, put a hand against the rock and almost fell. Ahwere caught him and lowered him back to the blanket.

"Don't try to get up," she said, looking worried.

Zeuxis shrugged her off and tried again. "I can't stay here," he mumbled, the words slurred. "The Keeper will be looking for me."

"Your Keeper's still in bed."

"The Romans will be looking for me, then."

"The Romans won't find you in here, don't worry. Grandmother's taken precautions." Ahwere frowned at the entrance again. "What do *you* think they're up to, Zeuxis? Are they really planning to invade Egypt?"

Zeuxis blinked. It was getting hard to stay awake. "You're as bad as Prince Ptolemy, interrogating me like this."

The girl looked hurt. "I'm your friend. I rescued you, remember?"

"If what you say is true, the ka-demon rescued me."

"Demons don't…" Ahwere shook her hair across her face. "Never mind. It doesn't matter what the Romans are up to. You can't leave until Grandmother's made the new curse safe, anyway. You've got enough food for a day or two, and the olives have magic in them to help you sleep so that the time will pass quicker. I'll bring more as soon as I can."

Zeuxis turned cold, beginning to suspect why he felt so sleepy. Without his promise, Lady Wernero must be trying to make sure he didn't drive in the next race by surer means. "You can't keep me here against my will!" he cried, struggling up again.

"I'm sorry." Ahwere touched his arm. "But it's for your own good. I'll leave you the lamp. Be careful with the oil, or it won't last. Don't try to follow me. Grandmother put a spell on the entrance." She backed towards the tunnel. "I really am sorry, Zeuxis. I didn't want it to be like this."

"Wait!" Zeuxis said, frightened now. He scrambled after her on all fours because his legs wouldn't support him. "What do you mean? Like what? You can't just leave me here!"

"I wish I could stay with you, I really do. But I'm worried about Grandmother. She might need my help with that second curse, after all. She says whatever the Romans are up to, we can't let them use you for their plans. I'll be back as soon as I can, I promise."

"But—"

Ahwere dragged the hem of her dress from his feebly clutching hands and stumbled away down the tunnel.

Zeuxis crawled after her, as if through thick sea mist. Halfway along, where the tunnel made a sharp turn, stars sparkled before his eyes. He put his head between his knees and took deep breaths, afraid he might faint. Nothing more happened when he stayed still. Only when he tried to follow Ahwere did everything fizz around him.

After several more attempts, he realized the spell would not let him go. He gritted his teeth, gave up and crawled back to the shelf. Too sleepy to make it back to his hard bed, he tugged down the blanket and wrapped himself in it, shivering at the thought of Ahwere's betrayal.

Never mind the spell the witch had put on the entrance. Ahwere, his *friend*, had sat there and watched him eat her grandmother's magic olives! She'd even passed him more.

Remembering how Prince Ptolemy had told him that the queen's charioteer Clytius used a feather to make himself throw up after eating, he tried putting a finger down his own throat. It did no good. Before his stomach had a chance to cramp, the witch's magic carried him into the dark.

Zeuxis drifted in and out of nightmares, his eyelids too heavy to open. Every time he knew himself to be awake, he thought about trying to crawl down the tunnel again. But he felt too weak to do more than help himself to water and more of the olives.

"Ahwere," he whispered. "Please come back. Please."

He had to escape before the next race. He *had* to. Ahwere had said there was a spell keeping him here... something magic... yet, if the witch was back at her house unrolling the curse, what was she using to keep the spell active? Maybe something Ahwere had brought, except that would have relied on him staying asleep until she came... of course, the amulet!

Desperate, his brain muddled with half-glimpsed demons, Zeuxis ripped off the little ankh the witch had given him, and flung it against the wall.

*   *   *

When Zeuxis next opened his eyes, the lamp Ahwere had left him had run out of oil, and his head felt clearer. It must have been night outside, for he could not see his fingers before his face – though which night, he did not know. Then he saw something that made him forget his other worries.

Two pinpricks of green. Eyes, watching him from the entrance to the tomb.

Zeuxis clutched the blanket to his chin, hardly daring to breathe. *I'm still asleep. This is a nightmare, that's all.*

The eyes disappeared and something large slithered away along the tunnel. Lady Wernero's spell sparkled briefly, glinting off a snake's scales. His ears popped, as if a seal had broken.

Cold sweat trickled down Zeuxis' spine. He waited in the dark for a long time, rigid, staring at the place where the monster had disappeared. But it did not come back. Finally, his throat dry with thirst, he reached for the water jar. It was empty. He must have drunk it all.

"Well, if I'm awake I need to find something to drink. And if I'm dreaming, the demon can't hurt me," he whispered, hoping this last part was true.

Clutching the jar tightly to use as a weapon if need be, he took a deep breath for courage. With a wild cry to frighten away anything that might be lurking in the tunnel, he darted for the entrance.

He had scrabbled from the tomb and fought his way through the vines that hid the entrance, before he realized

Lady Wernero's spell had not stopped him. His hands were no longer numb, letting him feel wet leaves, dripping after recent rain. Clouds raced across a sky vast with stars. The air smelled of sea.

He was awake, most definitely.

Zeuxis cast a terrified look at the shadows behind him and ran.

It wasn't easy getting back into the city. The guards at the Necropolis Gate didn't know him like the ones on the Canopic Gate. They were suspicious of his ragged appearance, thinking him one of the beggars who roamed the suburbs stealing from the holiday villas along the lakeshore. Zeuxis had to talk fast to persuade them he was the lighthouse boy and had driven the chariot for the Whites last race day. This almost made things worse, because most of the guards were Blue supporters and still angry about the wreck that had let the Red team win. Another argument began over what had caused it: whether it had been a curse, or simply the Green charioteer's trickery.

Luckily for Zeuxis, an officer who had been on duty at the Hippodrome came down from the battlements to see what all the fuss was about. After holding a torch close to Zeuxis' face, he grunted. "It's the lighthouse boy, all right," he muttered, shoving Zeuxis in the direction of the market place. "Hurry back to your island, Boy! You should be tending to your duties, not driving chariots all night for them Roman scum!" He spat in the direction of the harbour, where the Roman galley was anchored.

Zeuxis did not argue. The guards obviously assumed he'd been doing some secret race training for the Romans outside the city walls, which was a lot easier than explaining the truth – he couldn't have told them exactly what had happened at the tomb, anyway, because he didn't know himself.

His route back to the island led past the Egyptian Quarter. Glancing at the unlit alleys, Zeuxis thought of Ahwere and the curse her grandmother had taken to unroll, the one Prince Ptolemy had said would trap those who tried to interfere. Did that extend to everyone who touched the curse, or just him?

He set his jaw. The last thing he wanted to do now was leave the torchlit main street to venture down some dark alley where Prince Ptolemy's men might be lying in wait for him, to say nothing of the demon from his nightmares. Besides, he didn't see why he should go running after Ahwere. She'd be all right. She had her precious grandmother and her spells. He'd bet all the Pharos' remaining fuel that the Egyptian girl wasn't worrying about *him*.

Still angry at the way she'd tricked him in the tomb, Zeuxis broke into a run. By the time he reached the Heptastadion, dawn had turned the sea silver. A second roadblock had been set up at the island end, manned by Roman soldiers, which gave him a bit of a jolt. But both sets of guards recognized him and waved him through. "You're in a lot of trouble, Lighthouse Boy," was all the Romans said.

Too breathless to reply, Zeuxis ran on around the headland to the lighthouse, still wondering what he was going to tell the Keeper to explain his nights off the island.

"Sorry, I forgot the time..."

No. Sounded too irresponsible.

"I got caught up in the trouble after the races..."

True, in a way.

"Prince Ptolemy trapped me in the Hippodrome with a curse, and then a witch imprisoned me in an Egyptian tomb with a spell, but a ka-demon from the other world came and freed me..."

Only if he wanted to be locked up in the lighthouse for his own good.

The thud of hooves and the sound of horses snorting in the cool air jerked him back to the present. He paused to catch his breath. He'd reached the sand track the Romans had laid for exercising their team. A single chariot was circling it in the dawn.

Zeuxis forgot his other worries and narrowed his eyes as the chariot came closer. The three grey fillies cantered perfectly together, tossing their heads against their bits, impatient to go faster. Their manes rippled against the sea, and their tails floated like banners. The white mare, harnessed on the inside, glowed in the grey light like a horse from another world. Marcus Suetonius, clad only in an old tunic and barefoot, had them balanced well. But as they came round the turn, Zeuxis saw the chariot dip under the Roman's weight, breaking the fillies' stride. They tossed their heads in protest.

Marcus muttered something and eased his team back to a trot. Zeuxis stared at the dark filly on the outside. Venus looked as sound as the others.

As the chariot came abreast, Marcus spotted him. He pulled up and gave Zeuxis a long look. The fillies fidgeted and blew down their noses at him, recognizing his smell. Zeuxis stroked Venus' neck and looked more closely at her leg to make sure.

"Yes, she's sound now," Marcus said. "The cut healed cleanly, like I hoped it would." He shook his head at Zeuxis. "Where have you been? Lucian thought you'd been scared off by that wreck in the Hippodrome and run away so you wouldn't have to drive for us again. It's been getting more and more difficult to cover for you. We were about to tell your Keeper."

"The Keeper doesn't know I've been away?" Zeuxis said. His spirits lifted slightly as he looked at the lighthouse.

Marcus pressed his lips together. "Lucian thought it best we didn't tell him until it was absolutely necessary. We've been looking for you all over – Mark Anthony's men have been scouring the city. No one knew anything. It was like you'd vanished from the face of the earth. We weren't the only ones looking for you, either." He gave Zeuxis a sideways look, and lowered his voice. "Prince Ptolemy's guard have been over here, asking questions."

Zeuxis swallowed in sudden fear. Venus threw up her head, sensing his nerves. "What did you tell them?" he asked, a little too sharply.

"Nothing." Marcus gave him a sideways look. "Don't worry, we saw them off. That's why we set up our own roadblock on the Heptastadion, since they'd obviously got around the queen's. Your Keeper agreed we couldn't have Prince Ptolemy's soldiers coming over here, upsetting the islanders." His tone became more gentle as he noticed Zeuxis' hands were trembling. "What happened to you after you went to the Hippodrome to collect the wrecks? Old Aelian found your donkey and the cart up there in the morning, but there was no sign of you."

Zeuxis took a deep breath. He felt like bursting into tears and telling the Roman everything. But he remembered the Keeper's warnings about not trusting them. Even if Lady Wernero proved wrong about the invasion, they were definitely up to something. "I'm not sure," he said carefully, looking at the dark filly again; sound, and in training again. He could still see the scab on her injured leg, but it looked more than a day old. "How long?" he whispered. "How long have I been away?"

Marcus frowned. "Long enough for Lucian to make enquiries about hiring another driver, and for me to start getting Venus trained up for the race. We'd almost given up on you."

"Given up on me?" Zeuxis' legs went weak.

Marcus smiled. "I'm teasing, silly. But it's been five days. Quite a lot has happened since you've been away. The queen's announced the next championship race in the Hippodrome and we've entered the fillies. Word's out that Prince Ptolemy's bought another chestnut horse to replace the one that was killed in the wreck – a bit of an unknown, since our spies have yet to see it in training, and we don't know who his new driver is. Queen Cleopatra's entered her black colts and that crazy stallion of hers, with Clytius driving, and the Reds are wild with ambition for Hippolytus because of his unexpected win last time. No one expects much of the Whites, so there's no pressure. You've still got a few days to get yourself and Venus fit."

Zeuxis looked at the Pharos. The glow of its fire was fading as the sun rose, but still served to warn ships away from the rocks. He breathed again. He was going to be allowed to drive in the next race – if the Keeper let him, after what had happened last time.

Marcus followed his gaze. "Don't worry about your lighthouse duties. Lucian and I have worked out a rota to keep your fire burning. We had a bit of a scare the night after the race, what with the storm breaking the glass and the rain nearly putting the flames out, but we're managing. All things considered, it'll be safer if you stay here on the island till next race day. Aelian and the other boys can collect the fuel. You probably ought to go and see your Keeper, though, before he crawls down the lighthouse stairs looking for you and breaks his silly neck. He thinks a lot of you, you know."

Still trying to catch up with everything Marcus had told him, Zeuxis almost missed the most important part.

"A storm broke the lighthouse glass?" he said. "That's never happened before!"

Marcus gave him a thoughtful look. "It was a bad one. Wrecked three merchant ships further along the coast, and brought down a tree through the roof of the Great Library. The rain ruined hundreds of priceless scrolls, apparently. You must have heard the wind?"

"I was underground," Zeuxis whispered. The night after the race, Marcus had said: the night the ka had come to the Hippodrome and 'rescued' him from Prince Ptolemy... What had the demon been up to in the five days before he'd seen it in the tomb?

Marcus rested a hand on his shoulder and said gently, "Want to tell me about it?"

Zeuxis opened his mouth, shut it again and shook his head.

The Roman nodded. "I understand. I'm sure you'd prefer to talk to your Keeper about such things. Just as long as you're still happy to drive for us? Lucian is having trouble finding a competent driver willing to work for Romans. I was getting worried I'd have to race the fillies myself!"

Zeuxis took a breath and ran his hand down Venus' grey neck. "You wouldn't have a chance," he said, keeping his tone light. "You're much too heavy on the turns."

"I know." Marcus paused. He said quietly, "Zeuxis, there's something you ought to know if you're going to drive for us in the next race."

Zeuxis looked up in time to catch the Roman glance out to sea in the direction of his homeland. He wet his lips and said, "I know you're here on Caesar's business. It doesn't bother me. I'm not Egyptian, or Macedonian like Queen Cleopatra and Prince Ptolemy. I'm a slave, a nobody. I never knew my mother and father. They abandoned me as a baby. The lighthouse is my home. I just want to win in the Hippodrome. It doesn't matter to me who sits on the throne of Egypt, as long as your Caesar still keeps the Pharos light burning and still holds the races when he's in charge."

Marcus stared at him in surprise. Zeuxis met the Roman's gaze, his heart thudding. What if the Romans decided he was too dangerous now he knew of their plans, and decided to get rid of him anyway?

"Only a fool would extinguish the Pharos light," Marcus said finally. His lips twitched up at one corner. "And I don't think even Caesar would dare close the Hippodrome. You Alexandrians are crazy about your chariot racing!"

Zeuxis avoided going up into the second tier of the lighthouse as long as possible. It had been one thing to keep the Romans' plans secret when he hadn't been sure what they were up to. But now Marcus had more or less confirmed Lady Wernero's suspicions, and he didn't know how much to tell the Keeper. Also, he wanted to talk to Aelian about the storm, but there was no sign of the old man. In the meantime, he kept himself busy tending the Roman horses and questioning the other boys about what had happened while he'd been away. Just past noon, with Aelian still not back, he made his way reluctantly up the lighthouse stairs and knocked on the Keeper's door.

The woman, Phila, opened it and shook her head at him. "About time!" she said. "He's been impossible since the storm that broke our light. I've had to give him sleeping potions to keep him from climbing out the window!"

The Keeper looked even paler than before, though he was sitting propped up in a chair with cushions, rather than on his bed. His broken leg stuck out at an awkward angle and he winced when he moved it. But his face broke into a smile when he saw Zeuxis, and he sent Phila away with orders that they weren't to be disturbed.

"Come and sit by me, Zeuxis!" he ordered. "I want to know everything. Lucian and Marcus won't tell me a thing! 'Resting' after your race, they said. Then helping to fix the glass in the light. Then out training the new filly with their team... I know when someone's lying to me! What's kept you so you can't come and see me? Did you get injured in that chariot wreck I keep hearing about, is that it? Were those cowardly Romans too afraid to let me see your bruises, in case I forbade you to race for them again?"

He reached forward and checked Zeuxis over, feeling his limbs for broken bones.

Zeuxis hid his blistered hands under his tunic. "I'm all right, Sir," he said, touched by his concern. "Really."

But the Keeper wasn't fooled. "Let me see your hands!"

Reluctantly, Zeuxis stretched them out for his master to examine. The Keeper's scarred fingers ran gently across his half-healed blisters. Then he noticed the fading weals around Zeuxis' wrists, evidence of his treatment at the hands of Prince Ptolemy's men. His eyes darkened.

"Have those Romans been keeping you from seeing me against your will? I want to know the truth, Zeuxis! These look like rope burns."

"They're... from the race!" Zeuxis said, thinking fast. "The Green charioteer's whip got caught around my wrist... er, wrists... and pulled me out of the chariot."

"Yes, so I heard. I also heard you climbed straight back in again and completed the race, when most other boys would have given up." The Keeper sighed. "I'm not going to forbid you to drive the White chariot next race day, if that's what you still want to do. A boy your age should be allowed a little fun before he gets too old to enjoy it. But when all this is over, and the Romans have gone home, I want you to promise me you will concentrate on your duties here in the lighthouse. You won't stay a boy for ever, Zeuxis. Charioteers' careers are very short, even if they don't come to a bad end, like that Blue driver's did."

He gave Zeuxis a hard look.

Zeuxis avoided the Keeper's gaze. "Thank you, Sir," he mumbled. "I promise I won't let the Pharos fire go out."

It wasn't quite a lie. He would do both – drive in the race *and* look after the fire. It would be hard work, but if the Romans continued to help him, and people like Ahwere and Prince Ptolemy didn't try to interfere, he would manage.

His master sat back and nodded. "I'm sorry I doubted you, Zeuxis," he said, passing a hand across his eyes. "It's just that my head still hurts, my leg's not healed yet, so I can't get down the stairs, and I don't trust those Romans. I had no choice but to give them permission to bring their men over to the island, but I know they're up to something. They forget I've a window with a good view. I've seen them signalling across the harbour at night, and out at sea I've seen other signals that aren't stars. I'm almost sure they have more ships out there, and Mark Anthony's sending some sort of messages from the palace, only I can't work out why." He leant forward again, his eyes fierce. "Have they mentioned anything to you about Caesar's plans for Alexandria?"

Zeuxis bit his lip, certain his guilt would show. "No, Sir."

That wasn't quite a lie, either. He'd overhead Marcus and Lucian talking about their plans, not the other way around.

He promised himself he'd tell the Keeper everything after the race was over. It wouldn't make that much difference, surely? Only a few more days. It wasn't as if he knew the details of the Romans' plans, anyway. Maybe, by then, he'd have found out more.

The Keeper sighed again. "No, of course not... you're only a lighthouse boy, after all. Why would they take you into their confidence? But keep your ears open, Zeuxis. If you hear anything strange in the next few days, anything at all, you come and tell me at once. Understand?"

Zeuxis nodded, not trusting himself to speak, and the Keeper smiled. "All right, you can go. I'm sure you're anxious to get back to driving those Roman horses."

Zeuxis wet his lips. "Er... there's something else, Sir."

"What?" The Keeper looked up sharply.

"The storm that broke the lighthouse glass, Sir, the night after the race... some of the boys think it wasn't natural. Did you see anything strange that night?"

The Keeper frowned at the window for so long, Zeuxis thought his master had not heard him. He started to repeat his question, but the Keeper waved him silent.

"There are stranger things walking this earth than we know, Zeuxis. Alexandria might be a modern city, but Egypt is an ancient country. Curses work here. Witches sell spells in the Egyptian Quarter. Many claim to have seen a snake with a man's head and glowing green eyes swimming in the canals. They call it Agathodaimon, and say that when bad things happen, like Romans invading our shores, it comes to the aid of Egypt."

A shiver went down Zeuxis' spine. *A snake with glowing green eyes.*

"But a guardian spirit would want to keep the Pharos fire burning, wouldn't it?" he whispered. "Why would it try to put our light out?"

The Keeper sighed. "I don't know about Agathodaimon. But if there is a Roman war fleet out there, maybe we should put the fire out ourselves."

Chapter 12

AMULET

ZEUXIS SETTLED INTO a routine that left him so tired at the end of each day, he was glad he didn't have to keep up with his lighthouse duties. Lucian and Marcus made him train with a whip, even though he never had to use it on the fillies because they responded so well to his voice and hands. They didn't need to explain. Zeuxis knew now that the other charioteers used their whips in a race for a lot more than hitting their horses.

Determined not to be caught out the same way twice, he practised the trick the Green charioteer had used on him, until he could coil his lash around a post set at the side of the track from a slow trot. Using it to snare the post at full gallop remained beyond him, but that didn't stop him trying. Every day after the Romans left, he took the fillies on an extra circuit to practise.

"Too busy for your friends these days, I see!" called a voice from the side of the track.

Zeuxis jumped and the stupid whip tangled around his legs for the third time that morning. At first, he thought one of the Romans had caught him trying the trick, and his cheeks burned with embarrassment. But it was old Aelian.

The old man did not often come out to the practice track these days, preferring to stay at the lighthouse with the donkeys. He disapproved of the amount of time Zeuxis was spending with the Roman horses, and had barely spoken a word to him since he returned.

Wondering what he wanted, Zeuxis untangled the whip and reined in the fillies. "I have to train for the race," he explained.

Aelian grunted. "Those Romans payin' you well, are they?"

"No... but if I win, I get a bag of gold from the queen."

"And that's more important than your friends and the Pharos fire, is it?"

"You don't understand!"

Angry at the way the old man made him feel inside, Zeuxis gathered up the reins and climbed back into the chariot. "It's only until the race," he explained. "Then I'll be back at my duties again. It's important to me. I *have* to do well in this race, Aelian. It might be the last chance I ever get to race a chariot in the Hippodrome, because afterwards—" He bit the words back before he could say too much.

Aelian gave him a narrow-eyed look. "That wild stallion of the queen's seems to have recovered from its scare. I saw it in the park today. Clytius was giving it a turn with them black colts. Looked like they were goin' pretty fast to me."

Zeuxis halted the fillies again. "Faster than my fillies?"

"I'm no expert, but it looked like they were slowin' up a bit on the turns."

Zeuxis' heart leapt. "I knew it! That stallion doesn't work well with the colts, does he? His stride will be wrong, because he's bigger than they are. And Clytius is heavy enough to tip the chariot on the turns if he goes round too fast! I know I can beat the queen's blacks. It's Prince Ptolemy I'm worried about... is that why you came out here? To tell me about the queen's horses?"

Aelian shook his head. He looked over his shoulder, then grasped the mare's rein. "Your little Egyptian friend's lookin' for you. The one that hid in my muck cart that day. She sent you a message."

Zeuxis' heart jumped again. "What message?"

"She wants you to go to her house. She seemed upset."

"I can't go." He felt awful, but he wasn't going to give Ahwere and her grandmother another chance to ruin his dream.

"But she's your friend, and it sounds like she's in some sort of trouble." The old man frowned at Zeuxis.

"Maybe... but I have to stay here until the race."

"That might be too late. Your friend said... it don't make much sense, but she said that curse you were holding the Hippodrome called on the same *ka* as the first curse. When her mother... no, her grandmother, that's right... unrolled it, the demon attacked her."

Zeuxis stared at him. "The ka-demon attacked Lady Wernero?" he whispered. "Are you sure she said it *attacked* her grandmother?"

"Well..." Aelian scratched his head. "I think that's what she meant. You know how I don't remember things quite right sometimes, but she seemed very upset about it. I think you'd better go see her, lad."

Zeuxis stared at the white city across the water. He set his jaw. "Why can't Ahwere come here, if she wants my help so badly? The roadblocks have never stopped her before."

"Her grandmother's sick from the attack," Aelian said, as if that explained it.

Zeuxis hesitated, remembering how Ahwere had said the Royal Guard confiscated her papyrus with the prince's curse against the queen written on it. Perhaps she was too afraid to come across the Heptastadion in case they arrested her? Then he remembered how she had betrayed him, imprisoning him in that tomb. It was probably another trick so that Lady Wernero could stop him from racing the Roman team.

He gathered up the reins again. "I've got more important things to worry about than a sick Egyptian woman," he said, hardening his heart. "I'll go and see Ahwere after the race."

Aelian gave him a disapproving look. "I wouldn't go relyin' on them Romans to replace your friends, if I were you. Once you're no longer any use to them, they'll cast you aside like an old sandal."

"Now you're beginning to sound like the Keeper!" Already feeling guilty enough, Zeuxis slapped the reins on the fillies' backs, and they leapt into a canter. He didn't slow them up until he was sure he'd left the old man and his lectures behind.

Old Aelian had probably got it wrong, anyway. Even if the ka-demon had attacked Lady Wernero, she was a powerful witch. She wouldn't have let a curse make her sick. He shook away the little voice that said the witch's spell on the entrance to the tomb must have failed for some reason. No, Ahwere was probably just trying to scare him into going to see her. The girl could wait. Then maybe she would be sorry for betraying him.

In the days that followed, Zeuxis practised on the headland circuit in all weathers. To take his mind off Ahwere, he tried swapping the fillies around to see if that made any difference to the speed of the chariot. Venus remained on the outside, with the mare on the inside. But it took several swaps before he felt happy with the positioning of Minerva and Maia.

On the last day of training Zeuxis pulled up, grinning, after a perfect circuit. Marcus raised an eyebrow as the fillies snorted sand from their nostrils. "Maybe we have a chance to take the queen's gold, after all!" he said with a chuckle, patting Venus' damp neck.

But Lucian scowled. "Just concentrate on what's important," he muttered. "Right! One more circuit, then take them in. Big race tomorrow. Are you nervous?"

Zeuxis shook his head, his mouth going dry.

"Liar!" Marcus said with a laugh, slapping him on the thigh. "Do you think this lighthouse boy might have some Roman blood, Lucian?"

Lucian grunted and said to Zeuxis, "You concentrate on the race. Stay on the outside and keep out of trouble until the final circuit, then go for it. The Blue and Green chariots will be taken care of. You'll only have to beat the Red."

Zeuxis frowned suspiciously at the Roman. "What do you mean, 'taken care of'?"

"You Alexandrians plant curses against rival teams, don't you? There'll be several buried against us, no doubt, after last time. We'll use Roman-style curses to counter them." He exchanged a glance with Marcus, who avoided Zeuxis' gaze.

"Roman curses?" Zeuxis said, going cold.

"Surer than your Egyptian magic," Marcus said with a reassuring smile.

"But I don't want to win by cheating..."

Lucian's face hardened. "Don't go all soft on us now, Lighthouse Boy! In chariot racing, there are no rules. You know that as well as anyone, after what that Green driver did to you last time. The prize money the queen's putting up is enough to feed the entire Roman army for a year. You charioteers might be just boys when you're training on the practice track, but in the Hippodrome, when those starting gates open, you are men. And the charioteer who crosses the finish line in front will be as much a god as Great Alexander who built this fine city of yours. Remember that."

Zeuxis' heart swelled with pride, and the last ripple of guilt he felt at ignoring Ahwere's plea for help vanished. *As much a god as Great Alexander.*

He could do it. He *would* do it.

Then he'd go and see what Ahwere wanted. Not as a boy frightened of nightmares and demons, but as a winning charioteer with the power of a god!

The guilt resurfaced as Zeuxis polished Ahwere's charm bells on the morning of the big race. He stared hopefully across the Heptastadion. Over the water, Alexandria's marble buildings were stained pink by the rising sun, but there was no sign of his friend.

He clenched his jaw and fastened the bells to the mare's bridle. "She'll be fine," he muttered to the horses. "What could I have done to help her grandmother against the demon, anyway?"

After bringing in the fuel from the Royal Stables, old Aelian appeared with some of the lighthouse boys in tow, and organized them into washing the fillies' manes and tails. They gave the mare Diana an all-over bath, and she danced and snorted as they led her round to dry off, sensing the excitement in the air.

After breakfast, the Keeper summoned Zeuxis and pushed a charm fashioned from a seashell into his hand.

"Hang it from your outside horse's bridle," he said gruffly. "And watch out for the Greens' tricks this time!"

Zeuxis turned over the shell and saw Greek letters scratched on the pearly surface. He couldn't read them, but he mumbled thanks, touched.

The Keeper waved him away. "It's a prayer to Serapis, to bring you back in one piece so you can keep the Pharos fire burning. Go! You mustn't be late at the Hippodrome, or they'll disqualify you."

Zeuxis ran down the lighthouse stairs, lighter than air, and harnessed the fillies with sweaty hands. Venus wore the Keeper's shell by her ear. The mare had Ahwere's bells, tinkling on their strings. At the last moment, Marcus appeared with a clean white tunic and two leather wrist guards inlaid with silver.

"Can't have our driver looking like he's just forked a load of muck," he said. "The wrist pieces will help protect you from tricks like that Green driver's last time."

Zeuxis slipped on the tunic and let Marcus strap the leather around his wrists, mumbling thanks. The linen felt soft and cool against his skin, much nicer than his scratchy old slave's tunic.

Marcus smiled. "Lucian and I have an invitation to join the queen and Mark Anthony in the royal box, so this is the last time you'll see us before the race. Stay close to your escort, and watch yourself. We don't want anyone getting to you or our horses before the race. Aelian's going with you as a groom and an extra pair of eyes.

Zeuxis looked at the old man in surprise. Aelian just picked up his roll of grooming tools, sat on the back on the chariot, and grunted. "Well, lad, what are you waiting for? Let's get goin'!"

Their journey through the city was frustratingly slow. The main route had clogged to a halt with people and horses and chariots, all making their way out to the Hippodrome. The queen's Royal Guard, resplendent in polished Macedonian uniforms, lined the Canopic Way on the look out for trouble makers. But there was free food and free beer and, with the races still to come, the crowds were excitable but not violent. The inevitable scuffles that broke out between rival supporters over bets were good natured and ended in laughter.

Zeuxis started to relax and enjoy himself. The fillies trotted with arched necks, their freshly-washed manes lifting in the breeze, and the silver on their harness glinting in the early sunshine. It was a perfect day for racing, not too hot, with a fresh breeze from the sea and no sign of rain. Several people cheered as he drove past. "There go the Whites! Luck for the Lighthouse Boy!" Someone at the crossroads even threw a lotus flower into the chariot.

"An admirer!" Aelian grunted. "Don't let it go to your head, lad."

Zeuxis' heart leapt in hope, and he stared round at the crowd. But the girl who had thrown the flower had brown curls, not black Egyptian hair like Ahwere's. He drove on, disappointed.

They joined up with several other chariots at the Canopic Gate. Hippolytus waved to him and called, "Ready for a rematch, Lighthouse Boy? It'll be easier if you stay in the chariot this time and let the horses do the running!"

Some of the other drivers laughed in a friendly fashion.

"I'll beat you today," Zeuxis called back to Hippolytus. "Now I've got rid of my slow old gelding."

"So you have!" Hippolytus swung his whip in a fancy pattern over his head, and announced to the other drivers, "Look out! The Whites are trying out a secret new horse on us!"

There were whistles of appreciation and a few comments about the new horse making no difference if Zeuxis tried to run the race on foot again. He laughed with them, and tried to copy Hippolytus' trick with his whip. Aelian shook his head as it tangled round one of their own wheels.

The chariots turned into the Hippodrome, dropped off their grooms at the entrance to the stables, and organized themselves for the parade. Clytius was already out on the course, trotting his black team on a circuit to please his supporters, blue plumes waving from the horses' heads. The black stallion pranced and snorted alongside the colts, looking fit and well. There was no sign of the Green chariot, and Zeuxis wondered if the prince had been unable to find a replacement driver after what had happened last time. Served him right.

He'd just bent down to help Aelian untangle his whip from their wheel when he heard hooves thudding closer and warning shouts from the guards at the entrance.

"Watch out, lad!" Aelian called.

The other chariots had gone after Clytius, leaving Zeuxis and the White team in the middle of the track, the whip still tangled round their wheel. The Green's prize chestnuts came cantering straight for him, fighting for their heads. The replacement horse on the outside was huge, leaping like a war-stallion with blood flying from the severe bit in its mouth. All four horses wore green plumes and strings of golden charms that swung into their eyes, making them even wilder.

Then Zeuxis saw the driver, and his mouth went dry. Clad in a green tunic glittering with gold, Prince Ptolemy himself crouched over the front plate of the chariot, his gaze fixed on Zeuxis and a sneer on his face.

The Green supporters cheered at the sight of their hero. "Prince Ptolemy!" they cried. "Ptolemy for Pharaoh! Up the GREENS!"

Aelian swore under his breath, jumped out and ran to hold the fillies' heads as the Green chariot thundered closer. But Zeuxis was faster. He freed his whip from the wheel just in time and wrenched on the reins to turn his chariot out of the chestnuts' path. The mare snorted as Ahwere's charms chinked against the golden bells of the huge stallion. As he charged past, Prince Ptolemy threw something at Zeuxis and hissed, *"You're going to do exactly what I tell you today, Lighthouse Boy."*

Zeuxis shuddered. But the prince was already gone, shouting at Hippolytus to get his "Red donkeys" out of his way. He took no notice of the tradition that let the Blues go first in the pre-race parade and drove his chestnut team up beside Clytius' blacks, so close that the two stallions – the queen's wild black and the huge chestnut – squealed at each other.

The crowd went wild. This was a treat no one had anticipated. Prince Ptolemy himself, driving the challenger team!

Clytius glared at the prince, and let his blacks break into a canter. Prince Ptolemy gave chase with his chestnuts. The other teams leapt about in excitement. In the royal box, Queen Cleopatra sprang to her feet, her face like thunder as she recognized her brother. Mark Anthony scowled at Ptolemy. But there can't have been anything in the rules to forbid the prince to drive his own chariot, for the queen reluctantly waved back the guards who had stepped forward to stop the parade.

The Green and Blue supporters yelled louder than ever, drowning each other's cries.

"Cleopatra for Pharaoh!"

"Ptolemy for Pharaoh!"

"Queen CLEOPATRA!"

"Prince PTOLEMY!"

Zeuxis hardly heard the roars of the crowd. He clung on to the fillies' reins, staring at the thing Prince Ptolemy had thrown at his feet. His heart twisted with fear, and guilt sat like a stone in his stomach.

"Steady, lad," Aelian muttered, trying to help hold the fillies. "If it's a curse he threw at you, kick it off and don't touch it. We have to get off this course before them two idiots come round again. Look at 'em! They think they're in a race already."

Zeuxis did not care. He threw down his whip and snatched up the little amulet on its broken thong, the prince's words echoing in his ears. *You're going to do exactly what I tell you today, Lighthouse Boy.*

"It's not a curse," he whispered, clenching his fist around the little Egyptian eye. The amulet was chipped at one corner. A long strand of black hair had caught around the metal. He touched the hair, going cold all over. "Prince Ptolemy's got Ahwere."

The demon takes her royal throne and her stolen gold

Using Prince Ptolemy to get around the witch's spells was clumsy, I have to admit, but he has neatly removed the Egyptian girl from the scene. I will deal with her later, when I have more time. The boy's tears are puzzling, since I have not touched him since the night of my summoning. But this strange human behaviour will have to wait, as well. Right now, I have more urgent business.

Another chariot race. Another shift in the balance of power. This time, nothing will stand in my way.

Chapter 13

RIOT

PRINCE PTOLEMY'S ARRIVAL had roused the crowd. Already, Blue and Green supporters were fighting in the upper tiers. The guard settled for keeping them trapped in their seats until the big race. But Zeuxis hardly noticed who won the early races. He sat with his back pressed against the wood of the end stall and his knees drawn up to his chest, clutching Ahwere's amulet and screaming inside.

He had to find her. He had to find out what Prince Ptolemy had done to her. But the Roman soldiers Marcus and Lucian had sent as his escort would not let him out of their sight. "They'll disqualify any driver who leaves the Hippodrome," said their commander. "We can't let you go chasing about the city after some girl."

"Please!" Zeuxis begged. "She's my friend and she's in trouble!"

But the Roman shook his head. "The White team must be in this race."

"Marcus can drive them!" Zeuxis said, desperate. "He drove the chariot in training... can't you ask him?"

The commander shook his head again, his face stony. "Marcus Suetonius is on important business for Caesar."

"Don't be stupid, lad," Aelian muttered. "You're their driver now, for better or worse. Besides," he added, "you were the one who refused to go to your friend when she asked for help."

Zeuxis flushed. "But I didn't know she was in danger, or I'd have gone straight away! Prince Ptolemy's got her! Please help me, Aelian. I can't concentrate on winning this race if I'm worrying about Ahwere."

Aelian made a face. "You were never going to win, anyway, lad. But if you can manage here on your own, I'll go to the Egyptian Quarter and see if I can find your friend's grandmother. She's meant to be a witch, isn't she? Maybe she'll be able to help, if she's not too sick."

Zeuxis gripped the old man's hands in sudden hope. "Yes, Aelian! Hurry!" He described the route to Ahwere's house as best he could, trying not to worry at the confused glaze that came over the old man's eyes. "Tell her I'll come as soon as I can. Tell her I'm... oh, never mind. Just go!"

The old man schuffled off, repeating the directions under his breath. When he had gone, Zeuxis felt more alone than ever. He kept breaking into a sweat whenever he thought of Ahwere, helpless and in Prince Ptolemy's power. Though at least while the prince was in the Hippodrome driving his chestnut team in the race, he couldn't be doing anything nasty to his friend.

His dark thoughts were interrupted by a shout from his escort.

"Halt!" said the commander, pointing his spear at someone approaching the stall.

"Get your spear out of my face, you Roman scum!" Prince Ptolemy's voice snapped from behind the wooden partition. "I want a word with the White driver."

Zeuxis froze.

The Romans' hands went for their swords, but the commander shook his head. He pressed his lips together and said, "I'm sorry, Your Majesty, but we've orders to keep our horses and our driver safe from rival teams until the race."

"I'm sure you can make an exception for the rightful ruler of Alexandria," Ptolemy insisted. "You're a long way from home, and I suspect your Roman masters have forbidden you to cause any trouble before the big race. Am I right?"

The Romans eyed each other and the commander frowned. Zeuxis could almost hear his mind working. *The prince is hardly more than a boy. We can overpower him, if necessary. What harm can he do?*

"I'm not here to harm your driver," Prince Ptolemy said smoothly, spreading his hands. "Why not ask the boy if he wants to talk to me? I think you'll find the answer is 'yes'. If not, I'll leave you in peace."

The commander looked over the partition at Zeuxis, one eyebrow raised. Zeuxis tightened his fist around Ahwere's amulet. The last thing he wanted was to talk to Prince Ptolemy again. But the Romans would help him if the prince tried anything, and he had to know if Ahwere was all right. Reluctantly, he nodded.

Prince Ptolemy smiled. He crouched calmly next to Zeuxis in the back of the stall. "Well, Lighthouse Boy? Did you get my little present?"

"Where is she?" Zeuxis whispered, his scarred finger tingling where the prince had threatened to cut it off the last time they'd met.

"She's safe – for now." The prince spoke quietly, too. "Whether she stays safe is up to you."

"You… you haven't hurt her, have you?"

Prince Ptolemy chuckled. "Oh, I was right, wasn't I? You care for her a lot. I wish I'd known about your pretty little Egyptian friend earlier! It would have made our last meeting so much more interesting."

"Ahwere knows spells!" Zeuxis said. "She'll put a curse on you!"

"Half Alexandria would like to put a curse on me," Ptolemy said. "Including my sister. But I think we both know who's in control here. I'm the one who summoned the demon, and my men have your girlfriend in a safe place. If I don't return in one piece from this race, they have orders to kill her. So it's in your interests to make sure my chariot doesn't crash. I need to win this race today."

Zeuxis shook his head, tears in his eyes, remembering Lucian's dark words about Roman curses. "But I can't stop a wreck! If there's a curse or something…"

"If your Roman friends have planted a curse of their own against me, then tell me where it's buried and I'll make sure I avoid it."

"It's not a curse." Zeuxis bit his lip, realizing he had no idea what Lucian and Marcus meant to do to cause the double Blue and Green wreck. He should have found out more. Too late now.

Prince Ptolemy's eyes narrowed. "What are they up to, then?"

"I don't know what they're planning!" Zeuxis said. "Please let Ahwere go! She's got nothing to do with this."

"Oh, I think she has," Ptolemy said. "I know what you did now, when you dug up my curse that night. You didn't throw it at Clytius, after all. I found it in your girlfriend's house, unrolled to steal its power, along with the one I planted to trap you. Very foolish. That old witch of her grandmother got what she deserved. It means I've got to work a bit harder at this than I anticipated, but my sister Cleopatra *will* lose her throne – and when she does, you and your Roman masters are going to learn what happens to those who challenge the rightful Pharaoh of Egypt." He clutched Zeuxis' wrist in a fierce grip. "As for your little Egyptian friend, if you don't tell me what your Roman friends have planned for this race, you'll never see her again."

Zeuxis felt sick. "I told you, I don't know!" he shouted. "They didn't tell me! Why don't you go and ask Mark Anthony?"

The Roman commander took a step towards them, frowning. "I think that's enough…"

The cheering in the Hippodrome rose to a crescendo and another Green driver returned to the stables waving a palm branch. Prince Ptolemy stood up, hands raised. He smiled down at Zeuxis. "Until the race, Lighthouse Boy!"

Zeuxis spent what little time he had left before the race trying to get the Roman commander to tell him if Lucian and Marcus had ordered them to do anything to the Blue and Green teams to 'take care of them'. But the commander simply said his orders were to see Zeuxis and the fillies safely into the Hippodrome. Then the chariots were filing out on to the course, and the commander boosted him up into the chariot, put the reins in his hands and passed him his whip.

The fillies shook their heads, impatient to get on with the job they had been trained for. Zeuxis took up the pull and bent his knees by habit as the chariot leapt under his feet. It seemed he had no choice but to go through with the race. But as soon as it was over, he was going to look for Ahwere.

"Luck, Lighthouse Boy!" called the Roman commander. "Don't disgrace us!"

Zeuxis did not reply. He knotted the thong and hung Ahwere's eye amulet around his neck, tucked under his tunic where it would be safe. Then he set his lips and steered the fillies down the course to the starting gates. He had drawn third position today. Clytius was on the inside again for the Blues. Ptolemy's chestnuts were between them in the second gate, and Hippolytus on the outside. At least the Red team did not have the speed to cut across, which was one less thing to worry about.

As the fillies went in, Hippolytus prodded him over the barrier with his whip and whispered, "The prince is up to something. Watch him."

Zeuxis gave the Red driver a tight look. "I know."

"Look out for yourself. The crowd's in an ugly mood today. Have you seen the sky? Something feels wrong."

The last thing Zeuxis had been worrying about was the weather. He glanced up. He'd thought the darkness around him was due to his fear for Ahwere. But thick clouds had gathered above the Hippodrome, putting out the sun. He shuddered, reminded of the storm that had smashed the Pharos glass. The fillies, picking up his unease, neighed and grabbed at their bits.

Prince Ptolemy's chestnuts were last into the gates, still fighting for their heads. The prince jerked at their mouths, relying on pain inflicted by the severe bits to control them. Clytius' black stallion reared, its eye rolling. The queen stepped to the edge of the royal box, gold glinting at her neck and wrists in the light of the torches her guard had lit. Glaring at the second gate, where her brother had taken the chestnut team, she raised the white cloth.

There was a hush as the crowd held their breath. Tension built inside Zeuxis to an unbearable pitch.

To save Ahwere's life, Prince Ptolemy's chariot must not crash, which meant Zeuxis must give up his dream and lose this race. But if he let the prince win, how could he be sure Ptolemy would let Ahwere go?

In the meantime, they had eight laps of the track. Zeuxis tightened his hands on the reins and fixed his gaze on the gate, a daring idea forming. In chariot racing, there were no rules. Prince Ptolemy would be out on the course without his bodyguards, just another driver, as vulnerable as any of them.

Zeuxis gripped his whip in a determined fist. He knew a few tricks now. He would *make* the prince tell him where Ahwere was. "Steady," he muttered. "Steady, Venus, steady Minerva, steady Maia. Diana, get up there! This is more than just a race... you have to trust me..."

Queen Cleopatra's gilded fingernails opened, and the white cloth fluttered down.

Zeuxis' ears hummed. His limbs turned soft, his head light and dizzy. The supporters, the soldiers, Ahwere, his work at the lighthouse... all belonged to a different world. Only the reins in his hands, the white tails in front of him, and the chariot beneath his feet, felt real.

The starting gate opened in slow motion to reveal the course shimmering under the storm clouds. The fillies leapt through the gap with perfect timing, and his wheels pushed the gate fully open as the chariot followed. Out of the corner of his eye, Zeuxis saw Ptolemy's chestnuts leap forward as well. Clytius had a good start, too, and Hippolytus' team was only a fraction behind. All four chariots surged out of the gates together, making the crowd roar in appreciation.

"Clytius for the Blues!"

"Prince Ptolemy for Pharaoh and the Greens!"

"Hippolytus! Hippolytus for the Reds!"

No one called for the Whites, but Zeuxis had more to worry about than lack of supporters. Straight away, Prince Ptolemy lashed his whip at Clytius' black stallion and tried to swing his team across to get the leading position on the course. But Clytius was ready for him, and the stallion must have had some training since Zeuxis had driven him in the park, for he laid his ears back and did not check his speed. Blue and Green chariots bumped the central barrier, locked together.

Remembering what had happened at the start last time, Zeuxis kept the fillies wide, one eye on Prince Ptolemy's whip. Hippolytus tucked his team in behind and shouted something he could not make out.

But the prince seemed fully occupied trying to run Clytius' chariot up against the barrier, for now ignoring both the White and the Red teams. Zeuxis took advantage of this to sort himself out. The fillies were galloping smoothly, still on the wide outside heading for the first turn. If he didn't get them in soon, he'd lose a lot of ground on the turns. He began to ease them across, saw the red lining of the nostrils of Hippolytus' team on his inside rear, and changed his mind at the last moment.

Gripping the reins hard, he forced the mare to run straight, leaving enough of a gap for the Red chariot to squeeze round on his inside. Hippolytus took the turn a little raggedly and bumped his wheel, but they both ended up on the other side of the course in one piece. The boy glanced across at Zeuxis and raised his fist in thanks before his team dropped back again, too slow on the straight to keep up.

Zeuxis found himself right behind the Blue chariot. Sand sprayed into his eyes, and the fillies' hooves clattered against the back of the Blue platform. Clytius scowled over his shoulder and made a rough swing of his whip to make them back off. The fillies threw up their heads, and Zeuxis swung them out again, looking for a gap. The Green chariot was in front by a neck. Ptolemy was obviously concentrating on getting the lead before the next turn. As the wheels unlocked, a small gap opened between the Blue and Green chariots. Zeuxis called to the mare for more speed, and headed his team into it.

His wheels struck sparks off the other two chariots as he came between them. Clytius yelled at him to get back before he killed them all. The queen's black stallion laid back its ears as the mare came alongside. Diana put her white ears back and held her ground.

The Blue supporters yelled in protest. But someone from the upper tiers called, "Whites! Go the Whites!" and the yells changed to cheers of encouragement as the three chariots raced neck and neck down the straight side of the course.

Dizzy with the speed and excitement of having the fillies at full gallop in a real race, Zeuxis' dream took over.

He was the White driver, pushing his team to take the lead at the next turn, the crowd screaming his name.

Then Prince Ptolemy looked across, bared his teeth and hissed, "Remember I have your friend, Lighthouse Boy!" At the same time, he hauled on the chestnuts' reins until his inside horse leant on Venus.

The dark filly squealed in protest and leapt forward in an effort to escape, tugging the others with her for a few fierce strides. Now Zeuxis was in front, but Ptolemy had reminded him of Ahwere's danger, and he lost the rhythm. The turn was coming too fast, and the other teams were still too close on each side of him. He'd never make it...

Ptolemy laughed and swung his chestnuts hard round, leaving Zeuxis no room to manoeuvre. On the inside, Clytius cursed and checked his team. The chestnuts streamed across in front of them both to take the lead on the next straight. The Blue chariot went round the turn on one wheel, scraping the post. Zeuxis felt his chariot tip, too, and the inside wheel came off the ground. He threw himself across to balance it, clung on to the reins and shut his eyes.

Luckily, the mare knew her job. Feeling the chariot start to lift, she checked her speed and hauled the fillies round until the wheel bounced back to earth. Then she went forwards again to take up the running. Zeuxis breathed a little easier. That had been too close.

Now he was racing beside Clytius and the black colts, hard on the Green chariot's heels, with Hippolytus bringing up the rear. Only the second circuit. Six still to go.

Clytius looked across at him and shouted, "You little idiot! What did you think you were trying to *do*? If you lose me this race, I'll make sure you never drive a chariot again!"

Zeuxis ignored him and concentrated on Prince Ptolemy's back.

"I know you can hear me, Lighthouse Boy!" Clytius yelled. "Get those Roman donkeys out of my way, or that fool Ptolemy's going to win this race and gain enough support in the city to take the throne of Alexandria from the queen!"

Zeuxis called for more speed, and the fillies responded. Slowly, they drew ahead of the blacks.

Clytius growled in fury and swung his whip. It caught Zeuxis across the cheek, a sharp slice that brought tears to his eyes and made him lose concentration. The Green chariot rounded the turn ahead of them. Clytius made another turn dangerously close to the post to steal second position. Zeuxis forgot to check the eager Venus and messed up, going too wide and too fast.

"Bad luck!" Hippolytus called from behind. Zeuxis tightened his hands on the reins. It hadn't been bad luck, at all. It had been his own stupid fault, and now he had ground to make up. He had to catch Prince Ptolemy. He *had* to.

Two more circuits pounded by, with no change to their positions. Ptolemy was driving like a madman in front, slashing his horses' rumps with his whip until bloody foam flew back into Zeuxis' face with the kicked-up sand. Clytius was right on the Green's heels, pulling out to try to pass on the straights, but being forced behind again at every turn. Zeuxis squinted, finding it hard to see with the sand in his eyes. The fillies didn't like it any more than he did, shaking their heads every time a large clod hit them. The crowd roared, half for the Greens, half for the Blues. He couldn't hear anyone shouting for the Whites or Reds any more.

"Come on, Venus!" he called. "Get up there, Diana, Minerva, Maia… faster, you have to go faster!"

The fillies tried their best. Now there were only three circuits left. Prince Ptolemy and Clytius were still fighting it out in front, trying every trick they knew, but evenly matched, Ptolemy's youth making up for Clytius' experience. It looked as if the chestnuts were tiring. The blacks were still full of running, and slowly crept up the inside until their heads were in front. The royal box flashed past again, Queen Cleopatra leaning over the balcony to yell advice to Clytius as he passed beneath.

"*Please*," Zeuxis hissed, his breath coming in gasps. "You *have* to go faster!" He made the clucking sound with his tongue that the Romans had taught him.

The fillies flicked back their ears and responded, creeping up on Ptolemy's outside, until the mare's nose reached the chestnut stallion's rump... then his girth... then his shoulder.

Zeuxis leant forward and changed his whip to his left hand. The turn was coming up fast. But he wasn't going to drop back this time. He knew exactly how fast he could go round the post now without tipping his chariot. He'd take the difficult route and overtake on the outside. *Then* he'd show them.

When Diana's nose reached the chestnut stallion's shoulder, Prince Ptolemy finally realized someone was challenging him and looked round. His eyes widened in surprise at seeing Zeuxis so close. "I warned you, Lighthouse Boy! Your friend will suffer!" He raised his whip and lashed at Zeuxis' arm.

Zeuxis ducked and swung his own whip, using the twist of the wrist he'd practised and failed so many times. As he did so, he closed his eyes and prayed to Serapis and Great Alexander and Anubis and all the other gods he could remember the names of. With the fillies going so fast, the turn coming up so quickly, and his eyes full of sand, it was clumsy. But the lashes tangled together and tightened around the prince's wrist. Ptolemy jerked backwards, and it felt as if someone was trying to rip out Zeuxis' arm. He clung on, bracing himself against the front of the chariot.

"Let go, you idiot!" the prince snarled, trying to tug his whip hand free. But Zeuxis' lash had caught him firmly.

Zeuxis set his jaw. "Not until you tell me where Ahwere is!"

Ptolemy scowled, trying to free his wrist with his teeth. "Your little friend's going to suffer for this!"

Zeuxis' heart pounded. "Where is she? Quick, the turn's coming up!"

Ptolemy frowned and gave his whip another wrench. But the lashes were firmly knotted together, his wrist neatly trapped between them. The wind whipped the prince's hair across his eyes and he shook his head in fury. The gold on his tunic had been dulled with sand and sweat, and blood dripped down one arm where Clytius' whip had caught him earlier. He looked as dirty and scruffy as the rest of them. Clytius glanced across, saw his rival's predicament, and laughed.

"If you lose me this race, I'm going to give your friend to my men tonight!" Prince Ptolemy hissed.

"TELL ME WHERE SHE IS!" Zeuxis shouted. He clenched his teeth. He couldn't hold on to the prince much longer, or he'd never get round the post himself at this speed.

Prince Ptolemy had seen the post, too. He paled and hauled one-handed on his reins. "Slow down, you fool… *the turn!*"

At the last moment, Zeuxis let go of his whip and hauled desperately on the fillies' reins. Prince Ptolemy's team, feeling their driver lurch to his knees, faltered and fell back a place.

Zeuxis' eyes stung with tears as the Green chariot swerved away from him. His gamble had failed. Ptolemy was not going to let him get close enough to try that trick twice.

As they came round the post, a howling wind splattered him with rain, until he thought he was back on the island. Why was it so dark in the middle of the afternoon? Torches flared raggedly from the tiers. For a terrifying instant, he lost sight of the course. A vision of his chariot crashing into the barrier flashed into his head.

"No," he hissed, determination returning. "I can't crash! I've got to find Ahwere."

The clouds parted to show him the Blue chariot half way along the straight, Clytius looking round to see what had happened to the rest of them. Hippolytus' team was behind somewhere. The fillies were racing out of control, chasing down Clytius' blacks. Zeuxis wondered what had happened to Prince Ptolemy. Then Hippolytus shouted, "Look out!" and a lash coiled around Zeuxis' neck from behind.

He put his hands to his throat, catching the whip before it could tighten.

"Got you, Lighthouse Boy!" Ptolemy hissed, jerking him off balance.

Zeuxis clung to the reins with one hand, terror lending him strength he hadn't known he possessed. He mustn't fall off! He'd be trampled under the Green team's hooves, which was clearly what Ptolemy intended.

The prince laughed, so intent on revenge he didn't seem to care any more about winning the race. "I'll teach you to trick me like that! After the race, I'm going to enjoy taking your mangled body back to show your friend."

Clytius glanced over his shoulder and used his whip on the blacks. The crowd cheered him on as he drew ahead. The Blues knew that all he had to do was take the last circuit steadily, and they'd win.

Half-blinded by sand and rain, choking with the lash around his neck, Zeuxis wasn't sure how it happened. But as the Blue chariot went round the next turn, he saw a cloud of darkness rise around it, and the black stallion's harness snapped. Clytius yelled as his inside wheel caught on the post, whipping the chariot round and sending it tumbling across the course in a spray of sand, snapping wood, and thrashing black legs. The stallion broke free and galloped for the stables. The colts were not so lucky. They went down, kicking and neighing, trapped in the wreckage.

Ptolemy abandoned his whip with an oath and hauled on his reins to avoid the wreck. Zeuxis almost fell forward under his own team's hooves as the pressure released from his neck. He hauled on his own reins and shouted at the mare. She leapt a piece of broken chariot, stumbled over the tightly curled Clytius, and somehow managed to swerve round the wreck, carrying the fillies with her. Ptolemy followed, one of his chestnuts stamping on Clytius' arm as he did so. The Blue charioteer shouted in pain. Zeuxis looked anxiously for the Red chariot. But Hippolytus was so far behind, he was able to slow up and avoid the wreckage. He even found time to wave at Zeuxis.

"Go, Lighthouse Boy!" he shouted. "You can do it!"

One circuit – with a shiver, Zeuxis realized he was in the lead. But thinking of the wreckage waiting on what would be the final turn of the race and of Ahwere in the hands of Ptolemy's men, he eased up. The fillies had lost speed, anyway, and Diana was lame after that wrenching turn, one white leg dripping blood.

Ptolemy caught up and passed him on his inside, teeth bared in an evil smile. "I'll deal with you later, Lighthouse Boy," he hissed over his shoulder. "Now get out of my way – I've a race to win!"

Blue supporters spilled on to the course behind them to drag Clytius clear and free his horses before the chariots came round again, and the guards let them do so because of the emergency. But as Prince Ptolemy rounded the final post in front of Zeuxis, Dameos ran out on to the course brandishing the black stallion's broken harness. "CHEAT!" he yelled after Ptolemy, waving the harness. "The Greens cut our harness! They cheated!"

In the royal box, as if he had been waiting for this, Lucian Flavius leapt to his feet and called in righteous indignation, "Cheats! Is this what Caesar can expect from Alexandria?"

The Royal Guard grabbed Dameos and tried to clear the course. But the three injured colts were still trapped in the wreckage, and the wind and rain slowed the rescue operation. The Blue supporters' mood turned ugly when they saw the harness. "Cheat! Cheat!" they chanted, taking up the cry. The Green supporters, hearing them accuse their prince of cheating, climbed over the barriers too, and a fight started in the middle of the course. The Guard drew their swords. Zeuxis glimpsed their blades glinting through the rain, and imagined what would happen when Prince Ptolemy ploughed into that lot at full gallop.

He urged the fillies round the post after the Green chariot. He had no idea how he was going to clear the course for the prince, but knew he had to try. Then, as he rounded the turn, he saw something that made him forget the drama ahead. The big chestnut's harness had been cut beneath his girth, where no one would see. Just one frayed strand held the whole thing together. He bet the black stallion's harness had been cut in the same way, to make it snap under pressure during the race. And he could guess who had done the cutting.

Roman curses are surer than your Egyptian magic.

Ptolemy grinned back at Zeuxis as the Green chariot drew further ahead.

"GREENS! GO THE GREENS! PRINCE PTOLEMY FOR PHARAOH!" roared the crowd.

Zeuxis squinted through the storm at the chaos around the wreck ahead of them, and his heart sank. If Ptolemy ploughed into that lot with his weak harness, he'd crash. Then Ahwere would die.

"Your harness!" he shouted, pointing at the frayed piece. "It's about to snap!"

Prince Ptolemy laughed over his shoulder. "Nice try, Lighthouse Boy! But lies won't help your friend."

"I'm not lying!" Zeuxis' stomach churned as the prince pulled out to avoid the wreck and the supporters. "Please, you must listen to me—!"

Too late.

Even as the chariot slowed, the chestnut's harness snapped exactly as the black stallion's had done last time round. The big horse went right, the other three left. Prince Ptolemy tried to keep them together, but he'd lost his whip, and his horses were not listening to him. His chariot hit a piece of wreckage, bounced once, and turned over.

A massive groan came from the Green supporters.

Supporters and guards scattered in alarm, and Zeuxis hauled his team wide. Wind howled around him, full of sand and rain and shadows. He could not see. Where was the finish line? Where was Hippolytus and the Red chariot? Where was Prince Ptolemy?

His ears filled with screams and the groans of injured men and horses. Then from the darkness came a trumpet blast, and Mark Anthony's battle-trained voice called,

"WHITES FOR ROME, GLORY FOR CAESAR!"

The sand cleared from Zeuxis' eyes, and with some relief he saw Prince Ptolemy – who must have decided to listen to him, after all – scramble on to the big chestnut horse that had survived the wreck. He headed it towards the exit, pursued on foot by the furious Blue supporters.

His stomach twisting in new fear for Ahwere, Zeuxis wrenched his chariot off the course and headed the fillies after the prince.

"Where are you *going*?" Hippolytus called, behind him. "The finish line's that way!"

"You take the prize money!" Zeuxis yelled back. "My friend's in danger! I've got to find her."

No one was watching the race, anyway. The crowd was fighting in the tiers. Ptolemy's bodyguard and the queen's Royal Guard were having a small war in the middle of the course. Soldiers and supporters choked the entrance, intent on killing one another. Cleopatra gave Mark Anthony a frightened look as he hustled her out of the royal box, and her Guard abandoned the course to the supporters and closed around their queen and the envoy to get them to safety. It was impossible to get through the crush with a chariot.

Zeuxis jumped out and unharnessed Venus with shaking hands. He knotted her reins so they wouldn't trail and made a leap for her back. But, upset by all the noise and people, she whirled in a circle so he could not get on her.

"Stand *still*!" he sobbed. "Prince Ptolemy's getting away!"

Just as he was about to abandon the filly and go after the prince on foot, there was the sound of hooves behind him, and Hippolytus cantered up with his team. He boosted Zeuxis up on Venus and slapped her on the rump. "Go, Lighthouse Boy! When you catch Prince Ptolemy, give him a punch from me!"

Zeuxis clung on to the Roman filly's mane as she carried him out of the Hippodrome through the struggling crowds. It was hard to tell supporters from soldiers. Everyone seemed to have a weapon of some sort, and people fought more furiously as blood stained the sand.

It was a riot, exactly as the Romans had planned.

Chapter 14

DARKNESS

ZEUXIS RODE AS fast as he could through the rioting supporters and the storm, imagining all the terrible things Prince Ptolemy might do to Ahwere in revenge for the trick he'd tried to play on him during the race. But the prince had a head start and the help of his men. By the time he and the filly reached the Canopic Gate, their quarry had vanished.

Inside the city, the chaos continued. The streets filled with angry people as news spread of the race that no one had won. Blue supporters accused the Greens of cutting Clytius' harness, and Green supporters accused the Blues of cutting Prince Ptolemy's. Even the normally peaceful Red supporters were furious, because Hippolytus had pulled up before the finish line. They blamed the Romans for losing them the race, having seen their champion follow Zeuxis off the course. Torches flared in the unnatural darkness. Someone had set fire to the Great Library, which sprayed sparks into the sky. This enraged the citizens still further, and even those who didn't support a team joined in the riot, looking for someone to blame for the loss of their priceless scrolls.

But that was not the worst of it. As Zeuxis got closer to the waterfront, he saw that the harbour was full of warships. And from the mast of the biggest galley flew the golden eagle of Rome.

"*That's* what Lucian and Marcus wanted the riot for," Zeuxis whispered to the filly. "To distract everyone while Caesar invaded the palace! They don't care if we all die. And I helped them, just because I wanted to win a stupid chariot race! Aelian's right, you can't trust Romans. And now Ahwere's in danger, too. Oh Venus, why was I so *stupid*?"

Venus shook her sweat-drenched head and snorted.

Zeuxis sighed as he turned the filly away from the waterfront. Lady Wernero and the Keeper had both tried to warn him, but he'd allowed his dreams to blind him. He should have guessed Caesar meant to invade during the race – it seemed so obvious now.

"I know, girl," he murmured. "You've done enough running for today, and so have I. We're not going to be much help to Ahwere if we get caught up in the fighting. Let's go see if old Aelian managed to find Lady Wernero."

The Egyptian Quarter was in a state of panic. It had stopped raining, but the wind blew sparks from the fires across the city, setting alight the reed roofs of the poorer houses. Men ran along the alleys, banging on doors. "The Romans are burning the city!" they yelled. "Flee for your lives!" Women stumbled out of their houses with bundles of belongings, babies wailed, and little statues of Egyptian gods lay in puddles where they had been dropped.

Zeuxis urged the filly through the press of people and the flames. Nothing looked the same as when he'd been here before. He took a wrong turn and found himself in an alley he did not recognize. Wind banged the unlatched doors of homes deserted by their families.

He gripped Ahwere's amulet and closed his eyes. "Where?" he whispered. "Where are you?"

Darkness swirled around him, and Venus shied at shadows. Zeuxis had to grab the mane to stay on. Clouds raced across the sky, stained blood red by the fires. The filly jumped again. If he wasn't careful, she'd throw him. Injured, he would be no use to Ahwere at all.

He slipped off the filly's back and rubbed behind her ears until she calmed. "Shh, girl... I'm sorry. Everyone's crazy tonight. If we head back to the Library, we can start again."

Taking the reins over the filly's head, he led her back through the alleys in the direction of the waterfront. But every time he thought he was getting somewhere, he came to a dead end and had to turn around. The streets became darker. Venus dripped sweat, shooting up her head and rolling her eyes at every noise.

Zeuxis tried another alley, which ended at the ship canal that led from the harbour to the lake behind the city. As he stared into the dark water, the back of his neck prickled. Steps led down to the towpath. Venus took one look at the shadows under the bridge and spun round, ripping the reins out of his hand.

"Venus!" he cried, as the filly galloped back up the alley. Then his breath caught in terror. Under the bridge lurked a darker shadow with glowing green eyes like those he'd seen in his nightmares.

Zeuxis wanted to follow the filly, but his legs wouldn't work. Trembling, he sank down on the top step and squeezed Ahwere's amulet tightly. The eyes watched his every move, but the monster did not emerge from its hiding place.

Zeuxis wet his lips, the amulet giving him strength. It hadn't attacked him yet. "You're the ka-demon Prince Ptolemy summoned, aren't you?" he whispered. "I've seen you in my dreams."

This must be another nightmare. The only trouble being that he didn't remember falling asleep.

The demon uncoiled and words breathed into Zeuxis' ears as if it were standing right behind him. *"You are the boy who interfered with my curse."*

"N-no," Zeuxis stammered, his spine prickling. "That was Lady Wernero—"

"Yes, the witch who tried to banish me from this world. I have punished her."

Zeuxis swallowed, remembering what Aelian had said

about the old woman being sick. "What have you done to her? Where is she? Do you know where Prince Ptolemy took her granddaughter... Ahwere?"

The demon laughed, a sound that sent gravel from the bridge splashing into the canal. "*The girl has lost her amulet. She is powerless against me now.*"

"NO!" Zeuxis staggered down the steps and got halfway to the bridge before his nerve failed him. He stopped, breathing hard. "If you've hurt Ahwere..."

The green eyes watched him in amusement. The demon's coils shifted with a sound like the sea.

"*Worry not, Human. I have more important things to do first.*"

Zeuxis closed his eyes in relief.

"*You are very brave for a human,*" continued the demon. "*Why did you warn Prince Ptolemy of the danger in the race? If he had not jumped out before his chariot crashed, he would be dead by now.*"

Zeuxis clenched his fists to hide the fact his hands were shaking. As much as he wanted it to be, this was no dream. "I warned him because otherwise Ahwere would have been hurt... oh, you wouldn't understand! Why are you here?"

He meant here, under the bridge, talking to him. But the ka-demon answered the bigger question.

"*I have come to fulfil the curse. Take the power of the false Queen Cleopatra, make her horses fall and her chariots crash, take her royal throne and her stolen gold, remove her name from the coins of this land... all this is done or soon will be, but I am puzzled. I have another task before I can take her to my world. Tell me, Human, who does your Queen Cleopatra love?"*

Zeuxis blinked. The question took him by surprise. He'd almost forgotten that part of the curse. It hadn't seemed important, compared with the rest – but perhaps it was more important than he'd thought?

"As queen of Egypt, she had to marry her brother Prince Ptolemy," he said carefully. "But she threw him out of the palace and planted a curse against him, so I don't suppose she loves him like women are meant to love their husbands and brothers."

"Interesting… husband and brother. Who else does your queen love?"

Zeuxis thought of the way the queen had whispered and blushed with Mark Anthony in the park. He eyed the ka, an idea forming. "You don't really understand love, do you?"

The demon rippled. *"Tell me what I want to know, Human!"*

"That's why you're here, isn't it? You can't fulfil your task and go back to your world, until you find out who Queen Cleopatra really loves! Even if I tell you, I might not be right. I don't know the queen well enough. It'd be better if I told you what love is, so you can work it out for yourself when you… take… her."

He shuddered as the demon shifted closer.

"I'll tell you!" Zeuxis said quickly. "But only if you promise to keep Ahwere safe in return."

The demon hissed and coiled in the shadows. Zeuxis held his breath and the amulet, sweating in terror. If he'd made a mistake, the ka would destroy him now and ask someone else.

There was a pause long enough to make him feel faint. Then the ka said,

"*You have a bargain, Human.*"

Zeuxis let out the breath. He'd been right. It couldn't talk to anyone else, only to those who had touched the curse. But Ahwere had vanished, and Lady Wernero was sick. So it needed him. Zeuxis the lighthouse boy, the nobody.

"I helped Prince Ptolemy in the race because I love Ahwere," he said. "That's what love is. Doing something you don't want to do, for someone else's sake."

The demon was silent for so long, he thought it had gone. But then its coils shifted again in the shadows, and it sighed like a rock cracking. "*I will have to think about this. Give me a name.*"

"Mark Anthony?"

The eyes glowed brighter. "*Ah yes, the envoy from Rome. If she loves him, he will die.*"

"But I don't know if I'm right!" Zeuxis said, chilled by the demon's tone. He added quickly, "Queen Cleopatra's very rich and beautiful. She's probably loved lots of people!" and then wished he hadn't, as the green eyes turned towards the palace.

"*Maybe. The balance of power is changing. I must go.*"

"Wait!" Zeuxis said, taking another step towards the bridge. He stopped as the eyes fixed on him again. It felt like walking into a wall of icy water.

"*No further, Human,*" breathed the demon. "*Unless you, too, want to come with me when I return to my world?*"

Zeuxis shuddered. "But Ahwere," he whispered. "I told you what you wanted to know. We made a bargain! You must protect her."

"*I must fulfil my other tasks first.*"

The demon gathered darkness, sucking it from the black water and from the night. It shrank into the shadows and its green eyes closed. Zeuxis could not move, imagining the monster creeping up behind him.

"Please!" he croaked. "At least tell me where she is…"

But the ka did not speak again. Instead, a small, black snake slithered out from under the bridge. Zeuxis' knees gave way as its scales scraped over his ankle – a touch like ice. As the snake entered the water, a cloud of darkness enveloped him.

The next thing he knew, Aelian's voice was calling him.

"Zeuxis? Zeuxis, lad, wake up!"

Zeuxis stirred, thinking he was back in the lighthouse, and shuddered with the memory of his dream. Then he opened his eyes and saw the canal.

He struggled to sit up, trying to remember what had happened. The storm had died down. The water reflected a pale dawn. Aelian was peering into his face. Venus stood behind him, her reins knotted over his elbow. She blew softly at Zeuxis through her nostrils.

"Thank the gods I found you!" Aelian said. "Hippolytus said you'd gone chasin' after Prince Ptolemy. If I hadn't recognized the filly grazing on the towpath, I'd never have thought of lookin' for you down here. What happened? Did you fall off?"

"Something like that," Zeuxis said, looking carefully at the bridge.

Aelian shook his head. "We have to get back to the island at once, lad. The soldiers are telling everyone to go home and stay there. Here, you'd better ride the horse… you don't look so good."

"Which soldiers?" Zeuxis asked, rubbing his ankle, which was still numb from where the snake had slithered over it in his dream. Had the Romans managed to take over the city, or were Queen Cleopatra's men back in control?

The old man tried to persuade Venus to walk under the bridge so he could get Zeuxis mounted. The filly snorted and refused to enter the shadows. Watching her, Zeuxis shivered. It must have been another nightmare, surely? He had fallen off and hit his head, probably knocked himself out.

"I'm not going back without talking to Lady Wernero," he said firmly. "Did you find her house all right? How is she? Did she tell you where Prince Ptolemy took Ahwere?"

Aelian pulled a face. "I'm sorry, lad. I got lost, what with all the people last night, and the storm, and everything. I did try, but I couldn't remember your directions. Then the soldiers came and the riot started. No one knew who had won the race, even, though I don't suppose it matters much any more. Your friend will be all right now the Romans are in charge. They've ordered Prince Ptolemy to disband his army and surrender. He'll be arrested soon, I shouldn't wonder. Come on, lad, let's go back to the island. At least there will be a lot of fuel around for the Pharos' fire. Maybe we can pick some up on our way back."

Zeuxis looked guiltily towards the sea. He'd almost forgotten about the lighthouse and the Roman invasion. But from here, the island and its Pharos were hidden behind buildings and shipyards. Fires still burned against the sky, so it was hard to tell if the Pharos light was running short of fuel.

He limped out from under the bridge and took the filly's rein. "You go back and check if the Keeper's all right. I have to find Ahwere."

Aelian shook his head, looking at Zeuxis' foot. "You can't go racing about the city on your own in that state. The Romans will soon find your friend, if she's with the prince's men."

Zeuxis frowned. "Where's Queen Cleopatra? Is she still with Mark Anthony? I saw fighting on the waterfront last night."

"All I know is there are Roman soldiers all over the city and they're arrestin' anyone who don't do what they say." The old man looked up anxiously as hooves clattered across the bridge, making Venus dance and whinny. "Quickly, lad, we don't want to get into no more trouble!"

Zeuxis closed his eyes. His ankle felt the same as his hands had done after holding the curse in the Hippodrome, the night Prince Ptolemy had tortured him and the demon had 'punished' Lady Wernero for interfering. "I'm already in trouble," he said. "I abandoned the race when I could have won. Marcus and Lucian will be furious with me. I can't go back yet, Aelian. I know the Pharos is important, but I already ignored my friend once. I can't just abandon her in Prince Ptolemy's clutches. Help me get to her grandmother's house – please?"

The old man muttered something about crazy youngsters who couldn't make up their minds who their friends were. But, still grumbling under his breath, he boosted Zeuxis on to the filly's back and led her up the steps into the alley.

It felt wrong to be riding when old Aelian was on foot. But Zeuxis' leg that the demon had slithered over last night refused to work and hung limply down Venus' sweat-crusted side. They passed a troop of Roman legionaries, running in formation down the main street with their spears and rectangular shields. But the soldiers did not bother them, and the few Egyptians abroad scuttled into their houses and slammed their doors.

By daylight, it was obvious where he'd gone wrong last night and they reached Lady Wernero's house unchallenged. The window blind was down, the door ajar. All looked dark within.

Zeuxis jumped off the filly, forgetting his leg didn't work. He staggered and Aelian tried to help him. He shook off the old man, stumbled through the door – and stopped in dismay.

The house looked as if a chariot race had been held inside it. Every last one of Lady Wernero's statues and chests had been smashed or overturned and their contents spilled across the floor. Her bunches of herbs had been ripped down, scattered and trampled. The Persian carpets were slashed to shreds. The stuffed crocodile that guarded the stairs had been hacked into pieces. Its head lay gaping at the door with one jawbone smashed. Shards of coloured glass glittered everywhere and an overturned lamp had left a blackened, smouldering patch in the corner. How the whole building had not gone up in flames, he didn't know. That had obviously been what the looters intended.

"Lady Wernero?" he whispered, afraid to venture any further into the shadows.

"Go on up, lad," Aelian said, picking up a table leg to use as a weapon. "I'll keep watch down here."

Zeuxis took a deep breath and crept up the stairs, using his hands to help.

At the top fluttered a linen sheet, painted with hieroglyphs. He had the same feeling as when he'd tried to escape the Egyptian tomb – a coldness that made his ankle ache and his hands tingle.

"Lady Wernero?" he called, gripping Ahwere's amulet for courage. "It's me, Zeuxis!"

The cold feeling passed and a draught fluttered the sheet. He heard someone breathing on the other side – heavily, and in pain. He lifted the sheet. The smell of urine hit him first, and he wrinkled his nose in distaste. Then he saw the witch, huddled under a blanket in the corner, her Egyptian skin a peculiar shade of yellow. He dropped to his knees beside her.

"Oh, Lady, I'm sorry I didn't come when Ahwere asked me to! Where is she? Do you know where they took her?"

The witch's eyes flickered open and her hand reached out to touch his wrist. "Lighthouse Boy?" she whispered. Her eyes closed again and she moaned, "You took part in the race, didn't you? I tried to stop the Romans using you, but my spell failed. It was the ka... too powerful for me... And now you hate me for imprisoning you in that tomb, but I had to try for Egypt's sake."

"I know why you did it." Zeuxis grasped the old woman's hand. "I know you didn't want me to drive for the Romans in the race, and you were right. Mark Anthony must have planned it all along, persuading the queen to let Caesar's team into the Hippodrome. But it's too late now. Where's your granddaughter, Lady Wernero? Where did Prince Ptolemy's men take her?"

The witch shook her head. "I tried to stop them, but the ka attacked me! They found the curses. Then they took Ahwere... Oh, my poor girl! And the ka got away..."

"Forget the demon," Zeuxis said, growing impatient. "Can't you use your magic to find Ahwere? I've got her amulet! Maybe you can use that to trace her?" He showed her the chipped Egyptian eye he'd knotted around his neck.

Lady Wernero shook her head. "Too late. I've failed. The Romans are in control. Egypt's day is over. The old magic will soon be gone for ever."

"It's NOT all gone!" Zeuxis shouted. "Not yet, anyway. The ka is still here. I spoke to it last night, down by the canal. It's gone after those Queen Cleopatra loves, so it's occupied for now. But if you don't help me, Ahwere's going to die! Prince Ptolemy's got her. Don't you understand? The Romans have ordered him to disband his army and give himself up. But he won't do it. He'll be crazier than ever."

Lady Wernero stared at him, her voice almost normal. "You *spoke* to the ka-demon?"

"Yes! I thought it was another nightmare, but it wasn't."

"But you're not even Egyptian! Didn't it try to hurt you? It half killed me."

Zeuxis rubbed his ankle. The numbness had worn off a bit since he'd come upstairs. "Not really. It told me it's come for Queen Cleopatra – and it'll probably kill Mark Anthony, too, because I told it the queen loved him. It might take some other people from the palace as well, except I don't think it really understands what love is yet. It said it punished you because you tried to banish it before it had finished its task. But I made a bargain with it, and it promised to protect Ahwere. So, you see, we've still got time to find her."

Lady Wernero stared at him with new respect. "You made a bargain with a ka-demon?"

"I know it was a crazy thing to do, but it was all I could think of to help Ahwere. Do you think the demon will keep its promise, or try to punish her like it punished you?"

Lady Wernero chuckled. "Punished me, yes, that's what it felt like all right…" She grasped Zeuxis' arms and, with a struggle, managed to sit up. "Don't look so worried, Lighthouse Boy. A demon is bound to keep any bargain it is tricked into making. That's why curses work so well when a summoning is successful. If the magic really hasn't gone, then maybe there is something we can try. Help me downstairs, and let's see if Prince Ptolemy's men have left me enough ingredients for a finding spell!"

While Zeuxis helped the witch search through the mess of her downstairs room for the things she needed, Aelian fretted at the delay. He grumbled under his breath about needing to get back to the lighthouse before the Romans took control of that, too.

Lady Wernero grunted as she dusted off some dried petals she'd just found in the corner. "That's the least of our worries. Did you see the soldiers stopping people going to pray to our Goddess Isis? They'll destroy our gods first. Then they'll destroy us. At least when Great Alexander came to Egypt, he respected our ancient traditions. Even Queen Cleopatra worshipped Isis, though she changed our traditions to suit herself."

"What will Caesar do to the queen?" Zeuxis asked.

"Probably make her his prisoner and parade her through the streets of Rome," Lady Wernero said. "Serves her right for refusing to share the throne with her brother in the traditional way of our Pharaohs!"

"What'll Caesar do if Queen Cleopatra and Prince Ptolemy refuse to disband their armies and surrender to him?" Zeuxis said.

"There'll be war, of course." To her collection of ingredients, Lady Wernero added a frayed thread from the carpet Zeuxis had been sick on the last time he was here. "They'll destroy our beautiful city between them. It'd almost be better to let Caesar take complete control than have our beautiful Alexandria destroyed by riots. There! I think that'll have to do. I can easily use a strand of my hair instead of Ahwere's... give me her amulet. The Eye of Horus is powerful. It might find her, even without the proper ingredients. These are hardly perfect conditions for a finding spell, but we should be able to cook something up."

Zeuxis sank down on the floor in relief and rubbed his numb ankle.

The witch crouched over her pile of rose petals. She took the eye amulet, twisting around it the thread from the Persian rug and the strand of hair she'd pulled from her head. Then she took a pin and pierced Zeuxis' finger so his blood dripped on the eye, dark drops in the gloom. The petals began to smoulder. Zeuxis dared not ask how she'd lit the fire, though he could smell the scented oil she'd poured on them. His eyes watered.

Lady Wernero instructed him to hold the amulet, cupped her hands around it, and chanted softly in Egyptian. The fire-glow made her look younger. The shadows in the room deepened. Even Aelian stopped grumbling and crept closer to watch. The back of Zeuxis' neck prickled. He imagined the ka-demon's green eyes watching them.

"Think of Ahwere," Lady Wernero whispered. "Think of what she means to you."

Zeuxis blushed, suddenly glad it was so dark in the room. It was more difficult than he thought. He conjured up an image of Ahwere as he'd last seen her, looking like a priestess in the tomb of her ancestors... Shivering, he shook that memory away, and replaced it with an earlier one of Ahwere ducking through the Gate of the Moon, her dark eyes teasing him as she said, *"You drove that chariot better than Clytius did."* That day, she'd been more beautiful to him than Queen Cleopatra herself.

"Good," Lady Wernero whispered, as the amulet in his hands grew warm. "It's working. I can see... *a carpet rolled around a girl with black hair—"* She shook her head in frustration. "I can't see her properly, but she is in a large room. There are powerful people present, and something else. I see… *a snake in a basket… a basket full of black snakes… a great darkness over Alexandria…* OH!"

She snatched her hands away and fell backwards against the wall, as if she'd been pushed. Zeuxis dropped the amulet, his ankle turning fiercely cold where the ka had touched him. Lady Wernero curled into a ball and moaned, her grey hair hanging over her face. The petals had burnt to ash.

"What happened?" Zeuxis said, scrambling across to help her up. "Lady? Where was the large room you saw? Is that horrid Prince Ptolemy keeping Ahwere prisoner inside a carpet, is that it? We have to rescue her!"

The witch shook her head, trembling and breathing hard. "I couldn't see, it wasn't clear enough. It's no good, Lighthouse Boy. The ka must have made me weaker than I thought. I need the proper ingredients. You'll have to go to the market and get them for me."

Aelian grumbled some more, but Zeuxis did not argue. Lady Wernero obviously wasn't strong enough to go herself, and they could check the Pharos light from the agora.

He listened to the witch's list of ingredients carefully, knowing he couldn't rely on Aelian's memory. They fetched Lady Wernero some water. Then, with Aelian mounted on Venus this time, and Zeuxis supporting himself with a hand on the filly's neck, they made their way to the waterfront.

*　　*　　*

Zeuxis had not been entirely sure there would be a market today. But when they reached the agora, they found Roman soldiers standing guard around a handful of stalls. The merchants seemed nervous, and so did the shoppers. The Romans were stopping everyone on their way into the square and searching them. Smoke from the smouldering ruins of the Great Library hung over everything, hiding the island from view, though he could hear shouting out on the water somewhere.

"We'll never find everything Lady Wernero wants here," Zeuxis said, his heart sinking.

"Maybe we'll get some of the things she needs over on the island," Aelian said, squinting through the smoke. "If them lazy boys have been using this invasion as an excuse to shirk their duties, I'm goin' to give 'em a right hiding when I get back. Your eyes are sharper than mine, lad. Can you see if the light's bright enough?"

Zeuxis peered across the Heptastadion, his eyes stinging. The roadblocks had changed hands. Romans guarded the one at this end, and the soldiers at the other end seemed agitated – no doubt because of the line of Roman ships blockading the harbour mouth. For a moment, he couldn't think what the queen's men were doing out on the island. Had Queen Cleopatra taken refuge there? Then the wind changed, the smoke cleared, and he realized the second set of uniforms were not those of the queen's Royal Guard.

"Those are Prince Ptolemy's men out there!" he cried, his heart thudding. "They must have captured Pharos

Island, and – oh, gods, Aelian – *the light!*"

Even in the blazing sun, the Pharos' fire should have been visible against the sea. But for the first time in Zeuxis' life, the lighthouse was dark and cold.

The beacon of Alexandria had gone out.

The demon removes her name from the coins of this land

Humans are full of surprises!

The boy not only survived the race, but he dared make a bargain with me. I shall remove him easily when he is no longer of any use, of course. That silly amulet will not save him from my power, any more than it saved the girl he wants me to protect.

My task in this world is drawing to a close. It should not take me long now to work out which of Cleopatra's friends I should destroy along with the queen. In the meantime, there is this small matter of the coins.

I had planned to put Prince Ptolemy's name on them. But the balance of power has changed, and I am still a bit puzzled about love. So until I discover more, I think it had better be Caesar's.

Chapter 15

CAESAR

THE THOUGHT OF all the time he'd wasted chasing around the Egyptian Quarter made Zeuxis' head spin. Prince Ptolemy had been holding Ahwere prisoner on Pharos Island all along! He dragged the filly towards the Heptastadion. Aelian, equally desperate to rekindle the lighthouse fire, urged her on with his heels.

"Halt!" The officer in charge of the Roman roadblock stepped in front of them. "No further, citizens! The island is out of bounds for security reasons. You may do your shopping, but then you must return to your homes and listen out for Caesar's announcements. We will restore order to the city as soon as possible."

"We work on the island," Zeuxis said, trying to lead the filly around him. "And the Pharos' fire has gone out! You have to let us across!"

This had little effect on the Roman officer. "We are aware that the Pharos light has gone out, but the small lighthouse opposite is still working and under our control, so there's no need for panic." He looked at Zeuxis' filthy, torn tunic and Aelian's dung-splattered work clothes, and his tone turned suspicious. "Where did you get the horse?"

"I... er..." Zeuxis licked his lips. If he told the truth – that he'd driven the White chariot in the race – the Romans would only ask awkward questions. But could he risk a lie?

"That's one of Marcus Suetonius' racehorses!" spoke up one of the soldiers. "I follow chariot racing, Sir. I'd know that filly anywhere. She's the fastest of his whole team. They must have stolen her!"

Instantly, the officer's attitude changed. He drew his sword and Venus shied as he seized her rein. "I think you two had better come with me, don't you?"

Zeuxis stiffened. They couldn't let themselves get arrested, or they'd be no use to either Ahwere or the Keeper.

"I drove the White chariot in the Hippodrome," he said quickly. "Then there was a riot and I lost the filly in the Egyptian Quarter."

"Sure you did," said one of the men with a chuckle. "You're still coming with us."

It was no good. They didn't believe him. Zeuxis glanced up at Aelian. The old man nodded slightly and twisted his hands in the filly's mane. "Yah!" Zeuxis waved his arms at the filly, praying that Aelian wouldn't fall off.

Venus squealed and leapt forwards as she had been trained to do at the start of a race, ripping her reins from the Roman officer's hand. The rest of the soldiers scattered. Aelian clung on as she jumped the roadblock, and her grey tail disappeared into the smoke that hung over the Heptastadion. In the confusion, Zeuxis sprinted after her.

"Oy, you!" shouted the officer, as Zeuxis scrambled over the barrier. "Come back here!"

Zeuxis did not look round. Seven stadia of straight, shimmering marble lay between him and the island, and his leg still felt numb. He heard the Romans' sandals pounding closer behind him. One stade was the length of an Olympic sprint... one and a half, and the smoke made it difficult to get his breath... two... His stomach clenched in frustration as the leading soldier knocked him down and wrenched his arms behind his back.

"Up with you, young thief!" he growled. "You're going to answer before Caesar for stealing Marcus Suetonius' horse."

"But I didn't steal her! I just wanted to get back to the lighthouse. You don't understand..."

As they hauled him back to the roadblock, Zeuxis tried to explain how he had driven in the chariot race and chased Prince Ptolemy across the city last night because the prince had kidnapped his friend. But the Romans were furious at losing the filly, and tightened their hands on his elbows. At least Aelian had got away. Zeuxis tried to see if the old man had reached the lighthouse safely, but his captors wouldn't let him stop long enough to look.

"That was stupid, boy," said the officer, tying Zeuxis' wrists behind his back. "Only the guilty run."

"But it's true I drove the White chariot for Caesar in the Hippodrome—"

The Roman slapped him across the mouth. "Save it for your trial, thief! You've got a lot of explaining to do."

Zeuxis tasted blood, and remembered what Prince Ptolemy had said about Romans crucifying criminals to make an example of them. He twisted his wrists against his bonds in sudden fear. Did they do that to boys his age? While the Romans marched him along the waterfront with grim expressions, Zeuxis dared not open his mouth in case the officer decided to crucify him anyway.

They found Queen Cleopatra's palace in a state of confusion. Slaves ran past, carrying platters of fruit and jugs of wine. Roman soldiers stood at every door and barked orders across the courtyards. A group of prisoners shivered on the quayside in chains, awaiting transportation to Rome. The big galley Zeuxis had seen last night had been brought into the royal harbour, where its eagle standard gleamed in the Alexandrian sunshine. Trampled rose petals blew across the steps in the breeze.

Zeuxis' neck hurt with twisting his head to take everything in. He had never been further than the royal stables before. He wished he could stop to have a closer look at everything. But his escort hustled him along the marble corridors and past the gilded statues and pillars, grim-faced. The officer had a word with the guards standing at the doors to a huge hall. The door had been left open a crack, showing torches flaring across rich carpets, crowds of people in colourful robes, and wall hangings glittering with golden thread. But Zeuxis hardly had a chance to see inside, before he was hauled past.

"Please let me see Marcus Suetonius, Sir?" he said, finding his voice at last. "He knows me." He cringed as the officer turned and raised a fist. "Or Lucian Flavius! Please, Sir, at least ask them if my story's true! They were at the races. They'll tell you why I had their filly with me last night."

The officer lowered his fist. "You know Lucian Flavius?"

"Yes, I was trying to tell you... I drove the chariot for the White team in the race. I drove for Rome! It was all Lucian's idea. Please, Sir, let me see him."

"It's just a wild story to save his skin," growled one of his escort. "This scruffy lighthouse boy's never driven a chariot in the Hippodrome in his life! He probably overheard Lucian's name some place and knows he's Caesar's favourite spy."

The officer frowned. "Lucian doesn't exactly advertise the fact."

"I have driven a chariot!" Zeuxis said. "Look at my hands if you don't believe me!"

The officer stepped behind him and ran his thumb thoughtfully over Zeuxis' blisters. He examined the whip weal on his arm and grunted. "He might be telling the truth, at that... if he hasn't bathed since last night's race, that *could* account for his appearance." He frowned at Zeuxis again. "If you did drive that chariot for the Whites, boy, then you're in a lot more trouble than horse-stealing! Caesar don't take kindly to those who disgrace his name by abandoning a race half-run."

Zeuxis' heart sank. "I had my reasons, Sir."

His escort scowled. "More likely the boy's a spy for Prince Ptolemy, Sir! We ought to torture him to get at the real truth. He's got more crazy stories in him than a bard."

Zeuxis turned cold. This was going from bad to worse.

"I'm not a spy..." he began, the fear returning, but the officer held up a hand. He glanced towards the hall, where voices rose and fell in argument. They were too far away to hear the actual words. Zeuxis thought they were speaking Latin, anyway.

"There'll be no torturing of prisoners until I say so," the officer said in the end. "The boy's asked to see Lucian Flavius. Find him, and then maybe we'll get to the bottom of this. In the meantime, better put him in here."

He opened a door to a storeroom and checked it for security. As an afterthought, he added, "Untie the boy. He's not going anywhere."

* * *

Zeuxis huddled in a corner of the storeroom with his back against a bale of cloth and his arms wrapped around his knees, straining his eyes to see the glimmer of light that came under the door. The Romans had not left him a lamp, and his imagination conjured up a snake's coils in the gloom.

"Ka-demon?" he whispered, wishing he had not left Ahwere's amulet with Lady Wernero.

But the demon did not appear. If it was in the palace, it must be busy elsewhere.

Zeuxis cursed himself for being so stupid as to try lying to the Romans. He should have told that officer at the roadblock the truth right away. Then they might have listened to him and helped him rescue Ahwere. Instead, he was a prisoner in the palace, helpless to aid his friend, or escape the ka-demon if it came for him.

He shuddered. What was Prince Ptolemy doing to Ahwere over on the island? Would his men let Aelian rekindle the light? What had they done with the Keeper? And what about Lady Wernero, back in her wrecked house in the Egyptian Quarter, awaiting the ingredients for her spell...?

Not knowing what was happening was terrible. He had to bite the backs of his hands to stop himself from screaming.

It seemed a very long time before the key turned in the lock. The door slammed open, and light blinded him. He squinted at the man who stood in the corridor. His heart fell a little when he saw it was indeed Lucian Flavius, and not Marcus as he'd half hoped. But he scrambled to his feet and bowed his head before the Roman.

"I'm sorry about the race, Sir—" he began.

"Do you know the boy, Sir?" asked the guard, interrupting.

Lucian waved the guard aside and frowned at Zeuxis. "Where did you get to after the race? Marcus isn't very happy at the way you abandoned his horses in the Hippodrome."

Zeuxis' heart filled with relief. He'd been afraid Lucian would deny all knowledge of the race that had gone so wrong. "I know it was a bad thing to do, Sir. But Hippolytus was there to look after them, and—"

Lucian cut him off. "The Red charioteer had enough trouble getting his own horses out of the Hippodrome in one piece, let alone ours! Lucky for you, the three you abandoned are now safe in the royal stables. Marcus has gone to check on them, and I'm informed the grey filly is back on your island. Marcus will be pleased to know she's safe. But first Caesar wants to talk to you, and you can't see the emperor of Rome like that. You stink. Come with me."

Lucian Flavius hauled Zeuxis to a marble room with a bath sunk into the floor, and instructed the slaves to scrub him and dress him in a clean tunic. This was not as much fun as Zeuxis thought it would be. The slaves were rough, and he discovered a hundred cuts and bruises he hadn't felt after the race. Also, he was still anxious about Ahwere.

Lucian strode impatiently up and down through the steam, snapping at the slaves to hurry up. He snapped at Zeuxis, too, when he asked questions. But he learnt that the Romans had blockaded the harbour mouth, and that soldiers had been sent across by boat to drive Prince Ptolemy's men off Pharos Island and capture the prince. Lucian didn't seem to know where Mark Anthony had taken the queen after the race. But it seemed that camels and mule carts, laden with treasure, had arrived at the palace as a gift to Caesar, which meant either the queen or her brother was about to surrender.

"I bet... it isn't... urgh... Prince Ptolemy," Zeuxis mumbled, as one of the slaves attacked the cut on his mouth with a sponge.

Lucian stopped pacing. He smiled. "You're not as stupid as you look, are you, Lighthouse Boy?" He examined Zeuxis with a critical eye and straightened the tunic the slaves had tugged over his damp hair. It had a border of vine leaves and was too big for him. "You'll do. Come on! Caesar doesn't like to be kept waiting."

Nervously, Zeuxis followed the Roman into the great hall. The crowd was thicker than ever. Most people seemed to be arguing among themselves. No one took any notice of him or Lucian. On a dais at the far end loomed two huge ebony thrones inlaid with gold. Their feet were carved like panthers. On one of them sat a powerful-looking Roman with a strong nose and glittering eyes, wearing a diadem of golden leaves and a purple-edged toga with a sword strapped over the top.

He was leaning over one of the arms, talking to a soldier who stood beside the throne.

"Julius Caesar," whispered Lucian, as if there could be any mistake.

Zeuxis' mouth dried with nerves. A long line of men and women snaked back from the throne, between the pillars. One by one, they dropped to their knees before Caesar and pleaded their case. Sometimes, the soldiers kicked them away, or hauled them off to the dungeons still yelling their innocence. Other times, Caesar broke off his conversation to speak a few words, or waved his hand, and they were led away into another room smiling in relief – presumably to get whatever they'd asked for.

Lucian hauled Zeuxis to the front of the queue, pushed him to his knees and cleared his throat.

"Your charioteer, Caesar!" he said.

The man who had conquered half the known world shifted on his throne. He spoke good Greek. "Ah, Lucian Flavius! I wondered where you'd got to. So, this is the boy who drove my White chariot in the Hippodrome and caused that convenient little riot?"

Zeuxis looked at the floor, dizzy with fear.

Caesar laughed and clapped his hands. "I've heard great things about you, Charioteer. Leaving the race before the finish and taking the Red charioteer with you, so no one won, and all the supporters got angry with everyone else – that was an excellent touch. Not even Mark Anthony thought of that! What reward do you want?"

Reward? Zeuxis glanced at Lucian and opened his mouth. No words came out. Caesar waited, tapping a finger on the arm of his throne.

"Is the boy mute?" he said, growing impatient. "Take him away, Lucian, and give him a bag of gold. I've a lot to attend to today... Oh, and make sure the coins have my head on them and not Cleopatra's, won't you? Hers will be worthless after today."

The men standing around the throne chuckled. But Zeuxis turned cold as he heard a whisper in his ear, "*Remove her name from the coins of this land... all this is done, but I am still here.*"

He looked carefully round the throne room, but he couldn't see the demon. He shook the words away. Lady Wernero's spell might not have seen where Ahwere was being kept, but it had seen her alive, and this was his chance.

"S-sir!" Zeuxis stammered, recovering his voice. "There is something I want."

"Well?" Caesar leant closer. "Out with it, then."

"Prince Ptolemy, Sir... he has an Egyptian girl called Ahwere with him. When you capture him, please can I have her?"

It did not come out right, not at all. The men around the throne laughed again.

Caesar looked amused. "Aren't you a bit young to be looking for that kind of reward?"

Zeuxis flushed, and Caesar sighed. "Very well, then. The girl is yours, Charioteer, as well as the gold." He waved his hand, and Lucian gripped Zeuxis' elbow to drag him away.

"Wait!" Zeuxis said. "Does that mean she's already here, Sir? Did Mark Anthony manage to capture Prince Ptolemy? Has the Pharos fire been relit? And what's going to happen to Queen Cleopatra when—?"

"Shut up, stupid!" Lucian hissed, dragging him away from the throne. "You're extremely lucky Caesar didn't order you executed for abandoning the race and disgracing his name. The emperor of Rome hasn't time to talk to a common lighthouse boy."

"But I didn't disgrace you, did I?" Zeuxis said, more confident now he knew he wasn't going to be crucified for horse stealing. "I caused the riot, and that enabled you to take over the palace. I'm not stupid. I knew what you were up to, well before that race started."

Lucian stared at him, eyes narrow. "Marcus told you our plans?"

"Not exactly…" Zeuxis bit his tongue, not wanting to get Marcus Suetonius into trouble.

Lucian scowled. "Lighthouse Boy, you're going the right way about getting your reward revoked—"

Before he could continue, the heavy doors swung back and a trumpet blew. A detachment of the queen's Royal Guard, escorted by Mark Anthony and his men, marched stiffly into the hall, followed by a line of slaves laden with the tribute Lucian had mentioned. Urns of olive oil; baskets of lotus blooms and spices; bolts of bright silk; gold; ivory; a pair of panthers growling at the end of golden chains; huge peacock-feather fans; dancing girls with oiled skin the colour of midnight... and in the middle, carried carefully between two huge black slaves, the biggest carpet Zeuxis had ever seen. It must have been heavy, for it drooped in the middle. Mark Anthony kept glancing at it, a crease between his eyes.

A carpet.

Zeuxis froze as Caesar's men parted to let the procession through, exclaiming at the richness of the gifts. The emperor straightened on his throne. He smiled as Mark Anthony approached the dais and went down on one knee.

"Queen Cleopatra sends these gifts to the great Julius Caesar, along with a request that you accept them as her apology for the Romans inadvertently killed and wounded by her men last night. She also begs that you accept the throne of Egypt..." The Romans' smiles widened in anticipation, only to turn to scowls as Mark Anthony finished, "...to rule at her side, in the traditional manner of the Pharaohs of this ancient land."

Uproar broke out in the hall as his words filtered through the crowd and their meaning sank in.

"...who does this proud Egyptian queen think she is...?"

"...insult to our Caesar, suggesting she is his equal...!"

The emperor held up his hand, and the noise subsided. "Where is the queen?" he demanded.

Mark Anthony rose to his feet and raised his chin to meet the emperor's gaze. He said in a tight voice, as if the words stuck in his throat, "She will be here shortly, Caesar – and she brings a gift more precious than any ever offered in tribute to a conqueror before."

Caesar's eyebrow raised. He looked more closely at the tribute the queen had sent, his gaze lingering on the panthers. "The animals will be useful in the Circus, but I see nothing here that I haven't seen before. Is this some kind of joke, Mark Anthony? Show me something we don't already have in Rome!"

Mark Anthony stepped aside. He nodded at the slaves carrying the carpet, and they laid it gently on the floor before the throne. Untying the loops that kept it secure, they gave the roll a hard push towards Caesar.

Rich reds, greens and blues flickered in the torchlight, blurring into human form. A sweet scent filled the hall like summer roses, and black braids decorated with little golden bells tinkled in the sudden silence.

All the hairs on the back of Zeuxis' neck rose. He caught his breath as a girl in a white dress with kohl-lined eyes rolled gracefully out of the carpet at Caesar's feet.

"AHWERE!" he cried, breaking free of Lucian's grip and rushing forward.

He didn't get far. Caesar's bodyguard closed up around the dais, and a hundred swords scraped out of their scabbards to protect their emperor.

But it quickly became obvious the girl rolled in the carpet had brought no weapon with her except her own beauty. Caesar waved his bodyguard back and stepped down from the dais. As Mark Anthony reached down a hand to help the girl to her feet, Zeuxis stared in confusion. The black hair was a wig... the girl's body more developed than Ahwere's... her skin not the dark copper colour of his friend's, but the pale flesh of a Macedonian princess.

"No," he whispered. "No."

Smiling in her way that dazzled men, Queen Cleopatra shook off Mark Anthony, brushed a coloured thread off her dress, and stepped towards the dais. Graciously, she indicated the throne Caesar had risen from, and took his hand in hers to lead him back up the steps. The crowd stirred and whispered. Caesar could not take his eyes from her. The queen smiled again and sat on her throne. Caesar sat beside her, still gazing at her in admiration. The entire hall sighed.

Zeuxis' eyes blurred with tears. "Lady Wererno got it wrong!" he moaned, realizing the mistake. "She saw the wrong girl!"

Then he caught his breath. In the shadows under Cleopatra's throne, in the cobwebs where no one else could see it, dark coils writhed. The ka-demon blinked its green eyes at him in amusement. Very slowly, it uncoiled and slithered across the dais to coil beneath Caesar's.

Zeuxis shivered and edged away, eyeing the soldiers. But they did not appear to have seen the demon. When Cleopatra leant across to whisper something in the emperor's ear, Mark Anthony's face twisted in pain. He fingered the hilt of his sword and, very quietly, began to draw the blade. Zeuxis held his breath.

No one else had noticed. The rest of the people in the hall were cheering – Egyptians, Alexandrians and Romans alike. They threw rose petals over their queen and their emperor. Music started up, and the girls who had come with the queen's tribute began to dance in celebration of the union. Cleopatra glared at Mark Anthony over Caesar's shoulder and shook her head. With a look of frustration, Caesar's envoy removed his hand from his sword. Darkness rippled beneath the thrones, and the ka disappeared.

Like everyone else in the hall, Lucian Flavius was staring at the queen, who still glimmered with the magic that had brought her out of the carpet. He shook his head in wonder as he took Zeuxis' arm again. "Well!" he said. "That surprised even me! Your queen must be a sorceress, to ensnare Julius Caesar with her charms like that. Now Mark Anthony's here, there's no point us hanging around any longer. Let's go to the stables and find Marcus. He'll want to know what's happened."

Chapter 16

PHAROS

Zeuxis did not argue. It seemed the easiest way of getting out of the palace so he could find Ahwere. Lucian Flavius was clearly well known to the Roman legionaries, for they were waved through every checkpoint without question.

As soon as they were outside, Zeuxis darted to the edge of the quay and stared across the harbour to see what was happening on the island. The sun, reflected in the water, dazzled him. But he could see that the Pharos fire had not yet been rekindled. Smoke coiled from the islanders' houses, and boats swarmed around the rocks like flies. Soldiers, sunlight flashing from their armour and weapons, fought on the headland where he'd trained the Roman chariot team.

Lucian came to stand beside him. "Prince Ptolemy's putting up more of a fight over there than we expected," he said in a grim tone.

"They're destroying our island!" Zeuxis said, his stomach twisting in anxiety for Ahwere. "*Please* let me go across, Sir! I think my friend's a prisoner over there, and probably the Keeper and all the lighthouse workers, too. We have to relight the fire before it gets dark. They've got your filly over there, too, remember?" he added.

Lucian pressed his lips together. "We'll recapture the island and get our horse back soon enough, don't worry – look, Ptolemy's men are already abandoning their refuge." He pointed to some small boats Zeuxis had not noticed, black specks disappearing around the headland under an unnaturally dark cloud that coiled after them like a ghostly flying snake.

The hairs on the back of his neck rose as he remembered how the ka had disappeared from under the thrones. "Why aren't your soldiers chasing them?"

"They have orders to secure the island and the Pharos first," Lucian said, frowning at the boats. "Though you're right... it's possible the commander hasn't seen them, with that cloud. Strange how it hangs over the boats like that." He shaded his eyes and watched the battle for a moment, then cursed under his breath and strode to the stables, calling for the grooms to bring him a horse. As an afterthought, he looked over his shoulder at Zeuxis. "Come on, then, Lighthouse Boy! I thought you wanted to go over there and rescue your friend?"

Marcus Suetonius joined them in the yard. He cut off Zeuxis' explanation of what had gone wrong in the race and boosted him up on one of the queen's horses. As they galloped along the waterfront and through the market place, Zeuxis tried not to think of what they might find when they got across to the island. At the Heptastadion roadblock, the officer who had arrested him blinked in surprise to see him mounted in such company, and pulled the barrier aside. Zeuxis couldn't resist a cheeky wave as he followed Lucian and Marcus through.

The roadblock at the island end was no longer manned. As they crossed the headland to reach the lighthouse, Zeuxis turned his eyes away from the dead bodies lying on the rocks. Mostly they were Ptolemy's men, but he saw more than a few dead Romans, too.

Lucian leapt off his horse in full gallop, ran to the edge of the rocks and shouted at the men on the ships blockading the harbour mouth. "The prince is getting away! He's got boats round the headland! After him, quick!" Meanwhile, Marcus galloped up to the lighthouse and shouted similar warnings at the men fighting around its base.

Eventually, the message got through. Two of the galleys from the blockade rowed out to sea after the fugitives, and legionaries formed up and ran to the far side of the island. But even Zeuxis could see they were too late. The battle here was over. The few remaining defenders died under Roman swords, and only the smoking shells of houses remained. One of the lighthouse storerooms had been set alight, and terrified donkeys brayed as boys ran in and out of the stables, letting them loose. Islanders ventured out of their doorways to stare at the Romans with accusing eyes. Someone threw a stone that hit Lucian on the arm.

He frowned and rubbed the bruise, but did not go after the thrower. Instead, he climbed the lighthouse steps and raised his arms for silence.

"Pharos Islanders!" he called. "Caesar is sorry your homes have been destroyed, but you must realize the destruction here is a direct result of Prince Ptolemy's resistance. If you cooperate with us, order will be restored as soon as possible. Queen Cleopatra of Egypt and Julius Caesar of Rome have come to an agreement. They will be joint rulers of Alexandria for the foreseeable future." He rested a hand on the hilt of his sword and watched the crowd warily.

A hush followed these words. The islanders muttered uneasily and turned their heads to look across the harbour at the palace. Then they realized a peaceful celebration was going on across the water, and started to nod and smile.

"Our queen's enchanted Caesar!"

"Queen Cleopatra for Pharaoh!"

"Down with Prince Ptolemy and the Greens!"

"Up the Blues!"

The Romans were busy watching the crowd for trouble and checking the buildings for the last of Ptolemy's men. Zeuxis urged his horse into the lighthouse and rode it up the spiral ramp at a fast trot until he reached the Keeper's levels. He abandoned the horse with a quick pat for its bravery and climbed the steps to the Keeper's room, breathless with fear at what he might find.

But if Ptolemy had been inside the lighthouse, he was long gone. A detachment of Roman soldiers passed him on their way down from searching the rooms and called, "If you're supposed to be helping the other boys light the fire, you'd best get up there double quick! That old man in charge up there is in a fierce mood."

Zeuxis smiled. It sounded as if old Aelian was all right, at least.

"Did you find a girl?" he asked the soldiers. "An Egyptian girl?"

But they shook their heads. "All the civilians are outside in the village. Only woman up there is some old hag who says she's looking after your Keeper – though that one's more in need of a priest, by the looks of him."

They clattered down the stairs. Zeuxis stared after them, his stomach twisting in fresh anxiety. *More in need of a priest*? He leapt the final three stairs and burst through the door without knocking.

He stared in horror at the man lying on the bed. The Keeper's skin had gone grey. His eyes were closed. His broken leg stuck out at an unnatural angle that made Zeuxis sick to look at it. The room smelt of a sickly mixture of urine and incense. The incense curled from a brazier in the corner, where the nurse the soldiers had mentioned chanted in Egyptian as she added things to the fire. Smoke, swirling in the sunlight that came through the round window, hid her face. But she was not the same woman who had tended the Keeper before.

"What are you doing…?" Zeuxis demanded. Then his breath whooshed out of him in relief. "Lady Wernero!"

"He's very sick," Lady Wernero said. "Prince Ptolemy tried to get your Keeper to tell him where you went after the race. The Keeper didn't know, of course. But that didn't matter to Ptolemy. He had his men break his leg in three more places. There's only so much a man's body can take at his age."

Zeuxis hugged himself as he imagined the pain of that.

"I've given him something to help him sleep," continued Lady Wernero. "But I'm afraid it's bad news. Prince Ptolemy fled the island, and he took Ahwere with him. Seems my seeing spell…"

"…wasn't quite right, I know. But it did work. You just saw the wrong girl." Zeuxis told her what had happened in the palace, when Cleopatra had rolled out of her carpet at Caesar's feet; how she'd enchanted Caesar so that he agreed to share the throne of Alexandria with her, and how he'd seen the ka-demon under the thrones.

Lady Wernero paled. "It seems Cleopatra is more of a sorceress than I thought! If she's enchanted Caesar as well as Mark Anthony, then things are just getting more complicated. If the ka now thinks it has to remove *Caesar*, the gods only know what'll happen to us all!"

Zeuxis crept across to touch the Keeper's cheek. It felt icy. He shuddered. "What's going to happen to the Keeper?"

Lady Wernero shook her head. "I've done my best for him, but he's dying. I think he only held on this long because he was waiting to see you."

"I... he said *I'd* be the new Keeper after him." Zeuxis hugged himself, shivering. "But I'm not ready, and Ahwere is still Prince Ptolemy's prisoner!"

"We'll get her back," Lady Wernero said. "At least we know she's still alive. I'll cast another spell and see if I can find out where Prince Ptolemy's taken her, but I'll be more careful this time. I don't want another brush with that ka."

Zeuxis took a deep breath. "Nor me... but we mightn't have any choice."

Lady Wernero's eyes narrowed. "What do you mean?"

"Caesar and Mark Anthony will go after Prince Ptolemy, won't they? If they do that, and the ka attacks them, Prince Ptolemy will win and we'll never get Ahwere back. But when I spoke to it under the bridge, the demon seemed confused about love. Somehow, we have to convince it that Queen Cleopatra loves Prince Ptolemy more than she loves Mark Anthony or Caesar. Then it will attack Prince Ptolemy, and we can rescue Ahwere." He eyed the witch uncertainly. "But it means we'll have to work with the Romans."

There was a silence. The brazier crackled, the incense making Zeuxis feel light-headed. Lady Wernero drew herself up, and for a terrifying moment he thought she was going to put a spell on *him*.

Then she sighed and said softly, "The Keeper told me you had no interest in politics, but it seems you've worked things out better than any of us. Much as I hate to admit it, in this case I think you're right. The last thing we want is Prince Ptolemy on the throne of Egypt, so I agree we have no choice but to use Caesar's strength to help get rid of him. I'll prepare my finding spell, and you can try talking to the ka again… Ah well, it's time I let your Keeper wake up, anyway."

Lady Wernero went to stare out of the window, and *something* sighed out of the room. The sun brightened. As the sleep spell lifted, the Keeper stirred.

Zeuxis clutched his master's cold hand. "I'm here, Sir," he whispered. "The race is over."

The Keeper's eyelids flickered open. He stared past Zeuxis, as if at something behind him. Then his eyes focused and the cracked lips smiled.

"Zeuxis lad," he breathed, and the icy fingers tightened. "I knew you would come back. Lady Wernero tells me the Romans won. I'm proud of you. Is the fire alight?"

"Aelian's up there with the boys, lighting it right now," Zeuxis said with as much confidence as he could manage. He didn't tell the Keeper that he had left before the finish of the race, so he hadn't won anything, and what Lady Wernero meant was that the Romans had won the city.

The Keeper relaxed. "Good. The Pharos must stay alight for Alexandria…" His broken leg twitched, and his face creased with pain. "…no matter who rules her. Do you understand, Zeuxis? Now you're Keeper, it's important you understand this."

Zeuxis nodded. He could not speak past the lump in his throat.

"You're free now, as I promised."

The lump almost choked him. "I don't deserve it," he whispered. "I let the Pharos' fire go out. I helped the Romans invade us. And I ignored my friend when she needed me… I was selfish and stupid. But I'll make up for it, I promise!"

The Keeper's fingers tightened again. "You'll make a fine Keeper of the Pharos, Zeuxis."

He smiled. Then his fingers loosened, and he breathed his last.

Chapter 17

LOVE

AFTER JULIUS CAESAR moved into Queen Cleopatra's palace, rumours flew around the city, growing wilder every day. Favourite ones claimed that Ptolemy had sent tomb robbers to steal the treasure from the pyramids at Giza; Ptolemy was hiring mercenaries to raise an army bigger than Great Alexander had brought to Egypt three hundred years ago; Ptolemy was raising a fleet to sail across the Mediterranean and attack Rome. Other rumours concerned the queen and the emperor. Cleopatra was pregnant with Caesar's child; Caesar was going to take her back to Rome and make her his empress; Mark Anthony was so jealous, he couldn't bear to be in the same room with Julius Caesar; Cleopatra's child was not Caesar's, but her baby brother's…

No one knew quite what to believe. It was true that, now Prince Ptolemy had been banished from Alexandria, the Egyptian priests had made Cleopatra marry her nine-year-old second brother in order to satisfy tradition. But a boy so young could hardly have made his older sister pregnant without a powerful spell, and in Zeuxis' opinion the child was far more likely to be Mark Anthony's – though no one seemed brave enough to mention that.

Zeuxis' new duties as Keeper of the Pharos kept him busy while Lady Wernero prepared her finding spell, though this took much longer than he had imagined. The witch said she needed to restore her house so that they would be properly protected when she made contact with Ahwere. This meant replacing all the things Prince Ptolemy's men had smashed, some of which could only be found in remote corners of Egypt. Zeuxis went half crazy imagining what Prince Ptolemy might be doing to Ahwere in the meantime. But, finally, Lady Wernero sent a message to say she was ready. Leaving old Aelian in charge of the lighthouse, Zeuxis and Lucian Flavius hurried to the Egyptian Quarter.

Evening sunlight cast long copper shadows between the houses. Most still had broken doors and burnt holes in their roofs from the night of the riot, but the families had moved back in. The jangle of sistrum rattles and the barking of dogs could be heard as they hurried through the narrow streets.

Lucian wore a drab-coloured cloak, which concealed his sword. "Things are still a bit sensitive here," he explained as they went. "Sometimes it's best to keep a low profile."

Zeuxis nodded, but he wished Lucian had brought some horses and men. When they reached the place where he used to tether Cleo, his mouth dried. Here, at the end of the witch's dark alley, he felt like a little boy again.

"What's wrong?" Lucian whispered, resting a hand on his sword and frowning into the gloom. "Why is there no one to meet us? Is it a trick?"

Zeuxis took a deep breath. He reminded himself he was Keeper of the Pharos now, and had Caesar's favourite spy to watch his back. "No, it's always like this." He pushed back his shoulders, marched into the alley and rapped on the witch's new door. As he did so, he saw it had been carved all over with tiny hieroglyphs.

Spells.

There was a pause after his knock, when he had a horrible fear Lucian might be right. What if the Egyptian resistance had decided to remove both Caesar's spy and the new Keeper of the Pharos who supported the Romans? Then the door swung inwards, and Lady Wernero silently held out an ankh amulet. The same one Zeuxis had cast away in the tomb? Impossible to tell. He took it without a word and looped it over his head. The witch was wearing Ahwere's chipped Eye of Horus. She and Lucian stared warily at each other. She did not offer the Roman any protection, and he did not ask. He kept his hand on his sword.

"I know why you need to be here, Roman," Lady Wernero said. "But if you interfere, the spell won't work. Sit over there and keep quiet, no matter what you see."

Lucian nodded to show he understood. He perched on the three-legged stool she indicated, his sword resting across his knees.

Zeuxis lowered himself to the mat in front of the smoking brazier and stole a look around the room. Statuettes of Egyptian gods watched from the corners, just as he remembered, though among them he spotted the Alexandrian god Serapis, and even some of the new Roman gods. Lucian raised an eyebrow when he saw them.

Lady Wernero caught him looking and gave the Roman a wry smile. "We're going to need all the protection we can get tonight," she explained.

A shiver went down Zeuxis' spine.

"Are you sure you want to try this?" the witch whispered, as she knelt opposite him on the other side of the brazier.

"Yes," Zeuxis said firmly. It was the only way he could think of to help Ahwere.

Lady Wernero gave him a searching look and nodded. "All right. Don't say anything until I've made contact. Then, if the ka comes as it's sure to do when it senses my spell, be ready. I'm not sure I can take another 'punishment' like the one it gave me last time."

Zeuxis watched as she added lotus petals to the brazier, followed by drips of a black liquid. The resulting hiss of purple smoke made his eyes sting. He closed them, while Lady Wernero rattled her sistrum and began to chant in Egyptian.

The spell went on for a long time. Zeuxis grew sleepy from the purple smoke. He heard Lucian shift his weight on the stool and stifle a cough. Then, without warning, the air rippled, and something *changed*.

At the same time, the witch's chant changed from Egyptian to Greek. "I see…" she whispered. "I see… I see… *many tents, beside a river, between the marshes and the sea…*"

There was a creak from the stool as Lucian leant forward in interest.

Zeuxis forced his eyes open. The purple smoke was now so thick, he could barely see Lady Wernero opposite him. Her hair, glimmering with silver, hung like a curtain across her face as she swayed from side to side.

"I see… I see… *another tent, guarded by soldiers, my girl sleeping on a carpet. There is something moving in her hair… a snake… a small, black snake…*"

Zeuxis breathed faster and a shudder went through Lady Wernero.

"Ahwere," she whispered. "Ahwere, can you hear me?"

Silence.

Then the air rippled again, and relief showed on the witch's face.

"Yes, my darling," she whispered. "Don't worry. We know where you are now. Just hold on a little longer. We're coming to rescue you as soon as we can. But take care when you get up, darling. I think there's a snake in your hair— ah!" She rocked back on her heels with a sudden cry, put her hands to her throat, and staggered against the wall.

Lucian leapt to his feet, knocking over the stool. He drew his sword, looking for something to fight.

Zeuxis clenched his fists and forced himself to stay on the mat. "Ahwere!" he called. "Can you hear me? Don't be afraid! I'm going to talk to the ka-demon and explain—"

The demon's hiss almost sounded like laughter. It coiled out of the brazier – a twisting, looming darkness pierced by glowing green eyes.

Lucian drew a sharp breath and stepped forward. Lady Wernero pushed him out of the way and snapped, "Careful, Zeuxis!"

Zeuxis hardly heard. The room faded around him and his ears hummed. He felt strangely calm. The Roman's sword would be no use against a spirit from another world, anyway, and Lady Wernero obviously could not control the ka. It was just him and the demon, as it had been under the bridge.

"*Why do you call me, Human?*"

"When we spoke before, I told you the wrong thing about Prince Ptolemy," Zeuxis said.

"*I know your queen has a new husband-brother now. That must be why I am still here.*"

"No! I mean, yes, she does have a new husband. But most women love their first husband much more than their second one." He didn't know if this was true, but it sounded good. He added quickly, "Anyway, Prince Ptolemy's still her brother, even if he's been exiled. Brothers and sisters love each other lots, even though they fight most of the time. It's perfectly normal." That, at least, was true. Sometimes, he thought of Ahwere as the sister he'd never had.

The demon's coils shifted in the smoke. "*The queen is at war with her brother, yet she still loves him? This is very strange.*"

"We are strange!" Zeuxis said. "We're human."

The demon considered this, then hissed, "*It is true humans are strange creatures. I will have to think about this thing you call 'love' some more.*"

"Wait!" Zeuxis said. "What about Ahwere? Is she all right? Prince Ptolemy hasn't hurt her, has he? What'll happen to her after you've removed all those Cleopatra loves?"

"*You ask too many questions, Human. But I will tell you, since I am here. I must remove all those who interfered.*"

Zeuxis' stomach twisted as he realized what the demon meant. It intended to fulfil both Prince Ptolemy's curses – the one against the queen, and the second one against those who interfered.

"No!" he said. "We made a bargain. You can't hurt Ahwere!"

"*After my other work is done, I will find a way round the witch's spells. Then our bargain will be no more.*"

This took a little time to sink in. But it was obvious, really. To break the bargain, the demon would simply need to remove Zeuxis.

"B-but you need me to tell you about love. Come back!"

"*Not for much longer, Human.*" The demon's amused eyes blinked out, and its coils faded into the smoke.

Zeuxis lunged after it without thinking. He yelled as his hands touched the hot coals. Lucian Flavius gripped his elbow and pulled him back.

"It's gone, lad," he said gruffly. "Don't summon it again, whatever you do. It seems your friend's grandmother isn't quite as in control of her magic as she'd like us to believe. I don't want to have to explain to Caesar how I lost his new Keeper in the Egyptian Quarter."

He glanced at Lady Wernero, who sat gasping against the wall with her amulet clutched between her gnarled hands, and lowered his voice. "If I hadn't seen it with my own eyes, I'd hardly have believed it. But that trick where you can speak to your friend through the smoke could be most useful. With a spy in Ptolemy's camp, we can keep an eye on his movements and lure him into a trap."

Zeuxis shuddered. The demon's departure had put out the brazier, and the smoke was clearing, along with his head.

He took a deep breath. "You can't use Ahwere as your spy! I'm not leaving her with Prince Ptolemy a moment longer. If you won't help me, I'll rescue her alone."

Lucian shook his head. "Don't be silly, lad. How do you think you're going to get in and out of Prince

Ptolemy's camp on your own? To say nothing of that demon I saw. Who's going to look after the Pharos if you get yourself killed? You're not just an unimportant lighthouse boy any more. You can't go gallivanting off to see your friends whenever you feel like it."

Zeuxis clenched his fists in frustration. He knew the Roman spoke sense. "But Ahwere..." he whispered.

"Ptolemy's unlikely to harm the girl while he thinks he can still use her as a bargaining tool. Once we know where his camp is, exactly how many men he has, and where they're positioned, Caesar will send me in with a strike force to get your friend back. Then Mark Anthony will finish off Ptolemy and his little army, once and for all. I promise you can come along, if you stay out of the way."

Reluctantly, Zeuxis nodded. At least he knew Ahwere would be safe until the ka's other tasks were fulfilled.

He pushed this uncomfortable thought away, and helped Lady Wernero up from the floor. "Where is she, Lady?" he asked, his throat still sore from the smoke. "Where did you see Prince Ptolemy's camp?"

"Yes," Lucian said, his gaze sharp. "Did you recognize the place?"

Lady Wernero sighed. "Pelusium," she whispered. "Prince Ptolemy is keeping my girl at Pelusium, on the other side of the Nile delta, and I saw thousands of tents hidden in the marshes nearby. It's not just a strike force you need to get her back, Roman. You need Caesar's entire army."

The demon takes those she loves away from her

The waiting is nearly over. All those involved are coming together in one place, at last.

Julius Caesar, Emperor of Rome... Mark Anthony, commander of Caesar's army... Prince Ptolemy, the queen's husband-brother.... the witch's interfering granddaughter... and the boy who dared make a bargain with a demon.

These marshy fields of the river delta are as good a place as any for my purposes. Soon I shall fulfil both curses, and my task in this world will be complete. But even a demon can't be everywhere at once, so I need to think carefully about who I take first.

All depends on the outcome of this battle.

Chapter 18

BATTLE

ZEUXIS STOOD IN Marcus' war chariot on a hill overlooking the battlefield, and stared past the pricked ears of the grey fillies. It felt good to be holding the reins again. Over the past few months the White team had raced in the Hippodrome and won several times, but with another driver, because Zeuxis couldn't risk his neck in a chariot race now he was Keeper. He would be too heavy to win, anyway. His body was shooting up at awkward angles by the day, and he'd only have tipped the chariot on the turns.

As the Roman trumpets blew across the glistening black mud left by the Nile flood, the fillies leapt as if at the start of a race. "Steady," he murmured. "Steady, Minerva, Maia... whoa Venus, good girl Diana."

Behind him, Marcus held on to the sides, grinning. "You haven't lost the touch, Lighthouse Boy. But remember this race is for Caesar and Mark Anthony to run, not us! We'll stay up here and watch until the battle is over. Then we can go down and find your girl. If she's still alive, she'll be in Ptolemy's camp."

Zeuxis grinned back. "Ahwere's alive," he said. "Don't worry."

That was about the only thing he could be sure of. Back in Alexandria, Lucian Flavius had encouraged Lady Wernero to contact her granddaughter regularly so that he could report Prince Ptolemy's movements to Caesar. Zeuxis hadn't always been able to escape his lighthouse duties to attend these sessions, but at least he knew his friend wasn't dead. Thankfully, the ka-demon seemed to be keeping its side of the bargain, and so far it had not attacked any of Queen Cleopatra's 'lovers' – though Zeuxis kept the witch's amulet around his neck night and day, just in case.

Marcus, who did not quite believe in Egyptian magic, touched his arm. "I hope so."

There wasn't time for further talk. The trumpets blew again as Prince Ptolemy's chariots raced across the fields towards the Roman line. The legionaries marched forward in their disciplined squares, shields locked together and spears ready. Zeuxis winced as Ptolemy's horses crashed against that barrier and fell in a jumble of legs and limbs. Screams and squeals of pain blew towards them on the wind.

Marcus grimaced. "Ptolemy's got no idea. He should have sent his infantry against us first."

The prince's foot soldiers gave a great yell and raced after the chariots, attempting a flanking manoeuvre. But it was obvious even to Zeuxis that by the time they reached the Roman lines, they were already exhausted from ploughing through the knee-deep mud churned up by the wheels.

With relentless single-mindedness, the Romans drove Ptolemy's surviving forces back to the river. A trumpet blast brought a great splashing of hooves as Mark Anthony's cavalry streamed along the bank to close the sides of the trap like a starting gate in the Hippodrome – but one from which Ptolemy's chariot would never escape.

Left with nowhere else to go, Ptolemy's chariots foundered in the mud of the riverbank. Some of the drivers cut the horses free of their traces and urged them into the water, trying to escape by swimming, only to be pierced in the back by Roman javelins. Others tried to get away along the bank, but were cut down by Mark Anthony's men. Zeuxis watched the prince's chariot anxiously. It seemed to be caught in a struggling knot of men and horses at the edge of the far bank. The sky, which had been blue when the battle started, boiled with storm clouds. Darkness hung over the battlefield, and a vast shadow swept towards the prince, eating up the ground with its coils.

The ka-demon.

Men of both sides looked up. In the confusion, Prince Ptolemy's chariot broke out of the trap and raced back along the bank towards the prince's camp, followed by that awful shadow.

Zeuxis broke into a cold sweat. He gathered up the reins.

"Zeuxis..." Marcus said in a warning tone. "It's not safe yet."

"Ahwere's in that camp! Prince Ptolemy's going to take her with him!"

He meant Ptolemy would take Ahwere with him into the world of demons. But Marcus assumed he meant to another camp. "Don't worry, Ptolemy won't have time to stop and collect any baggage. As soon as Caesar's secured the field, we'll go down and find her, I promise."

"That'll be too late! You don't understand! The demon's going to kill Caesar and Mark Anthony, too."

Even as he spoke, the shadow darkened, stretched out, and opened its huge mouth. An unnatural wind whirled along the Nile, foaming the water and billowing the tents. Prince Ptolemy looked over his shoulder and whipped his horses faster. Ropes snapped and tents took off into the sky. Sand roared down from the desert in a great wave, swallowing up the fields. Even Caesar's disciplined legions broke off fighting and looked round in sudden fear.

Zeuxis shouted to the fillies and they responded by leaping down the slope towards the battlefield, spraying his face with dirt kicked up by their hooves, just as they had done in the race nine months ago.

"What are you doing?" Marcus yelled, clinging to the sides as Zeuxis drove the chariot straight across the middle of the battlefield after Prince Ptolemy. "No, not *that* way...!"

The storm raged around him. Zuexis' ears hummed. The knots of fierce fighting, and the cries of dying men and horses, seemed to belong to another world.

He was in the Hippodrome, chasing Prince Ptolemy's chariot down the final straight. He crouched over the front of his own chariot, calling to the fillies for more speed. The crowd roared, "Zeuxis! Zeuxis for the Whites!"

Marcus gave up trying to persuade him to stop, and drew his sword to keep Prince Ptolemy's remaining men away from the chariot. The fillies threw up their heads and slowed as they drew closer to the vast ka-shadow. Prince Ptolemy had to slow down and fight his way through the Roman legionaries Caesar had sent round to cut him off, but he was still closer to the camp than Zeuxis. He vanished into the wreckage of tents, shouting for his guards. They dragged a small, struggling figure out of the chaos towards the prince's chariot.

Zeuxis screamed at the fillies. "Faster! Faster!"

More mud splattered his eyes. He couldn't see. He wiped them with his arm – and while he wasn't paying attention, all four horses reared, nearly tipping them both out of the back of the chariot. Marcus shouted something. Zeuxis threw himself forward and slackened the reins so he didn't pull the fillies over backwards.

Suddenly, Prince Ptolemy was right there in front of him with Ahwere kneeling in his chariot. He had his whip coiled tightly around her neck, and he was laughing under the demonic clouds.

"Lighthouse Boy!" he shrieked. "I have your girlfriend! Tell your Roman friends to back off and let me out of their death trap, or I'll break her little neck."

"Let her go!"

Zeuxis yelled at the fillies, but they would go no closer. Above Ptolemy's chariot hung the ka-demon, enormous and black, billowing up in a towering cloud. As it roared down towards them, Marcus muttered a prayer and ducked. Ahwere closed her eyes and began to chant under her breath in Egyptian. Zeuxis didn't blame her for praying. She must be terrified. As Ptolemy looked up, he seemed to notice the demon for the first time. His eyes widened as the ka's ghostly coils tightened around him and lifted him out of his chariot.

"No, no, not ME, you fool! The queen! I summoned you to take my sister, Cleopatra—"

You were her first husband-brother. I must take all those she loves away from her.

"Don't be ridiculous! She never loved me... Don't you understand love?"

The boy has reminded me. I made a bargain with him, so the girl must stay for now.

To Zeuxis' relief, the whip uncoiled from Ahwere's neck and twisted itself around Ptolemy's.

"You made a WHAT?" Prince Ptolemy stared down at Zeuxis in helpless fury as he realized the demon had no intention of letting him go.

I will deal with the others and your sister later. We must leave now.

"No-o-o!" screamed Ptolemy. "NO-O-O!"

His cries faded as the ka coiled up into the storm above the Nile, up and up, dragging the prince after it. With a great, sucking roar, wind and cloud and flying mud and sand twisted up from the battlefield to follow the demon and its human prisoner. Ahwere's chant finished on a loud cry. There was a deafening thunderclap and the prince's body fell out of the sky into the middle of the river, where it disappeared in a vast plume of spray.

The fillies, who had reared up in terror, came back to earth shivering and sweating. Ptolemy's chariot fled a short way down the bank, then slowed and came trotting back towards them. Ahwere held the reins, panting slightly, a triumphant smile on her face. Marcus let go of the sides and stared up at the sky, then down at the surface of the river, which was blue and calm again. In the middle, face down, floated Prince Ptolemy's body.

"I won't ask what just happened," Marcus said in a shaky voice. "But I think we can safely say Caesar won the day."

Zeuxis had eyes only for his friend. Clad in a filthy dress, with her hair hanging loose around her face and mud on her legs, he thought she had never looked so beautiful.

Her eyes gleamed as he drew up beside her. "About time!" she said. "I thought you'd never come."

"Ahwere..." Zeuxis said, his voice cracking. "I'm sorry I didn't come to help when your grandmother was sick and you needed me. I'm sorry I was so stupid and helped the Romans invade Alexandria. I thought I didn't care, because of not knowing who my parents were, but I *do* care. Whoever they might have been, Alexandria's my home now, and you... I mean, we—"

Ahwere leant across to touch his lips with her finger. "And I'm sorry about how I tricked you in that tomb. Grandmother isn't always right. She thought you would betray us because you weren't Egyptian, which is silly. But the ka's gone now. I sent it back to its own world. So at least we don't have to worry about the demon coming after us any more."

Zeuxis frowned at her. "What do you mean?" Then he remembered the chanting. "That wasn't just a prayer you were chanting in Prince Ptolemy's chariot, was it?"

"You don't think I sat around all these months in Prince Ptolemy's camp just twiddling my thumbs, do you? Grandmother and I have been working on a foolproof spell to banish the ka back to its own world, once and for all. We were waiting for the right time to cast it, that's all."

Zeuxis' stomach lifted. "You mean the ka's gone for good? But what about the rest of the curse? It was supposed to take all those Queen Cleopatra loves – Master Anthony and Julius Caesar, at least – and then it's supposed to end Cleopatra's life, and come after those of us who interfered. Do you mean we're safe? All of us?"

He glanced round at the Roman soldiers, and his heart sank slightly. "Does that mean we're stuck with Caesar for good?"

Ahwere smiled. "From what I hear, the Roman Caesar and Queen Cleopatra aren't making too bad a job of ruling Alexandria. Even Grandmother admits she got it wrong. The Romans didn't come here to destroy Egypt, after all."

"Certainly not!" Marcus interrupted, overhearing. "Your grain fields are much too valuable for feeding Caesar's empire."

Zeuxis wet his lips. "But are you *sure* the ka's gone? It might have just removed the prince and then gone back to Alexandria to destroy the queen, before coming for the rest of us."

Ahwere made an impatient sound. "Do you want me to bring it back, just to prove I can make it go away again?"

"No!" Zeuxis said, and she laughed.

"Lighthouse Boy, I do believe you're just as scared of me as Prince Ptolemy was! He thought I was a witch, and didn't dare hurt me in case I put a spell on him."

Zeuxis opened his mouth to tell her about the bargain he had made with the ka that had kept her safe from Prince Ptolemy, and probably prevented it from striking back when she banished it from the world. Then he smiled and shook his head. Ahwere did not need to know about that.

Instead he said, "I'm not just a lighthouse boy any more. I'm Keeper now."

Ahwere smiled again and touched his wrist. "I know. Grandmother told me. Prince Ptolemy said you were too busy to care about me any more, but I knew you would come. And I heard how you held your own against the Greens and Blues in the Hippodrome. If it had been a fair race, you would have won."

"There's no such thing as a fair race," Zeuxis said as he climbed out of the chariot. "I know that now."

Marcus took over the fillies' reins and ordered a passing legionary to take Ptolemy's chariot back to camp. The rest of the Romans busied themselves with tidying up the tents and the spoils ready for Caesar's inspection.

Shyly, Zeuxis took Ahwere's hand and they walked together along the riverbank. She did not pull away. He felt a lot older than the night he'd dug Prince Ptolemy's curse out of the Hippodrome. Hard to believe it had been less than a year ago. "The ka's really gone for ever?" he said, checking the sky to make sure. No more nightmares.

Ahwere nodded. "I promise."

"So curses won't work any more?"

"That depends."

"On what?" He stopped and pulled his friend round to face him. He wondered if he dared kiss her.

Ahwere's look was sly. "On what you believe. Neither Mark Anthony nor Julius Caesar are going to live for ever. And the last part of the curse didn't involve the ka itself, did it? *Send your serpent to end her wretched life,* remember? We Alexandrians will have our city back in the end." She eyed him sideways. "Who your parents were doesn't matter to me, Zeuxis. It never did. Grandmother says, now the Romans are here, we'll all have mixed blood soon."

As Zeuxis hesitated, not sure what she meant, she heaved a sigh and planted a kiss firmly on his lips. Then she tugged her hand free and ran along the bank, laughing.

The demon sends its serpent

That is positively the last time I enter into a bargain with a human! Who would have thought the boy would dare trick a demon? Making me promise not to harm the girl so that, when she cast her silly spell to banish me, I could do nothing except obey. No doubt it has something to do with this thing they call love. At least I managed to take Prince Ptolemy with me. I scared *him*, all right.

And the rest of the curse? Did I reach across the worlds and complete my task?

You will have to make up your own mind about that. Just remember humans do not live for ever. When all those the queen loves are gone from the human world, the way will be open for me to proceed.

I shall not come myself, though. You can summon me all you like. I have been humiliated by two humans a zillionth of my age, and a demon does not fall for that trick twice.

HISTORICAL NOTE

When Julius Caesar returned to Rome a year later, Cleopatra and her new-born son accompanied him. But the Romans were not happy when Caesar announced his plans to marry the Egyptian queen, and they assassinated him in the senate. Cleopatra returned to Alexandria, where she murdered her second husband-brother and joined forces with Mark Anthony, who still commanded part of the Roman army.

Mark Anthony and Cleopatra ruled Egypt for nine years, until the new Caesar, Octavian, declared war on them. In 30BC, after five years of fighting between Rome and Alexandria, Octavian defeated the Egyptian forces. Rather than face capture, Mark Anthony fell on his sword and died in Cleopatra's arms. Cleopatra, mad with grief, sent for a basket of poisonous snakes and allowed them to bite her, thus ending her own life.

GUIDE TO ZEUXIS' WORLD

Zeuxis and Ahwere lived in Alexandria on the northern coast of Egypt during the major riot of 48BC, when the city was ruled by Queen Cleopatra and her brother Prince Ptolemy. It was a time of civil war, which the Roman emperor Julius Caesar took advantage of to seize power. At that time, Alexandria housed people of many different nationalities (Egyptians, Greeks, Macedonians, Judeans), and chariot races in the Hippodrome had the status of today's football matches, with frequent riots caused by fighting between the supporters of the different teams.

Agathodaimon	Snake-bodied demon with a man's head, believed to be the guardian spirit of Alexandria.
agora	market place
amulet	A charm against evil.
ankh	a powerful amulet in the shape of a cross with a loop at the top.
Blues Reds Whites	Chariot racing teams. By tradition, Blues were the royals, and Greens were the challengers. In this story, the Whites are supported by Rome, and the Reds by native Egyptians.
Caesar	Emperor of Rome. In this story, the famous Julius Caesar.
chariot	A two-wheeled vehicle that could be drawn by one, two, or four horses, usually harnessed side-by-side. A racing chariot was a special light frame made of wood and leather, just big enough to carry the driver and very fragile. War chariots were much tougher and could carry more than one person.
Charms of Safe Running	Silver bells hung from a horse's harness to counteract curses.

colt	A young male horse.
curse	A piece of soft lead, inscribed with the words of the curse, rolled up and fastened with a nail. Curses were often planted in the Hippodrome against rival chariot teams to make them crash.
Eye of Horus	The 'Egyptian eye', often worn around the neck as a powerful amulet.
filly	A young female horse.
Great Library	The Great Library of Alexandria was world-famous and housed many irreplaceable scrolls. When Julius Caesar invaded, it was burnt to the ground, and many of the scrolls were lost.
Heptastadion	The sea wall connecting the city of Alexandria to Pharos Island, so called because it was seven stadia (about 1400 metres) in length.
hieroglyphs	Ancient Egyptian picture-writing.
Hippodrome	A race track for chariot racing.
ka	An ancient Egyptian spirit, being the "animal soul" of a human, which takes its own form upon death. The ka in this story is

Agathodaimon, the demon-spirit of Alexandria.

lotus
Native Egyptian flower – a large, sweetly-scented lily coloured blue or white.

mausoleum
A tomb.

obelisk
A needle-like stone pillar erected to mark a significant place, or in memory of an important event or person.

Pharaoh
King (or Queen) of Egypt. By ancient tradition, the Pharaoh was expected to marry his sister, who then became his 'sister-wife'. In later times, this tradition was carried on by the Macedonian rulers of Alexandria, so that Queen Cleopatra had to marry her brother in order to satisfy the Egyptian priests.

Pharos
The largest and most famous lighthouse of Alexandria, which stood on an island connected to the mainland by a sea wall. The Pharos was one of the Seven Wonders of the Ancient World, and gave its name to other lighthouses all over the world.

scroll
An ancient 'book' (a rolled sheet of papyrus).

Serapis   The main god of Alexandria – a mixture of the Egyptian god Osiris and the Greek god Zeus.

sistrum   An Egyptian rattle.

stade   An ancient measurement – the length of a Greek stadium. About 600 feet, or 200 metres.

DISCOVER MORE ADVENTURE
AND MAGIC IN THE ANCIENT
WORLD...

THE
SEVEN FABULOUS WONDERS

THE GREAT
PYRAMID
ROBBERY

Magic, murder and mayhem spread through the Two Lands, when Senu, the son of a scribe, is forced to help build one of the largest and most magnificent pyramids ever recorded. He and his friend, Reonet, are sucked into a plot to rob the great pyramid of Khufu and an ancient curse is woken. Soon they are caught in a desperate struggle against forces from another world, and even Senu's mischievous ka, Red, finds his magical powers are dangerously tested.

000 711278 5

www.harpercollinschildrensbooks.co.uk

THE
SEVEN FABULOUS WONDERS

THE
BABYLON
GAME

Tia's luck starts to change the moment she touches a
dragon patrolling the Hanging Gardens of Babylon.
At the Twenty Squares Club Tia wins every game –
could the dragon have given her a magical power?

But Tia discovers her lucky gift brings great danger.
While the Persian army prepares to attack her home,
she and her friend, Simeon, must fight their own
battle. Will Tia's magic save the city – or destroy it
altogether?

000 711279 3

www.harpercollinschildrensbooks.co.uk

THE
SEVEN FABULOUS WONDERS

THE
AMAZON
TEMPLE
·QUEST·

Lysippe is an Amazon princess with a mission. Her tribe has vanished and her sister is fatally wounded. Only the power of a Gryphon Stone can help, but Lysippe has a problem. She has been enslaved by the sinister Alchemist, and he is after the Stones too…

Lysippe and her friend, Hero, plan a daring escape from the slave gang and claim sanctuary in the mysterious Temple of Artemis. But can they decipher the Temple's magical secrets before it's too late?

000 711280 7

www.harpercollinschildrensbooks.co.uk

THE
SEVEN FABULOUS WONDERS

◄THE►
MAUSOLEUM
MURDER

Alexis has a magical gift, but it's not one he wants. It hasn't helped him find his father, who has mysteriously disappeared, or freed him from his hard-hearted stepmother. Alex's home is under seige, and he can't do anything about *that* either. But when Alex and his best friend meet Princess Phoebe, things start to change. Together, they must unlock the murderous secrets of Halicarnassos. Magic is the key, but there may be a high price to pay for bringing statues to life...

0 00 711281 5

www.harpercollinschildrensbooks.co.uk

THE SEVEN FABULOUS WONDERS

THE OLYMPIC CONSPIRACY

Sosi's brother Theron is in training for the Olympic Games. When he is injured, only Sosi can help him – but he gets more than he bargained for when he takes Theron's place. Who is trying to sabotage the Games, and why? And what's so important about the sacred fire and the Statue of Zeus? Sorcery, plotting, poison and a power struggle at the Olympic Games...

0 00 711282 3

www.harpercollinschildrensbooks.co.uk

THE
SEVEN FABULOUS WONDERS

When an earthquake strikes and the Colossus of
Rhodes collapses, humans come face to face with an
ancient race of sea creatures – the telchines. At the
centre of the struggle is Aura, half-telchine and half-
human, destined to reveal an ancient prophecy. But
what is the strange Gift that everyone wants? And
who can Aura trust?

0 00 711283 1

www.harpercollinschildrensbooks.co.uk